A WIND IS BLOWING

MONICA EDWARDS

Girls Gone By Publishers

COMPLETE AND UNABRIDGED

Published by Girls Gone By Publishers
The Vicarage, Church Street, Coleford, Radstock, Somerset, BA3 5NG
www.ggbp.co.uk

First published by Collins 1969
First published by Girls Gone By Publishers 2009; New edition 2023
Text © the Estate of Monica Edwards; Monica Edwards: The Person,
The Places and the Books © Joy Wotton 2007; A New Focus: Locations
in *A Wind is Blowing* © Joy Wotton 2009; A Personal Introduction © Sally
Bourne 2009/2023; Preface © Shelley Edwards 2009; A Wind Blown
Out or A Change of Tack © Sean Edwards 2023; A Bittersweet Farewell
© Joyce Bailey 2023; Appendix: The Author's Notebook © The Estate of
Monica Edwards; introduction to Appendix © Brian Parks 2009/2023;
Publishing History © Clarissa Cridland 2023; Note on the Text © Rich
Curler and Sarah Woodall 2009; Alison Neale 2023.
Design and Layout © Girls Gone By Publishers 2023

Cover design by Ken Websdale
Typeset in England by GGBP
Printed and bound by Short Run Press, Exeter
ISBN 978-1-84745-321-1

CONTENTS

Monica Edwards and Vashti

MONICA EDWARDS: THE PERSON, THE PLACES AND THE BOOKS

THE AUTHOR

Monica Edwards was born Monica le Doux Newton on 8 November 1912 in Belper, Derbyshire. She was the second daughter and third of the four children of the Revd Harry Newton (died 1939) and Beryl Frances le Doux Newton, née Sargeant (died 1970). As a child she attended Beecholm College, Thornes House School and Wakefield High School. In 1927 her father left St Andrew's Church, Wakefield, and accepted the living of Rye Harbour, Sussex. Monica's elder sister was sent to school and her two brothers had a tutor, but she herself ran wild in Rye Harbour for three months, picking up much material for her future novels as, to quote her *Dictionary of National Biography* entry by Josephine Pullein-Thompson, she 'sailed with fishermen, rode shepherds' ponies, and helped at a riding school'. So far as is known, she did not indulge in smuggling. 'If you wanted to find Monica,' an elderly resident told John Allsup, 'you looked around the net sheds, she'd be there working with the fishermen'.

In January 1928 Monica was sent to St Brandon's Clergy Daughters' School, Bristol; she disliked the school and left at Easter 1928, but in the mean time a good English teacher had encouraged her to write.

On Thursday 15 November 1928 the *Mary Stanford*, the Rye Harbour lifeboat, was lost with all 17 hands. Monica was just 16, and the disaster made a deep impression on her. Her father, Harry Newton, reported that on receipt of the SOS message the crew and launchers turned out with such speed that 'it was as if they had slept with their clothes on' (*The* Mary Stanford *Disaster*, p14). He later saw the *Mary Stanford* capsize as he looked out from the vicarage windows, although in *Storm Ahead* the incident is witnessed by Meryon rather than the vicar. Monica walked the seashore, helping to identify the bodies of the crew as they were washed up. Her mother, Beryl Newton, said in a radio interview: 'And I think I shall never as long as I live, forget the vicar kneeling on the beach, and the women of the village kneeling with him, and the rain coming down like knitting needles.' Monica's father and John Fowler, the vicar of Rye, officiated at the mass funeral on Tuesday 20 November. Mrs Newton later recalled the intense emotion and complete silence that occurred as the men were lowered into the grave: 'Tears stained the faces of hardened lifeboatmen as they quietly bade their last farewell to their former colleagues. "You could have heard a pin drop, there wasn't a sound."' (*The* Mary Stanford *Disaster*, p29). A memorial to the lifeboatmen stands in the churchyard at Rye Harbour today. Years later, when her own daughter Shelley was 16 years old, Monica drew on her vivid memories of the event in her account of the lifeboat disaster at Westling Harbour in *Storm Ahead* (1953). The storms of October 1931 at Rye Harbour when the village was flooded may have coloured her writing of the book, and 20 years later the accounts of the Lynmouth Flood Disaster of August 1952 may also have stirred memories.

One of Monica's friends was William (Bill) Edwards, nearly ten years her senior, with whom she worked on an acrobatic tumbling routine, reminiscent of Meryon's antics at the pageant in *The Midnight Horse*. Her parents felt she was too young to marry, perhaps because Bill's background may not have been socially acceptable to them, and suggested a separation until she was 21. Just two days after her 21st birthday in 1933, Monica married Bill Edwards in Rye Harbour Church. A maternal cousin, Richard Talbot, vicar of Reigate, officiated at the ceremony. Monica and Bill went on to have two children, Shelley and Sean.

Bill with Sean

In 1946 the Edwardses were living in a semi-suburban house near Woking, longing for the real country. By then Monica had begun to write children's books, the first two of which were published in 1947. *The Unsought Farm* (1954), the first of her autobiographical books, tells the story of how they came to buy Pitlands Farm, a ruined 14th-century farmhouse with 70 acres of land a mile outside the village of Thursley, Surrey, following a brief Sunday viewing two days before the sale. Bill was working, so Monica went to the sale at the Lion Hotel in Guildford. Absently attending to the auction while reading Pamela Whitlock and Katherine Hull's new book *Crowns* (1947), she suddenly realised that 'the hammer was literally coming right down' and 'said two words—my only bid—while the hammer was dropping' (*The Unsought Farm*, p20). Those two words were 'three thousand', a jump of £250 from the previous bid, which, Monica reported the auctioneer as saying, 'crabbed the sale'. She went home to inform her family of their good fortune: 'The house is in ruins … There's no water, no light, no drains, no bathroom, and the Other Place is at the bottom of the garden'

Monica with a calf at Punch Bowl Farm

(p22). They renamed the farm Punch Bowl Farm and moved there in November 1947, and Shelley rode to school on her black pony Tarquin—yet another incident from life that was reflected in Monica's books as the young Thorntons rode to school. Monica's description of this ride in *The Unsought Farm*—'into the rugged heath and pine land of Highcomb Bottom; through the great jungle of the Devil's Punch Bowl and over the notorious Gibbet Hill and Hindhead Common' (p25)—is more fiction than fact, however, as Shelley's actual route was more direct. Life at Punch Bowl Farm, and the practicalities of real-life farming, fed into many of the books, mainly in the hard work carried out by Dion and the other Thornton children, but also in the description in *No Entry* of the way in which Mr Merrow puts Castle Farm out of bounds to everyone during a foot-and-mouth epidemic.

As mentioned previously, 1947 saw the publication of Monica's first two novels, both in different ways pony books. In *Wish for a Pony*, the first of 15 stories set in and around Westling Village (in real life the industrial village of Rye Harbour), Dunsford (Rye), Winklesea (Winchelsea) and Romney Marsh, Monica drew on her experiences growing up as the daughter of the vicar of Rye Harbour, for the series' heroine, Tamzin Grey, is also the daughter of a vicar. It is in many ways a classic pony story, where the young heroine and her best friend, Rissa, not only win through but ultimately win ponies (although Rissa has to wait for hers until *The Summer of the Great Secret*). In later life Monica was to regret that *Wish for a Pony*, her best-known work, labelled her as a writer of pony books. The more discerning reader was never deceived by this for, as Margery Fisher points out in *Intent Upon Reading*: 'Though ponies play their part in the stories, they are not the object of adulation or of excessive care. Sometimes they are used as casually by the girls as their boy companions in adventure use their bicycles' (p187, 1964 edition). The other book, *No Mistaking Corker*, is the conventional story of a family caravanning holiday, notable chiefly as the first of the 11 Punchbowl Farm books and for introducing us to the Thornton family.

Monica's membership of a number of societies reflected not only her interests but also the subjects of her books. She was a member of the Society of Authors, the Royal Horticultural Society, the International Camellia Society, the Burmese Cat Society (as one would expect) and the National Farmers' Union.

During most of the 1950s Monica produced two books a year and also wrote for *The Elizabethan* (later *Young Elizabethan*), *The Children's*

Newspaper, *Woman's Journal* and the BBC's *Children's Hour*. She was co-recipient of Foyles' Children's Book Club Author of the Year in 1957, and in 1960 she was voted Children's Writer of the Year, jointly with the creator of the Biggles books, Captain W E Johns. She wrote a film script, *The Dawn Killer*, based on her novel *Killer Dog*, for the Children's Film Foundation. At least 12 of her books have been translated into foreign languages, and *A Wind is Blowing*, as is only right when one considers its central theme, was transcribed into Braille.

Monica Edwards's penultimate book, *The Valley and the Farm* (1971), relates her husband's terrible tractor accident on 27 August 1968, which ended in the decision that they could no longer run the farm. They sold it, but kept Monica with granddaughter Kitty

Smallbrook Valley and the Little Orchard, where they built a bungalow named Cowdray Cross. Monica's final book, *Badger Valley* (1976), is a record of the many days and nights she spent watching and photographing badgers in the valley.

Bill Edwards died in 1990. Monica's sight began to fail, but Jill Goulder, who interviewed her in the mid-1990s and corresponded with her about the real-life Tamzin, Meryon, Rissa, Roger and the

Thorntons, found her 'slim, straight and so quick and confident in her house that you would never realise that she is almost blind' (*Folly* 18). Monica Edwards died on 18 January 1998, and her ashes are buried with Bill's in Smallbrook Valley, which she left to the Woodland Trust.

THE BOOKS
The Linked Books

Over half the books are set in and around Rye and Rye Harbour, on the Sussex part of Romney Marsh, where Monica Edwards lived as a young adult. As so many authors have done, Monica thinly disguises the reality. Rye becomes Dunsford, Camber Castle becomes Cloudesley (or Cloudesly) Castle, after admiral Sir Cloudesley Shovel, Rye's industrial district of Rye Harbour becomes the fishing village of Westling, and the nearby small town of Winchelsea acquires the quaint yet comical name of Winklesea. The other books are set at Punchbowl Farm, based on Punch Bowl Farm at Thursley, Surrey, the farm Monica and her husband bought in 1947.

Some of the paperback editions issued by Armada were cut. For example, in the episode early in *Dolphin Summer* where Tamzin nearly drowns, the hardback contains more detail about Rissa's distress as the incident unfolds. There are similar cuts concerning emotional response in *Spirit of Punchbowl Farm*, and it would appear that Armada decided to sacrifice girlish emotion in the interests of getting on with the adventure. The text of *Storm Ahead* appears to be the same in the hardback and Puffin editions, although the captions have been altered.

An author's note opposite the Contents Page of *Strangers to the Marsh* makes it clear that 'this book is meant to come, in sequence of time, just before *Hidden in a Dream*'. Brian Parks points out that Monica's notebooks also make it clear that *No Entry* and *The Nightbird* are meant to precede *Storm Ahead*, even though they were written

11

afterwards, and that *No Going Back* began life as a retrospective novel, set before *Operation Seabird*. Finally, the events of *A Wind is Blowing* cover the months August–October and begin before the plot of *The Wild One* which opens in September. The books have been listed here in publication order.

1   *Wish for a Pony* (Collins, 1947). Romney Marsh. The first story of Westling, and Tamzin and Rissa's 'pony book'.

2   *No Mistaking Corker* (Collins, 1947). Punchbowl. A family caravanning holiday introducing the Thorntons.

3   *The Summer of the Great Secret* (Collins, 1948). Romney Marsh. Tamzin and Rissa take up smuggling, and Lesley cannot walk.

4   *The Midnight Horse* (Collins, 1949). Romney Marsh. Meryon and Roger are introduced, and a pageant is staged (reminiscent in some ways of Noel Streatfeild's *Party Frock*, 1946).

5   *The White Riders* (Collins, 1950). Romney Marsh. Eighteenth-century smuggling methods are brought into play as Tamzin, Meryon, Rissa and Roger save Cloudesley Castle and Castle Farm from becoming a holiday camp.

6   *Black Hunting Whip* (Collins, 1950). Punchbowl. The Thorntons buy a farm—modelled on the Edwardses' own farm at Thursley, Surrey. Also a timeslip story about Dion.

7   *Cargo of Horses* (Collins, 1951). Romney Marsh. A violent story about horse smugglers in which the farmer's wife at Castle Farm more than proves her mettle.

8   *Punchbowl Midnight* (Collins, 1951). Punchbowl. Focuses on the loss of a calf and the accident that leads to Tamzin's first visit to Punchbowl Farm.

9   *Hidden in a Dream* (Collins, 1952). Romney Marsh. Meryon falls on a breakwater and knocks himself out, and the friends camp out in the Martello Tower at Westling Harbour.

10   *Spirit of Punchbowl Farm* (Collins, 1952). Punchbowl. Another

timeslip story, thought by many to be Monica Edwards's finest novel.

11   *Storm Ahead* (Collins, 1953). Romney Marsh. The 1928 *Mary Stanford* lifeboat disaster at Rye Harbour, experienced by Monica Edwards in her youth, is re-experienced by Tamzin and her friends, with Lindsey from Punchbowl Farm.

12   *The Wanderer* (Collins, 1953). Punchbowl. Dion is annoyed by a runaway horse, but Lindsey wants to save it (the plot of the unwanted animal recurs time and again in the Punchbowl books).

13   *No Entry* (Collins, 1954). Romney Marsh. Foot-and-mouth disease threatens Castle Farm, but the four friends come to the rescue.

14   *Punchbowl Harvest* (Collins, 1954). Punchbowl. The story of the harvest, surprisingly enough, and Dion's pet fox.

15   *The Nightbird* (Collins, 1955). Romney Marsh. Westling fishing is under threat, so Tamzin and friends create a ghost ship and frighten off the French poachers.

16   *Frenchman's Secret* (Collins, 1956). Punchbowl. The Thorntons make friends with children from the mill—and then the dam breaks.

17   *Operation Seabird* (Collins, 1957). Romney Marsh. Meryon becomes an engine driver as an emergency strikes the little Romney, Hythe & Dymchurch Railway; an oil slick threatens the local seabirds, and Tamzin and Co mount an operation to save them.

18   *Strangers to the Marsh* (Collins, 1957). Romney Marsh. A pair of hoopoes prepares to nest in Cloudesley Castle, and Jim's accident in Mermaid Street leads the friends to establish a local newspaper to raise money.

19   *The Cownappers* (Collins, 1958). Punchbowl/Romney Marsh. A cow is smuggled back to its rightful owners in France.

20   *No Going Back* (Collins, 1960). Romney Marsh. Meryon helps Jim Decks buy a hearse and falls in love with Tamzin—but she decides she is too young for a serious relationship.

21   *The Outsider* (Collins, 1961). Punchbowl. Lindsey, with Tamzin and Co visiting, becomes involved with a wild deer.

22   *The Hoodwinkers* (Collins, 1962). Romney Marsh. The discovery of the drowned village of Old Winklesea, the usefulness of Bob-a-Jobbing and the advent of the Young Socialists.

23   *Dolphin Summer* (Collins, 1963). Romney Marsh. Tamzin makes friends with and saves a local dolphin.

24   *Fire in the Punchbowl* (Collins, 1965). A Punchbowl story involving Roger and Rissa. A long hot summer leads to a heath fire.

25   *The Wild One* (Collins, 1967). A Punchbowl story involving Roger and Rissa. Yet another animal escapes—this time a puma—and Dion wants to dispose of it. Lindsey disagrees.

26   *A Wind is Blowing* (Collins, 1969). Romney Marsh. Meryon suffers a terrible accident, and his career as a doctor is threatened. A very stark book, focusing entirely on Meryon and Tamzin.

Autobiographical Writings

Monica Edwards's autobiographical writings provide a great deal of background information to her Punchbowl Farm books, but they also shed light on the Westling books, not least in their pictures of many of the leading characters.

The Unsought Farm is the first, and the best for those seeking the real-life background to the Punchbowl novels. It explains how Monica went to an auction and absentmindedly bought a farm while reading a book. *Badger Valley* is especially good for its natural history observation of badgers at night.

The Unsought Farm (Michael Joseph, 1954)
The Cats of Punchbowl Farm (Michael Joseph, 1964)
The Badgers of Punchbowl Farm (Michael Joseph, 1966)
The Valley and the Farm (Michael Joseph, 1971)
Badger Valley (Michael Joseph, 1976)

Other Writings

Joan Goes Farming (Bodley Head, 1954). A career novel.

Rennie Goes Riding (Bodley Head, 1956). A career novel.

Killer Dog (Collins, 1959). Is Glen really a killer dog?

Under the Rose (Collins, 1968). A complex family adventure story involving the abduction of a horse.

THE REAL ROMNEY MARSH

Over the past one hundred years or so, Rye appears to have been the town of choice for more writers than almost any other. Many of these writers were inspired by the location. Monica Edwards, of course, lived at Rye Harbour. Malcolm Saville, whose holiday adventure stories most closely resemble Monica Edwards's books in spirit, set several of his Lone Pine books and a short story in Rye and Romney Marsh, and his characters often walk down the same streets as Tamzin, Rissa, Meryon and Roger. Joan Aiken wrote a novel about a murder at Jeake's House on Mermaid Street, where her father, the writer Conrad Aiken, lived. E F Benson, a mayor of Rye and one of numerous writer-residents of Lamb House over the years, set many of his Mapp and Lucia books in Rye (renamed Tilling), and Tom Holt wrote a couple of sequels, in one of which Mapp challenges Lucia by introducing the game of *Monopoly* to the town.

Smuggling has a long history on the Marsh, and the ineffectiveness of smuggling officers has been celebrated not just by Monica Edwards but also by Georgette Heyer in *The Unknown Ajax*, and by Russell Thorndike, brother of the actress Sybil Thorndike, in his seven Dr Syn books about a smuggling parson who was Rector of Dymchurch.

In *A Gift from Winklesea* Helen Cresswell set stories in a renamed Winchelsea, as did Rumer Godden in *A Kindle of Kittens* and Beatrix

Potter in *The Faithful Dove*. Elinor Brent-Dyer set her Skelton Hall books on Romney Marsh. The following writers also lived in and around Rye and Winchelsea: Viola Bayley, Nancy Breary, John Christopher, Joseph Conrad, Patric Dickinson, Ford Madox Ford, Radclyffe Hall, Jane Aiken Hodge, Susan Howatch, Alison James, Henry James, William James, Sheila Kaye-Smith, Malcolm Lowry, Spike Milligan, H G Wells and, of course, John Ryan—the creator of Captain Pugwash. After London, Edinburgh and Bath, Rye is surely the British town most cited in literature.

Getting Around

The 313 bus service runs from Rye Railway Station down to Rye Harbour roughly every forty minutes (Mondays–Saturdays, except public holidays), making for easy access to the real Westling village. Alternatively, it's a forty-minute walk, crossing the river at the Strand in Rye to Winchelsea Road, then left down Harbour Road. One can stick to the pavement (it's shared with a cycle path, so be wary of bicycles), keeping the River Rother (so named in both the books and reality) on the left; or for those with strong shoes on, just after you pass the lock and private road on the right, next to the triangular cycle path sign there's a tiny footpath entrance hidden in the bushes that takes you on a more picturesque route, mirroring the road but without the traffic and industrial vista that's grown up since Monica Edwards's time. The path emerges just before the church at the end of Harbour Road, and watch out for a good view of Camber (Cloudesley) Castle en route.

For an easy three-mile walk, suitable for pushchairs if you keep to the concrete on the seafront, catch the bus down to the Hard and begin by walking west towards the Rye Harbour Nature Reserve (well worth a visit), and its new Discovery Centre and café, then onwards to the isolated old lifeboat house, scene of the launch of the lifeboat in *Storm Ahead*, about a mile and a half from the village itself. In real life, the *Mary Stanford* was launched from the old lifeboat house on 15 November 1928 in a valiant attempt to rescue the crew of the ss *Alice* of Riga. This is an exposed walk, but from May onwards it is well rewarded by good coastal vegetation, including viper's bugloss, sea kale, the yellow-horned poppy, valerian and the sea pea. The Nature Reserve contains hides from which a watch is kept in season on the little tern, a rare breeding bird in Britain, which has a major colony at Rye Harbour.

Retrace your steps, and at the junction of Main Street (now unlabelled as such, and known as the continuation of Harbour Road) and the road to the Nature Reserve you will pass on the left Martello Tower No 28, where Tamzin's family and friends camped out in *Hidden in a Dream*. Frenchman's Beach Caravan Park by the Martello Tower is unlikely to have inspired Monica with the title of *Frenchman's Secret*. Brian Parks says that in a letter to him, Monica stated that she heartily disapproved of the site. The title comes from the real-life Frenchman mentioned in *The Unsought Farm*, and from Frenchman's Hill and Frenchman's Lane, adjacent to Cosford Mill.

Walk past the Old Vicarage, which closely resembles Geoffrey Whittam's illustration in *Dolphin Summer* but not Anne Bullen's drawing in *The Summer of the Great Secret*. Tamzin's attic window and the drainpipe down which she climbed on so many unauthorised occasions can be seen very clearly. A low wall represents the southerly boundary of the Vicarage garden, and a car park now occupies the shingly area where the fishermen used to dry their nets. After reverting to a private house back in 2005, the Old Vicarage is again a bed-and-breakfast, for those who would like an opportunity to see inside.

The Vicarage at Rye Harbour was built in 1901, owing to the generosity of local benefactor Mrs Lucas Shadwell. *The Romney Marsh Companion* by Brian Parks contains interesting plans of the ground and first floors of the house. When the house was put on the market in 2009, the estate agent's plans showed that the attic floor contained not only Tamzin's bedroom but also a second bedroom. The house retains many of its original features, including tiled floors and large wooden sash and casement windows.

The Old Vicarage, 2022

Continue along the seafront towards Camber Sands (the fictional Dunsmere Sands). Keep on along the Hard, passing on the left the Old Ship Inn, the Watch House, Rose Cottage and Harbour Lights, and pausing at the William the Conqueror Inn (opened c1860), where you will fail to find either old Jim Decks, the ferryman, or the splendidly named Hookey Galley. On the right is the harbour mast (almost lost forever in 2020), close to Jim's hut and the new lifeboat house. Following the loss of the *Mary Stanford*, the station was first temporarily closed, and then permanently so in 1929, and Rye Harbour did not have a lifeboat again until 1966. For the purposes of fiction, and perhaps of tact, the lifeboat house in *Wish for a Pony* is placed on the Dunsmere side of the river, as far away from the old lifeboat house as it may be.

William the Conqueror Inn, 2021

Turn back along the Hard and turn right just before the Old Vicarage up Main Street. On the left, now built over, is the Grey family's tennis court, and on the right is Smiling Morn's shop. Continue up Main Street, passing Tram Road on the left (named after the tram that ran from Rye to Camber Sands from 1895 to 1939). The Rye and Camber tram terminated at a stage opposite Rye Harbour village, from where old Jim's ferry could be hailed, so Tamzin and Rissa could cross over to Dunsmere Sands (Camber Sands), the Hillocks Riding School and Jury's Gap (its real and fictional name). The Rye Harbour ferryman ran two boats in the 1920s, one with a keel for use at high tides, and the other flat-bottomed for low tides.

Continuing up Main Street, walk past Mary Stanford Green, named after the lost lifeboat, and proceed north. On the left is the Village Hall, also known as the Sailors' Institute, but both the old Post Office on the right and the garage opposite, where Fritz from Punchbowl Farm filled up with petrol in *The Cownappers*, have now gone. Close by on the right is the Church Mission Room, which plays so important a part in *Storm Ahead*. The Vicar discusses with Old Jim just which buildings will not be flooded out: "'The Mission Hall stands higher than most in the village [this is certainly true] [...] And the Sailors' Institute, and of course the vicarage'" (*Storm Ahead*, Chapter 3). On the left is The Inkerman or Inkermann Arms (now closed), which is called the Sea Serpent in *Storm Ahead*. Stonework Cottages follow and then Dickson's (or is that Diccon's?!) School—a long walk from the Vicarage for a small boy—soon follows, on the outskirts of the village, by 'the little boat-shaped church', Rye Harbour Church itself.

Rye Harbour's Church of the Holy Spirit was built in 1849 by the landowner William Drew Lucas Shadwell of The Hall, Fairlight.

After his death his widow, a temperance campaigner, converted the Old Ship Inn into a private house and also provided a reading room, hoping thus to distract the men from the public houses, and built the Old Vicarage. Close by the vestry door are two yew trees, from one of which Jimmy Decks may have taken the branch of yew that so nearly poisoned Cascade in *The Summer of the Great Secret*—and gave Lesley Frampton the will to walk again. There is a tablet to the

Inside Rye Harbour Church

lifeboatmen inside the church, a gift from the people of the Isle of Man, and the mass grave lies in the churchyard.

Main Street becomes Harbour Road, and one can either catch the bus back to Rye (or Dunsford), or follow the footpath on the left just after the sandworks, remembering Tamzin's night-time ride through the floods in *Storm Ahead*.

Staff at the Discovery Centre can point out routes through the Nature Reserve, but Camber Castle is best approached from Rye rather than Rye Harbour, owing to the preponderance of dykes and ditches. There is no vehicle access. From Rye, walk down to the Rye Harbour junction, turn left, cross the bridge and immediately turn right along the private road. Where the footpath forks at Castle Mill Cottages, take the left turn along a track and go through the gate. The castle is in front of you on the right, about half a mile away. Keeping the River Brede on the right, follow the raised bank around in a right-hand curve until you encounter a gate on your left beside a small ruined shed. The castle will now be visible across the marshland ahead of you.

Camber Castle is run by English Heritage and is now occasionally open to the public, after being closed for many years. Commissioned by Henry VIII as part of the South Coast defences against the French, it was completed around 1540. It was built as a fortress rather than a castle residence, and was abandoned in 1643, since the sea had receded; it now lies over a mile away. The walls are still 'flamed with yellow wallflowers' (*Strangers to the Marsh*, Chapter 6), but no hoopoes can now be seen. Camber Castle is where Penny and Jon first meet David and the twins in Malcolm Saville's *The Gay Dolphin Adventure*, and it is interesting to compare the different uses the two authors make of the location. By continuing along a footpath south of the castle you reach Castle Farm, although the original farmhouse has been rebuilt.

Trains run between Rye and Winchelsea (Winklesea), and the 100 bus service also operates hourly from Rye Station to the New Inn in Winchelsea. This is where Meryon lived 'at the house with green shutters next but one to Winklesea Rectory' (*The Midnight Horse*, Chapter 5). The town was rebuilt inland in an unusual grid pattern, by Edward I in the late 13th century, Old Winchelsea having been mostly destroyed by a storm in 1287. In the church, a Book of Remembrance and a hassock commemorate the local author Malcolm Saville, and a stained-glass window by Douglas Strachan, dedicated on 6 July 1929, commemorates the men who died in the *Mary Stanford* disaster.

Joy Wotton, 2007
(The section on The Real Romney Marsh updated and expanded by Alison Neale, 2022.)

BIBLIOGRAPHY

Carpenter, Edward *Wrecks and Rescues off the Romney Marsh Coast* 1985

Clark, K M *Many a Bloody Affray* Rye Museum Publication No 8, 1968

Contemporary Authors Nos 9–12 1974

Copson, Belinda 'Romney Marsh and Punchbowl Farm: The Books of Monica Edwards' *Folly*, 7, November 1992

Cridland, Clarissa 'Monica Edwards' *Book and Magazine Collector*, 191, February 2000

Dickinson, Alan *Around Rye in Old Photographs* 1989

Fisher, Margery *Intent Upon Reading* revised edition, 1964

Foster, Jim *Adams' Rye Guide* 1934, revised edition by Kenneth Clark, 1993

Goulder, Jill 'Dream Hero: Monica Edwards' Real Characters' *Folly*, 18, July 1996

    'Whose Childhood?—More about Monica' *Folly*, 21, July 1997

    'A Picture of Meryon' *Folly*, 22, November 1997

Goulder, Jill, with Sue Sims 'A Farewell to Monica' *Folly*, 23, March 1998

Holy Trinity Rye Harbour Marriages 1903–1940: Hastings and Rother Family History Society n.d.

Horner, Richard *Rye Shipping* 1993

Hutchinson, Geoff *The* Mary Stanford *Disaster* revised edition, 1993

Kirkham, Jo, editor *Bygone Rye Harbour* 1992, revised edition, 2006

Kirkham, Jo *The Story of Rye College* 2008

Kirkpatrick, D L, editor *Twentieth-century Children's Writers* 1978

Parks, Brian *The Monica Edwards Romney Marsh Companion* 2006

Pratt, Malcolm, and Gooders, John *The Antient Town of Winchelsea* 2003

Pullein-Thompson, Josephine 'Monica le Doux Edwards' *Oxford Dictionary of National Biography* 2004

Rye Harbour: Your Guide to a Shingle Nature Reserve n.d.

Rye Ramblers *Country Walks Around Rye* 1995

RX Wildlife: Wildlife Sites from Hastings to Romney Marsh n.d.

Saville, Malcolm *Portrait of Rye* Mark O'Hanlon, 1999

Saville, Malcolm *The Story of Winchelsea Church* East Sussex County Library, 1986, revised edition by Robert Hargeaves, 2004

Sibson, Penny 'Double Vision' *Souvenir: The Journal of the Violet Needham Society,* 10, Spring 1989

Wallace, Una D. *Douglas Strachan: Stained Glass Artist, An Appreciation by his Daughter* n.d.

Wigram, Jeniffer 'A Visit to "Westling"' *Souvenir,* 26, Summer 1994

The Inkermann Arms

A NEW FOCUS: LOCATIONS IN
A WIND IS BLOWING

There is no denying that *A Wind is Blowing* is a difficult book. It opens happily enough with Tamzin and Meryon shopping in Dunsford High Street but moves swiftly into bleak tragedy. At times, its spare text reads almost like an outline of the story. There are fewer supporting characters—Old Jim, Hookey Galley, walk-on parts from Smiling Morn and Mrs Venus. A weak plot device concerns the casual introduction of two characters who are killed within 17 pages of their first appearance (*A Wind is Blowing*, pp 163-177.) And there is the startling absence of the other main characters of the series: "Rissa and her cousin Roger were away at a Surrey farm and the pony was with them. Tamzin had never missed her more." (p103). These events are chronicled in *The Wild One*. Phone calls between Westling Vicarage and Punchbowl Farm are rare in the books, but one can hardly believe that Tamzin's close friend Rissa and her cousin Roger would not been told of the accident and hurried to offer support. The reason is of course that although *The Wild One* opens in September, it was written before *A Wind is Blowing*, which opens in August.

Much of the action of the book takes place away from the familiar settings of Dunsford (Rye) and Westling (Rye Harbour). The book is largely set in Winklesea (Winchelsea), which features mainly as Meryon's home in the other books, and abroad in Barcelona. *A Wind is Blowing* may end on a positive note, but even young readers are left wondering whether Meryon's sight will ever truly recover enough for him to become a doctor with "everything as it was always going to be" (p215).

The manuscript of *A Wind is Blowing* was completed following Bill Edwards' appalling tractor accident on 27 August 1968, which Monica described in her penultimate book, *The Valley and the Farm* (1971). Following the accident, "I found myself completely unable to work at writing" *A Wind is Blowing* (*The Valley and the Farm*, Michael Joseph, 1971, p72). Her words about Bill's accident echo Tamzin's thoughts: "Something terrible happens and life seems almost to go on in the same way, so much that is normal must be done; but really it is all changed, one knows this, and it will never be the same again." This, and the absence of Geoffrey Whittam's usual line drawings, give *A Wind* a very different emotional tone to that of her previous Westling book, *Dolphin Summer*.

Other contributors of articles have written about corneal transplants and blindness, so this introduction focuses on the new settings of this story in Winchelsea, Rye and Barcelona.

The scene towards Rye Harbour from the viewpoint where Tamzin and Meryon look out over the Marsh

THAT DAY IN DUNSFORD

Late in the book, Meryon's mother refers to "That Day" (p198) in Dunsford, but it is hard to pinpoint exactly where the attack took place. Tamzin has been shopping and meets Meryon and his

converted hearse Emma at what appears to be the eastern end of the High Street, close to Hilders Cliff or Eastcliff and above the Belvedere viewpoint. All that we know about the bank, however, is that it has a "bare brick wall" (p95) and some steps down which the bank robber and his victim can fall. There are several candidates. The bank is presumably above the Land Gate, the ancient entrance to the town, since the last sentence of chapter 1 has Meryon being driven "straight down through the Land Gate . . ." (p96) towards the hospital. At the time of writing, Rye had several banks—and there must have been more then, whether then is the 1930s of Monica's childhood or the 1960s when *A Wind is Blowing* is set.

Two of several possible banks in Rye High Street where the raid could have taken place

The Land Gate is one of the ancient gateways into Rye built by Edward III. It was erected in 1329 and has a chamber over the arch and two towers. It once had gates, a portcullis and a drawbridge, suggesting that the town was then protected by a moat, making it a formidable barrier to any French wishing to break into the town. The erratic clock was erected in 1863 as a memorial to Queen Victoria's husband Prince Albert. George Chambers' 1887 guide to Rye comments wryly, "the good citizens who subscribed did not

27

Rye High Street
The medieval Land Gate at Rye

spend much on the decoration of their Albert Memorial clock".

The viewpoint or lookout was given to the town in 1935 by E.F. Benson when mayor of Rye. He immortalized Rye as Tilling in his Mapp and Lucia books, and the lookout offers any "well instructed tripper" (*A Wind is Blowing*, p92) a fine view "across the bright river with its little yachts and fishing boats, over the wide grazings flecked with sheep" towards Westling and Cloudesley (Camber) Castle. Malcolm Saville says that with the help of the telescope you can see "Dungeness Lighthouse, the noble tower of Lydd Church which was badly damaged in the last war and, on a fine day, the white cliffs of Dover" (*Portrait of Rye*, Chapter 3).

OFF TO BARCELONA

Barcelona is the setting for some of the most significant scenes in *A Wind is Blowing*, offering the reader a chance to experience life abroad. It is both a city and also a part of Catalonia, a maritime province in north-east Spain. The city is on the Mediterranean coast and is bordered to the north by the Pyrenees and the Sierra del Cadí. Meryon's aunt and uncle, Lucy and Ben, meet their death in a plane crash in the Sierra del Cadí while flying back from Algiers. The Sierra del Cadí (8,322 feet/2,536 metres) are a chain of mountains, close to the Pyrenees, which form a natural border between France and Spain. They are mined for coal, iron, copper, gold and salt.

Barcelona is today the second largest city in Spain, most famous for being the host city for the 1992 Summer Olympic Games and for its many buildings by the Art Nouveau architect Antoni Gaudí, including the cathedral of the Sagrada Familia. En route to Gatwick Airport, Tamzin and the Fairbrasses are given a lift by an actor who has a small part in a film called *The Bulls of Vilanova* (p184), which I have not been able to trace. This may have been a documentary about bull-fighting or the bull-running festival where bulls are let loose to run through the streets of Vilanova. On arrival in Barcelona they are held up on the way to the hospital in traffic on the Avenida de Jose. This is a wide road linking a number of villages around the coastal part of Barcelona and is today known as the Gran Via de les Corts Catalanes.

Seeking permission to use the corneas, the Fairbrasses and Tamzin visit the coroner's house "in a little street near ... the Parque de la Ciudadela" (p194) in the Gothic quarter of the city. For many years, this was the only park in the city. Ciudadela means "Citadel" and reflects the fact that it was built in the former grounds of the city's fortress. Its design is based on that of the Jardin de Luxembourg in Paris. It includes Barcelona Zoo, various buildings from the old fortress including the govenor's palace and the arsenal, and a *Monument to Walt Disney* by Núria Tortras erected in 1969, the year *A Wind is Blowing* was published.

In the days following Meryon's operation, the Fairbrass parents and Tamzin explore "the great port, full of shipping" and "the old zig-zag market and shopping streets, the *Ramblas*, where every kind of business and trade flourished, and you could buy cage-birds, fruit, books, clothes, or a Spanish guitar" (p204). Las Ramblas or La Rambla is a series of short streets in central Barcelona, now a pedestrian mall and popular for shopping with locals, tourists and pickpockets alike. Its name derives from the Spanish or Catalan for an intermittent water flow. The Spanish poet Federico García Lorca declared that La Rambla was "the only street in the world which I wish would never end". It contains the Liceu, Barcelona's world-famous opera house, a street market known as the Mercat de la Boqueria and the Font de Canaletes, the city's most famous fountain.

The Cathedral

The actor who gives Tamzin and the Fairbrasses a lift to the airport explains they must visit St George's Fountain in the cathedral garden in Barcelona, where people throw coins "to bring blessings for the blind" (p184). Tamzin thinks of it as "a kind of Mecca to which she had travelled, a pilgrim from afar" (p200). She asks if they can visit it on the day after the operation, and drops in her coin. The mossy fountain stands in the cloisters built in 1380–1451. It dates from the 15th century and is crowned by a small iron statue of St George (Sant Jordi) with the dragon. At the feast of Corpus Christi in early June there is a custom of blowing an egg and letting it spin on the fountain. The cathedral itself contains the chapel of St Lucy (Santa Llúcia), the saint of sight and vision. On her saint's day, 12 December, the blind come to pray at her chapel.

The cloisters are entered through the Portal de Santa Eulàlia; Monica Edwards explains the flock of geese in the cloisters is consecrated to St Eulalia. Eulalia was 13 years old when she was subjected to 13 tortures and martyred in ancient Rome during the reign of Emperor Diocletian; she and St George are the co-patron saints of the city, and the cathedral is dedicated to her. Like the sacred geese of Juno who helped save Rome from the Gauls in 387BC, the geese of Barcelona have guarded the cathedral and its treasures from attack since the medieval period by means of their general aggressiveness and loud cries. The cathedral was begun in 1298 and completed by 1448, apart from the main façade and dome, which were added in 1898 and 1913. The choir stalls date from 1340 and are decorated with the colourful coats-of-arms of the Barcelona Chapter of the Order of the Golden Fleece, an order of chivalry. They are indeed very beautiful, although "nobody wanted, on this day, to see the sights" (p200).

WEST TO WINKLESEA

Winklesea (Winchelsea) is first mentioned in *The Summer of the Great Secret* where Tamzin recalls that "Shepherd Tewmell had to come from Winklesea" (Chapter 11) because Taverner's Cottage, the tied cottage that came with his job, was haunted. It is mentioned throughout the Westling books, but usually with reference to the house where Meryon lives with his parents. It is frequently compounded with Winchelsea Beach, a village that now lies a couple of miles distant from the hilltop town. For example, in *Hidden in a Dream*, Meryon is said to have swum from Winklesea before his concussion.

Very few episodes in the series before *A Wind is Blowing* are set in Winklesea, with the exceptions of *The Midnight Horse* and *The White Riders*. Meryon and Rissa share the task of driving "Through the New Gate and into Winklesea, terrified of sudden discovery as they drove through the town, but every citizen was indoors out of the gale and most probably asleep in bed" (*The White Riders*, Chapter 16).

Winchelsea is one of the seven ancient Cinque Ports. Hastings, Romney, Hythe, Dover and Sandwich were the original Cinque Ports, and Rye and Winchelsea were added late in the 11th century. The first Winchelsea

Sign of the New Inn at Winchelsea showing the grid pattern of the town

stood on a low-lying island, some three miles south-east of Iham. Its exact location is not known, but the town was very vulnerable to sea damage. It was partly submerged by a very high tide in October 1250 and virtually destroyed in the Great Storm of 1287. A new town was built high on the hill of Iham in the reign of Edward I. The town was planned on a grid pattern—originally there were 39 squares—based around a great churchyard and church in the centre of the town dedicated to St Thomas à Becket of Canterbury.

The chief drama of *The Midnight Horse* focuses around the Winklesea pageant of scenes from Sussex history. Mike Merrow reports that it is "going to be a slap-up affair with hundreds of performers and that" (*The Midnight Horse*, Chapter 2) in aid of Hastings hospitals. The pageant runs "for the whole of the first week in August. Winklesea went mad for it. All the sober little town was hung with flags and bunting and streamers" (Chapter 11).

The third episode of the pageant concerns "the Defence of Winklesea, and all were in the fighting except Sara, who was a Winklesea girl giving warning of the approach of French ships in the bay" (Chapter 11). "The kindly Rector of Winklesea took the part of the Abbot of Battle who was called so imperiously by the French, fresh from the sack and burning of the sister port of Dunsford, to defend the town if he could" (Chapter 11). This is presumably the attack of 1377, when the Abbot of Battle Abbey, Hastings, led his own men to the defence of Winchelsea while Rye burnt. The attack was made during the Hundred Years War by the Castilian fleet of Admiral Sánchez since Castile was then allied to France, so French soldiers may have been among the attackers. It was probably during this attack that the parish church was burnt to the ground.

Winchelsea was vulnerable to attack for very many years. It was a walled city and three 14th-century gates survive to this day—Strand Gate, Pipewell Gate and New Gate. Winchelsea and Rye were last attacked by the French in 1449, but fear of invasion continued. In 1794, Winchelsea was garrisoned at the outbreak of war with France, and again in 1940 during the Second World War.

Winchelsea appears throughout the series, most frequently as Meryon's home or because of its hill: "Riding up the steep hill into Winklesea Tamzin looked down over the green world where she had been riding. The sheep now were like a million button mushrooms as far as she could see" (*The Hoodwinkers*, Chapter 19). Also in *The Hoodwinkers*, Meryon goes babysitting in a house opposite the church and Rissa scrubs out a wine cellar. Mrs Venus's sister-in-law lives in Winklesea and Rose Jarvis is the girl who served in the grocer's shop on Winklesea High Street (Chapter 11).

There are several references to the Town Records. Meryon takes pride in "his sea-going ancestors; especially, perhaps, of one, Tonkin Fairbrass, who had been a notorious pirate, as could be read by anyone in the Winklesea Town Records." (*Operation Seabird*, Chapter 1). In *The Midnight Horse*, Meryon explains that "when he had sons of his own he meant to christen them all Tonkin (Chapter 5). Tamzin finds this rather muddling.

In more modern times, various well-known people have been associated with Winchelsea. The Pre-Raphaelite John Everett Millais painted *The Random Shot* and *The Blind Girl* here. The comedian and author Spike Milligan lies in the churchyard. In 1896 the actress Ellen Terry bought a house in Winchelsea, and the writer Ford Madox Ford moved there in 1901. Children's writer Malcolm Saville, creator of the Lone Pine books, lived here, and a plaque to his memory was erected on Chelsea Cottage where he lived from 1971–82. His ashes are buried in the Garden of Remembrance at Winchelsea Church.

The Search for Meryon's House

Meryon lived at "the house with green shutters next but one to Winklesea Rectory" (*The Midnight Horse*, Chapter 5). In *The White Riders*, Tamzin and Rissa drive via Strand Gate and "drove down Rectory Lane under a shower of brown and golden leaves." They draw up at Meryon's gate and find that "Both boys were in the field beyond the house playing bicycle polo with a croquet ball and mallets" (*The White Riders*, Chapter 2). In the last 40 years trees have grown up, and much of the land in Winchelsea is in private hands, making it hard to pinpoint exactly where Meryon's house was—

Rectory Lane, Winchelsea

always supposing, of course, that it was a real house and not a fictional creation.

It appears that Meryon's house is on or off Rectory Lane, but not in the centre of the town. A reference in *No Going Back* has Meryon and Roger "driving the hearse along the narrow lane from his home into Winklesea" (Chapter 11), and since he passes three cars on the way this suggests the house lies a little way out of the main town. They get caught in a funeral procession, turn into Dead Man's Lane ("scene of an old and bitter massacre by the raiding French", and then into Winklesea High Street. The boys eventually "turned down towards the Strand Gate, with its hawk's-eye view of the western reaches of the Marsh. Meryon's attention was absorbed in negotiating the ancient gateway, whose stone arch straddled the road right on the corner, but Roger could lean forward and look out across the green spread of fabulous grazings."

In *A Wind is Blowing*, we learn that the garden has a south wall and that the view from the garden shows Camber/ Cloudesley Castle, Redshanks' Pool,

The Strand Gate

Dunsmere and Dungeness. Tamzin says: "Castle [presumably Castle Farm] flock is lying in the shade of the walls, but there's a flock at Redshanks' Pool, changing pasture" (Chapter 9). At the end of the book Tamzin and Meryon "look out at the marsh": Tamzin "was staring away to the sea, beyond Cloudesley Castle" (Chapter 18). The following passage indicates the route to his house from Castle Farm and Dunsford:

> Mrs. Fairbrass took the sharp bend at the bottom of the Strand Hill and changed down as the Rover leapt to the steep gradient. … At the hilltop the car turned under the arch of the immensely strong stone Strand Gate that had stood there through six centuries. … Mrs. Fairbrass wove the big car through the traffic of the little town's main street. … She cut-in and was shouted at near the ancient church. … the Rover took the right-angled turn out of the street to a quieter lane. … She turned into the drive of the Fairbrass house and pulled up." (Chapter 12)

The house itself is described as old: "The orange-red tiles of the roof came halfway down the walls as well, in the Sussex tradition. The woodwork was all white, and an evergreen magnolia climbed round the south windows, holding up its white globes among polished leaves" (Chapter 3). Unfortunately, if one ignores the presence of the magnolia, this description fits a number of houses in Rectory Lane quite well.

Tile-hung houses seen from the churchyard in Winchelsea

Possible site of Meryon's house

Putting all these clues together, and drawing on conversations with Tom Ashmore and other parishioners at Winchelsea Church one Sunday morning, we left church and headed south-west through the churchyard, keeping Wesley's Tree, where he preached his last sermon in 1790, to our right. We left the churchyard by the exit at the crossing of German Street and Back Lane. We headed west along Back Lane and turned left into Rectory Lane, seeking out Dead Man's Lane (marked on maps as Hogtrough Lane) and the site of St Giles' Church and the Old Rectory on the right, where we found a house that would do very well as the Fairbrass house. Please respect the fact that this is a private house.

Winchelsea Church

The Church of St Thomas the Martyr of Canterbury was founded by King Edward I in the 13th century, and it was planned on a grand scale. It stands in two acres on the crown of the hill and was intended to be the most magnificent church in the neighbourhood. Stone was imported from Caen in Normandy, marble from West Sussex and from the ruins of Old Winchelsea. Much of the church was probably destroyed in the raid of 1377, and only the chancel and chapels survived.

St Thomas the Martyr, Winchelsea

Winchelsea, then a larger town than Rye, had at least two other churches, including St Giles and St Leonard (at Iham). *Strangers to the Marsh* records that "Roger was at Winklesea, a church old and bloodstained too: the town still talked of the dark day in the third Edward's reign when three thousand Norman raiders surprised the citizens during Mass, dragging them from their worship with a very great slaughter, so that a near-by street is still called Dead Man's Lane" (Chapter 15). This was the attack one Sunday in 1359, when the French killed many members of the church of St Giles, now the site of the Old Rectory. For the sake of her story, or not unnaturally confusing St Giles' with St Thomas', Monica Edwards has sent Roger to morning service in a church that no longer exists.

The decay of Winchelsea as a port led to the decline of the church. The 17th-century diarist John Evelyn records that he found "forlorn ruins" there. From 1850 onwards considerable restoration work was carried out, and St Thomas' Church today is a harmonious building of medieval mastery and bright glass. Embroidered hassocks, including one to Malcolm Saville, remind one of the Monica Edwards hassocks in Guildford Cathedral.

Right: Part of Douglas Strachan's window commemorating the *Mary Stanford* Lifeboat Disaster

Below: detail showing the tiny lifeboat battling with the waves

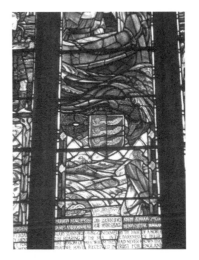

Douglas Strachan (1875–1950), who designed the windows for the Scottish National War Memorial in Edinburgh Castle and for the Palace of Peace at The Hague, worked on several windows in Winchelsea Church. According to his daughter Una D. Wallace, they visited the church while on a motoring tour in the 1920s. When they went into the church his daughters exclaimed, "Daddy, look at all those lovely empty windows for you to fill." A week after they returned home, Strachan was commissioned to fill some of the windows in the church.

The first window to be completed was that over the sedilia in the south wall commemorating the *Mary Stanford* Lifeboat Disaster of 1928. The central light shows Christ stilling the tempest, on the right is St Augustine of Canterbury landing in AD597, and on the left St Nicholas, patron saint of sailors and children. Panels above show the pelican and phoenix—symbols of self-sacrifice and Resurrection. At the bottom of the window, across all three panels, runs a dramatic story—a small lifeboat forges its way through angry seas, watched anxiously by figures on the shore. The window, plus five others,

39

were dedicated together in May 1931, in a magnificent ceremony officiated over by the Archbishop of Canterbury and the Bishop of Chichester, with the world-famous Temple Choir in London singing "Heraclitus". Monica's father, the Revd Harry Newton, was Vicar of Rye Harbour until September 1936, so one imagines that he, and perhaps his wife and daughter, attended the service. Many years later she was to commemorate the men of the *Mary Stanford* in *Storm Ahead*, perhaps her most significant work.

Joy Wotton, 2009

Mary Stanford Memorial

A PERSONAL INTRODUCTION

If you are about to read this book you will probably know that it deals with the subject of corneal donation and the possibility of restoring sight through a corneal transplant. During 2008 there were 2,634 corneal transplants in the UK.* All of those who had their sight restored will be aware that they owe this gift to the surgeons and other medical and nursing staff who performed the operation, to the donors who generously allowed their corneas to be used after their death and to the next of kin of the donors, who gave consent for the donation to take place. Two people, though they will probably never know this, also owe their restored sight—to some extent at least—to Monica Edwards!

Let me explain. It may take a while, so if you're in a hurry, just skip this bit and go on to Shelley Edwards's fascinating preface. Read this later, or not at all. I'm not a professional writer, and, although I loved her books and read as many of them as I could get hold of as a child, I'm not an authority on Monica Edwards and her writing. I never had the privilege of meeting her. I'm just an ordinary woman with a rather sad tale to tell. I'm honoured to have been asked to tell it here.

I first read *A Wind is Blowing* in the early 1970s. I was about 12 years old at the time, at secondary school at Folkestone in Kent, where I borrowed the book from the school library. It was my first introduction to Monica Edwards's writing. I loved it! Over the next few years I borrowed Monica Edwards books from the school library and the public library in Folkestone and read and reread them. I

* Statistics prepared by NHS Blood and Transplant from the National Transplant Database maintained on behalf of transplant services in the UK and Ireland.

tried to buy some with Christmas and birthday money, but by that time many of them were already out of print. Staff at bookshops in Folkestone and Canterbury had sometimes not even heard of Monica Edwards. Did I mean Monica Dickens? I managed to buy Armada copies of several of the Punchbowl Farm series, and over the years I acquired very battered copies of *The White Riders*, *Cargo of Horses* and, much later, *Wish for a Pony*. I loved all of them.

The Romney Marsh books were and still are my favourites. I didn't know that 'Dunsford' was Rye or that 'Westling' was Rye Harbour, but I had visited Romney Marsh sometimes with my parents and my two brothers. We had a relative who had a farm there, and every summer my brothers would go camping on the Marsh with the Boy Scouts. I also remember being taken on the Romney, Hythe & Dymchurch Railway, which is mentioned in *Operation Seabird*. It's hard to explain just why I loved those books so much or why the memory of reading them all those years ago is still with me. I envied Tamzin and Rissa for their ponies (my own horse-riding adventures did not start until much later). Tamzin was my favourite character. I loved her for her honesty and courage. Meryon, of course, was a true hero—good looking, funny, level headed, intelligent yet unassuming. What more could a girl want!

Perhaps I was unusual in that I began at the end of the Romney Marsh series with *A Wind is Blowing*. I think one of the reasons this book made such an impression on me was because my grandmother, one of my favourite people in the world, was partially sighted. Her sight was affected first by cataracts, and then she lost the sight of one eye completely due to a detached retina. Despite several eye operations the surgeons were unable to improve her sight significantly. She bore her disability with great courage and even cheerfulness. What irked her most was having to rely on others to do things for her. Like Meryon, she was fiercely independent. I understood that nothing could be done to restore her sight, but it seemed a dreadful thing to me that there were people who could have had their sight restored, but who were blind just because, as Meryon tells Tamzin, "'There are never enough corneas to go round. There's a waiting list.'" Reading *A Wind is Blowing* convinced me that having a donor card was the right thing for me to do.

In 1969, the year *A Wind is Blowing* was first published, corneal transplants were far less common and the operation was a more complicated and difficult procedure than it is today. We live in a very different world 40 years later, but still there are never enough donated corneas to go round. There's still a waiting list. People who could have their sight restored still remain blind while they wait for a cornea to become available, but today the transplant itself is usually a comparatively straightforward operation, performed in about an hour.

Most of us are in favour of organ donation, it seems, in theory at least. Yet, so often, registering to be a donor or carrying a card and discussing our views with our families is something we don't get round to. Even when a person has filled in the card and registered to be a donor, at the time of their death their next of kin may also be asked to give consent, usually while shocked and distressed by this very recent bereavement. And nowadays, in order to protect the potential recipient from the risk of AIDS, the next of kin of the organ or tissue donor must answer a number of questions concerning the 'lifestyle' of the donor. Some of these are of a very intimate and personal nature, and to have to go through all this just minutes or hours after someone you love so much has died is very distressing.

I know this because I was in just that situation myself in January 2008. My husband, Dave, had been diagnosed with renal cancer the previous November. His diagnosis was a tremendous shock. He had been suffering from rheumatoid arthritis for about ten years, but apart from that he was fit and well, still managing to work full time at a demanding job and still enjoying life. After his diagnosis it was suggested that, as one kidney was still apparently healthy, his life might be saved by an operation to remove the diseased kidney combined with chemotherapy. Just before Christmas, however, we were told that even if the proposed treatment went ahead his disease would still be terminal, and that without treatment he would probably live until the summer. In fact his disease was more advanced than anyone knew, and his condition deteriorated rapidly. We lived in a nightmare world, attempting to come to terms with this horrendous news and, worst of all, trying to explain it all to our four children: our eldest son was 16 and our next son 14, and we had twins, a girl and a boy of 11. I witnessed Dave's suffering for the next few weeks, helpless to do anything to alleviate it. The drugs he was prescribed helped with the pain but did not make it go away, and the side effects were horrible and terrifying. Early in the New Year he was admitted to hospital, initially to have his drugs stabilised. Five days later he died there while I held his hand.

Memories of that terrible time still haunt me more than a year later. The doctor who attended my husband at the time of his death explained to me that because of the way he had died the only body parts suitable for donation were the corneas of his eyes. Dave and I had discussed organ donation years before, and were both in favour of it. He carried a donor card. I was told I would need to answer some questions over the phone so that the retrieval of the corneas could go ahead the next day.

I was utterly distraught and grief stricken, and exhausted from lack of sleep and the shock and trauma of the last few weeks. Since Dave's admission to hospital I had been torn between wanting to be with him all the time and the need to try to comfort and care for our children. The hospital was 80 miles from where we lived and I had been rushing from home to hospital and back again over the last few days. It was my birthday, too—it seemed a strange coincidence that my husband had left the world on the same date that I had come into it (I was 48 years old and Dave was 53). All I wanted to do was get away from that hospital, go home and be with the children, break the news to them, weep until I could weep no more, and then seek oblivion, if only temporarily, in sleep. The last thing I needed was to have to wait around and answer a string of questions. I was tempted to say I couldn't do it. At that stage I had no idea whether the corneas would be suitable for donation. The possibility that through my staying at the hospital and answering all these questions someone somewhere might one day regain their sight seemed remote. However, although it was some thirty-five years since I had read it, the memory of *A Wind is Blowing* came back to me. Surely Tamzin would have had the strength to do the right thing rather than the easiest thing? I was very fortunate in that the doctor, all the nursing staff and the transplant coordinator who asked the questions over the telephone handled everything with great sensitivity and compassion. I managed to get through all the questions and give my consent.

The transplant coordinator wanted to know if I would like to be informed about the outcome of the corneal donation. Would I like to be told whether the corneas had been suitable for donation, and, if so, whether the transplant operations had been successful? My initial reaction was that I did not want to know. I had played my small part and everything was now out of my hands. Then it occurred to me that I would have to tell the children about the donation. We had kept them informed about everything to do with Dave's illness from the start, told them as much as they could understand and tried to answer all their questions honestly. Perhaps they would be comforted by the thought that something positive had come out of their father's death, if it all worked out of course. Even if it didn't they would know that their father and I had done our best, done what we believed to be the right thing. So I asked to be informed by letter. I was told that it would be at least six weeks before I had any news. Provided the retrieval went ahead successfully, the corneas would be stored at the Manchester eye bank for up to four weeks.

In fact it was more than three months until we had any news. Then in mid April I had the long-awaited letter:

> I'm pleased to be able to tell you that both corneas were successfully transplanted. As a result of David's generosity two people have now had their sight restored. One cornea was transplanted into a 29 year old lady from the midlands and the other was allocated to a 28 year old female from the north of England.

I read the words over and over again. So, it had worked! It was the best news I could possibly have had. All the same, alone in the house, with the children away at school, I sat at the scrubbed pine kitchen table and wept for a long time. Our three Labradors and the cat eyed me with concern from their place on the window seat.

Later I emailed the transplant coordinator to let her know how pleased I was. 'My husband was a great one for hoarding anything that might one day come in useful,' I wrote. 'I am sure he would have been delighted to know that a part of his body that would otherwise have been discarded had benefitted two people in this way!'

I also wrote to the wonderful doctor at the hospital where he died. It was she who had thought to ask me about our views on donation when Dave died. Had she not done so it would never have happened. I would not have had the presence of mind to think of it at that time. She was kind enough to telephone me after she received my letter to tell me how pleased she was.

The children were pleased, too. I had explained to them about the donation just after Dave's death. When they got home from school I was able to tell them about these two young women who could now see again. I wanted them to realise what a wonderful thing it was that had happened. I also needed them to understand that when I die I want my organs and corneas to be donated, though I was careful to stress that I hoped that would not be for a long time! Our children are now my next of kin. I wanted to reread *A Wind is Blowing* myself and to read it to the two younger children. Our twins had celebrated their 12th birthday in February and were about the same age as I had been when I first read it.

So began my search for a copy of the book. I knew that it was out of print, but in my ignorance I had no idea how few copies had been printed in the first place, or that, because it was so rare, copies were now collectors' items and changing hands for a lot of money. Dave had managed to find me several books which were out of print through Internet searches, and they had not been too expensive. I could not find a copy of *A Wind is Blowing*, though. Kind friends promised to look out for it in charity shops and second-hand book shops in Kent. I discovered that there was a small publishing firm called Girls Gone By who had republished some of Monica Edwards's books, but it seemed that *A Wind is Blowing* was not one of them. I emailed them asking if they had any plans to republish this book, and I was very pleased to hear from Clarissa Cridland that they did intend to, but not for more than a year. I wanted a copy to read now. I emailed Clarissa, explaining why I so much wanted a copy of the book and asking her to let me know if she happened to hear of a second-hand copy.

I then discovered John Allsup's website, [which sadly, in 2023 no longer exists]. I was astonished to learn how many fellow Monica Edwards fans there are. Still unaware that second-hand copies were selling for several hundred pounds on the Internet, I put a message on the Guestbook, asking if anyone had a copy of *A Wind is Blowing* they would be prepared to sell or even lend me. I explained that I wanted the book to read to my children 'for a special reason'. Almost immediately I had an email from a generous reader. She could not bear to sell her treasured copy, she said, but she would be happy to lend it to me. Delighted and very touched by her generosity I emailed her back, thanking her for this kind offer and explaining why I so much wanted to get hold of a copy of the book. I received a very kind message back by email and then the book itself, carefully wrapped in tissue paper! Strangely I also had an email from Clarissa that same day, apologising for not replying to my last one earlier, and saying how sorry she was to hear of my husband's death and that she would let me know if she heard of a second-hand copy of *A Wind is Blowing* for sale. I replied with the good news that I now had a copy of the book to read on loan, and told her that I would order the GGBP edition once it became available and that I also intended to order some of the Monica Edwards books that they had already published.

That evening I read the first chapter of *A Wind is Blowing* to my twins. I had read to all my children long after they could read for themselves, simply because we enjoy sharing books so much (some years earlier I had read my two older boys my falling-to-pieces copies of the Punchbowl Farm books). I read a chapter aloud to the twins each night. Needless to say, I had also read the whole book myself within a day of its arrival! By that time I had realised how much money it was worth. I'd promised that I would take the greatest care of it, and so I did, wrapping it back up in its tissue paper as soon as we had finished reading, and putting it away in a drawer in my bedroom each evening. My twins enjoyed it, becoming engrossed in the story as I had done all those years ago. I believe it made them think about what it would be like to be blind and what a difference being able to see again would make to someone's life. Once we had finished the last chapter I wrapped the book up in its tissue paper for the last time, put it in a padded bag together with thank-you notes from all of us, and returned it to its owner by Special Delivery. How relieved I was when she emailed me to say it had arrived safely!

So many memories came back to me as I read the book. Inevitably there were sad ones, remembering the evening of Dave's death and all those questions … but so many happy ones, too! Of childhood visits to Romney Marsh, and of learning to ride later as a young adult. I was never much of a

Our Wedding Day

horsewoman, but I loved my riding and it was a wonderful way to see the Kent countryside. And then came the later memories, of the time after I met Dave. We were not quite childhood sweethearts like Tamzin and Meryon. We met when I was 19 and he was 25, but that seems young when looked back on from middle age. I was smitten from the start! He was good looking, funny, level headed, intelligent yet unassuming … I had given up my long fair plaits by that time! I remembered trips out in the little fishing dinghy Dave kept beached at Hythe, and how as we fished we would look back at the coast and Romney Marsh, with the towers and spires of churches visible above the grazings dotted with the famous Romney sheep. Later we had bought the first dog we owned together, a very lively Springer Spaniel puppy, from some people near 'Winklesea'. I remembered a visit to 'Dunsford', walking up the steep cobbled hill and peering into antique shop windows. We had gone riding over the marsh from stables at Ruckinge. Dave was much better on a horse than either Meryon or me! I remembered gazing down at Romney Marsh, spread out before us, from the walls of Lympne Castle, just as Meryon and Tamzin had from the garden wall of his house (we were seeing it from the Kent side rather than the Sussex side, of course). Then there were memories of our last visit to the Marsh, of taking the children on the Romney, Hythe & Dymchurch Railway in the spring of 2001 and eating fish and chips beside the Royal Military Canal at Hythe afterwards.

Dave with our first son, Richard

Since childhood I had loved reading, and it had been a comfort and a solace in times of trouble. I had always had the ability to lose myself in a good book, and this had provided an escape and a respite when I had suffered previous bereavements. This time, though, my grief was all consuming and completely overwhelming. I lacked the ability to concentrate enough to read even the most lightweight of fiction. I would quite literally 'lose the plot'! I turned the pages, but I was totally unaware of what I had read, unable to remember who the characters were or care what was happening to them. Yet I had read and enjoyed *A Wind is Blowing*. Out came my dog-eared Armada paperbacks and I reread them all. I also managed to collect and read all the delightful GGBP editions with their interesting introductions. Some I clearly remembered reading before and others I was coming to for the first time. Brian Parks's *Romney Marsh Companion* also held my attention from start to finish. Here was a brief escape from my grief and my worries over all the practical difficulties I was facing.

As well as reading the books I was a frequent visitor to John Allsup's website. Reading through the comments in the Guestbook made it obvious what a huge influence Monica Edwards's writing had had on so many lives. It seemed I wasn't the only 'grown-up' still avidly reading her books, either! Looking back I wondered about the way reading her books had affected my own life, not just through my recent experiences but much earlier. Once I started earning my own money almost the first things I spent it on were riding lessons and a Siamese kitten! I wondered whether it was reading *Black Hunting Whip*, the story of the Thorntons buying the beautiful but dilapidated Punchbowl Farm and gradually turning it into a wonderful family home, that had made me long to do something similar. Fortunately it was a dream Dave shared, though he didn't read that book until years later. In 1989, ten years after we met and a year after we married, we managed to start to make that dream come true. 'A ruined farmhouse with seventy wild acres' was way beyond our means, but we moved to Scotland and bought a row of derelict farm cottages with one acre of rather boggy land. We kept hens and I grew vegetables. Like the Thorntons, for a while we had no electricity or gas, and the water came from a well where every bucket had to be drawn up! For the first 18 months we lived in a small touring caravan with our Winklesea spaniel, while builders replaced the leaking roof and rebuilt two extensions which were falling down and beyond repair. We did a lot of the work ourselves,

Our cottage in Scotland, after restoration

51

and 18 years later, when Dave was diagnosed with cancer, we had at last got it just about as we'd always wanted it, a comfortable family home. Just like the Thorntons we had four children by that time, too.

I feel I owe a debt of gratitude to Monica Edwards for all the enjoyment her books have given me and for the part they have played in my 'healing process'. Without the memory of *A Wind is Blowing* that awful evening at the hospital I might never have had the strength to give consent for the corneal donation. I think I would have regretted it for the rest of my life if I had not done so. My husband lives on, not only in our memories, but in some way

Sons Richard and George, aged about seven and five, with the catch of the day

through his eyes being used to help others. That thought has given me great comfort and satisfaction. I sometimes wonder what Monica would think if she knew about all this happening ten years after her death. I hope she would be pleased.

The subject of organ donation is an emotive one. When Dave and I were young and healthy and expecting to have many more years of married life ahead of us, it was easy for us to joke that anyone was welcome to whatever bits of us would be of use when we died. It seemed to us a really useful type of recycling! This was something we tried to do in our everyday lives long before the whole concept became fashionable as it is today. As we renovated our cottage we reused materials as much as we could. The old bricks from a dividing wall that we had removed to make two small rooms into one large kitchen were used for the fireplace I built to house the Rayburn (my first attempt at bricklaying!). The beam we used over the top of the bricks was a piece of timber we found washed up on the shore. Dave built a much more impressive fireplace in the sitting room from local stone we found lying around the place. When our eldest son grew out of his cot and needed a proper bed we bought recycled timbers at a local scrap yard and Dave made one for him. He did the same for our second son when the time came. Many of our clothes

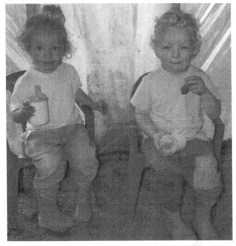

Twins Annis and Patrick having a picnic in the polytunnel in my vegetable garden

and books came from charity shops. Dave had a genius for mending things, and nothing was thrown away if it could be repaired and still be of use to us. Visits to the bottle bank were incorporated into shopping trips, and I enthusiastically made marvellous compost from all our vegetable waste and the contents of the henhouse whenever it was cleaned out. We tried to be as self-sufficient as we could. As well as the vegetables I grew, and eggs from our hens, our diet was supplemented by fish that Dave caught and rabbits he shot.

When my husband died I tried to explain to our children that the part of him that was truly him, his soul or his spirit, had gone, though

I did not know where. The part that we were going to bury, his body, was not really him, just what was left behind after the important bit had left it. What happened to it did not really matter, though it should be treated with respect because it had once contained a human soul. Although I honestly believe that, going through with the decision to allow the corneal donation and the thought of all that it entailed was not easy for me at the time.

For various reasons some people are totally opposed to the idea of organ or tissue donation. I would never try to persuade anyone who feels this way that they should change their mind. However, many people have never given the matter any serious thought. I believe that all of us should give it careful consideration, so that we can discuss our thoughts and hopes with our loved ones. Anyone who is interested in the subject and would like to know more can visit www.organdonation.nhs.uk, a site that I found most helpful while I was writing this. I was especially moved by the 'Life Stories' of some of the recipients of donated corneas. One story was of particular interest: that of a young man whose sight had become so poor that without corneal transplants he would have been unable to fulfil his dream to become a doctor. He is now fully qualified and working as an anaesthetist. I wonder in what field of medicine the fictional Meryon would have worked after his years at Cambridge?

Sally Bourne, 2009

Postscript, 2023

It's now fifteen years since my husband's death and the corneal donation. Our children are all quite grown up. We moved house ten years ago and renovated an old farmhouse where I have a little flower farm and a tiny business, Flowers of the Forest selling my cut flowers. No horses, but a dog, a cat and various poultry.

PREFACE

During the mid 1960s I joined the trend for sending taped letters, or tapesponding as it was known. I sent tapes to both blind and sighted people. A few years later, Mother was incubating a heroic plot for Meryon. Well, it's obvious really—but I won't give away the story.

Rissa and Roger were bundled off to Punchbowl Farm so that Mother could concentrate on Meryon's tragedy. She became deeply involved in a lot of interesting research. Meeting Mr Ashman, the dedicatee, proved the most inspirational. I heard so much about him, how he navigated his way around his vegetable garden, and had trained his two guide dogs. I don't know how she came to hear of him, but it was unusual for Mother to go and meet anyone.

On visits to the farm I told Mother all about my own tapesponding experiences. Notes must have been taken, probably at leisure in the garden after I'd gone, as there was little need for surreptitious note taking on 'shopping lists' by then. She heard all about the difficulties of my first attempts at talking into the mike and then playing it back disbelievingly ("'That can't be my voice!'", as Tamzin exclaims—(see p119). My own children hid behind the door and recorded my singing practice—so embarrassing. Mind you, the sound quality was not enhanced—but I couldn't have been *that* tinny.

The arrival of the first 'small padded packet' (see p120) was as exciting for me as it is for Tamzin. It came just after the children had gone to school; so there I was, sitting over the remains of breakfast, watched by two anticipatory dogs. This first tape was from a gentle married couple, both blind.

My second tapespondent was a young, blind bachelor called John. I invited him, with his Labrador, to lunch (peas were a poor choice) and collected him from the station. It was John's story of the over-helpful woman forcefully trying to direct him, and then tripping over, that Mother used for Meryon and Mrs March (see 157). I can well understand the feeling and the fall, having followed John up Guildford's North Street ('Meg set such a pace'). The crowds parted like the Red Sea as the three of us tore up the steep hill.

The tall and ginger Simon was Mother's invention. He notices that "'[a]ll the rooms have a different kind of sound'" (p140). Just what I found: it seems obvious, but it was still a surprise at the time and it made me more conscious of acoustics.

It was John who commented about the birdsong on my first tape to him that I had recorded outside, as Tamzin does. I hadn't even noticed it, but then I was concentrating hard on what I was saying, so I wouldn't have asked 'Do you know what that bird is?'. Mother had mentally segued to waves and seagulls. She was very good at identifying birdsong and tried to instruct me. (I'm still trying to remember the bird that sings the repetitive 'squeaky pram' song.* There's one in my road to taunt me and to remind me of her.) One summer's day at Kew Gardens with my children I rushed the wrong way up the spiral staircase in the Palm House, mike outstretched, in pursuit of a blackbird. Playing it back, sitting outside on the grass, we were thrilled when we realised nearby birds had joined in. Years later, my stroll around a German park was enhanced by liberal birdsong, until I spotted the speakers in the trees and realised it was 'piped'. I was amused to read that Americans have stopped using taped birdsong in their golf broadcasts since they were rumbled by twitchers.

Mother must have gone round, as I did, 'catching' suitable sounds:

* After I wrote that I resorted to Googling birdsong and managed to identify the squeaking bird. It's a metallic, two-note song. No doubt about it—that's a great tit!

'The digging made satisfying cracking and crumbling noises' (see p117); "'I never knew how many sounds there are until I started thinking about them'" (pxx). I took my tape recorder down to the stream in the valley to record a rippling background for my letters. At home the doorbell spurred the dogs into frenzied barking, breaking into my tape like fireworks. My father wanted such a tape as a burglar alarm for the dog-less bungalow. Mother, no doubt thinking of the cats, vetoed the idea.

Mother did own a large reel-to-reel tape recorder that she used for music. When Tamzin began her tape to Meryon with guitar music, it was with one of Mother's favourites. "'The man who wrote it was blind from three years old, the *Radio Times* says. He's called Rodrigo, and the music is the *Concerto de Aranjuez* …'" (see p118).

But Tamzin's account of the drifting willow herb seeds—"'You could think they were a fleet of flying saucers, the way they look with the sun behind them—very bright and round. You could easily think they were miles away …'" (see p116)—was far more mundane than Mother's original and excited account to me. That hot afternoon she had uncharacteristically lain down on the sloping side of Barn Field, looking dozily skywards. She was profoundly shocked when she saw a huge flying saucer hovering overhead, 'very bright and round'. Safely back in the farm kitchen, she gradually returned to normal as she told me how she had felt. Then she talked about the illusions of scale and distance. It's a wonder she didn't start writing science fiction.

In retrospect, Tamzin's 'running commentaries' for Meryon seem prescient. The grown-up Tamzin/Lindsey/Shelley did exactly the same for both parents after they lost their sight.

My father's attitude to his blindness was different from Mother's. He relished the kindly attention he got from complete strangers, especially at agricultural shows. His white stick, white hair and attendance at the show marked him out as a blind retired farmer, keen to reminisce. His official white symbol stick was quickly found to be useless, as the wretched thing was not weight bearing, but folded, as it was designed to do, whenever Dad leant on it. He was disgusted, found a proper stick and somehow painted it, and much else, white. The result was safe and effective. He was always keen to extract any concessions, regarding each one as a victory.

Mother also made sure she took advantage of such offers, but taking her to a ploughing match at Singleton was a far more serious affair. She had always loved heavy horses and duly stroked one or two, but it was obvious that such a sunny, bright day was, for her, dark in more than one way. In my mind I can see the photos I took of her that day but no longer have.

Her attitude to driving was alarming. There had been a narrow miss with a manned wheelbarrow that she had not seen until almost too late. She casually explained that it was like driving in a mist. I

My parents when retired, with a neighbourly dog

was horrified, both by the fact that legally she could go on driving (unlike in some other countries) and by her reasonable-sounding answer to my remonstrations: 'But people do drive in the mist.' A personal mist, I insisted, was quite different.

I'm sure that she was influenced by the thought of Mr Ashman when she eventually applied to the Guide Dogs for the Blind Association for a guide dog. This reversed the situation in the book. Meryon says: '"I had the offer of an Institute trained dog"'; Tamzin answers: '"You turned it down, of course."' I contacted the RNIB but they don't keep records of unsuccessful applicants indefinitely, and were unable to help.

That Mother wrote so engagingly about Meg was both surprising and funny—she, who never really took to dogs. I think she adapted some cat behaviour, such as the pouncing and the bringing of presents.

This is the only book without illustrations, and despite my endless annotations it is difficult to recap on events when required. There are no chapter titles either—no help at all. Nor is the cover even approximately accurate. Brian Parks quotes John Allsup in *The Romney Marsh Companion* as saying that 'Jawdokimov was apparently not well briefed on the Romney Marsh geography', a circumspect and apposite comment.

I do remember letters going to and from Collins about various artists on occasion, though not especially about this book. Mother was pernickety over correct detail. We had arguments over photographic representation versus artistic. She disliked Victorian paintings, especially of exaggerated views, and sentimental themes. (Victorian buildings were equally unappreciated. Maybe she was too close to that era.) She would examine each proposed illustration minutely, commenting on such things as the details of bridles. She often complained about hooves being 'blocky': there was good reason why I, like Tamzin, drew horses standing in long grass.

However, I think the real reason for the lack of illustrations in this book was that Collins felt it would be less trouble, and cheaper, to try without. Tunnicliffe, for instance, was considered expensive and they were reluctant to use him again.

There once was a scheme to put all the books on disc, and I often think how useful a computerised search function would be. But then there is Brian Parks, Mother's biographer, who is a multi-book search engine.

In Chapter Eleven I came across a little scene I remember so well: myself, when about Tamzin's age, in our stable with Tarquin (14.2 hands) resting his black head on my shoulder until his long jawbones dug in uncomfortably. I came up to tell Mother, whose hand and mind must have reached towards the kitchen drawer. She kept that note for about 19 years, and changed

Myself on Tarquin

the pony to Banner (p169). Banner was loosely based on Red Clover, my younger brother's pony, and was only 13.2 hands high. That 'small scruffy brown pony' could not have made such a gesture naturally, especially as I was already quite tall (see the photograph on p61).

When I was about Tamzin's age I had been puzzled to hear Mother telling friends how she had learned not to worry. What about? And what was her method for not worrying? I didn't understand at the time. But then I didn't know about the death of her 'best pal', Charlie Southerden, in the lifeboat disaster. 'Do you know that I have *never*, *never*, in my whole life, gone through such a day of terrible anxiety, grief and sorrow … He was only twenty-two, and so full of life, and as strong as a young lion.' So when Diccon complains of Tamzin's 'grasshopper' behaviour (p105) when she is acutely worried about Meryon, Mother was reliving part of those times. Both Charlie and the real Meryon were dark haired and attractive, and Mother loved them. They both died tragically early.

Mother watching Sean feed Red Clover, while I look on from above, feet dangling

There were other worrying times, of course. I remember how painful was the decision to remortgage the farm, after having worked so hard to pay it off. Both my parents hated to be in debt of any kind. Hire purchase was anathema to them: money should be earned before it was spent. I feel just the same.

In reading this book I realised I had become emotionally involved from the first chapter. Like Tamzin on Cascade, when chasing the blue car to intercept Meg, I galloped through the story. I flew across tide-creeks, and anything else that got in my way, until I reached the end. That I knew how the story ended didn't slow me down in the slightest.

I can so well visualise the jackdaws inhabiting the old stones in the ancient ruins of Cloudsley Castle. Maybe I'll go to visit them next spring. There are many pairs nesting in the local chimney pots here in our small market town. The male sits on top of the pots while his mate is deep inside, but drops inside for the occasional visit. It must be a squeeze in there. The fledglings eventually emerge looking as bedraggled as anyone might, having been dragged up in a chimney pot, and fly for the first time to our power lines. It must be so much more civilised in a ruined castle.

The 'stranger's' ball-bearings in the saucer trick belonged to an old friend of the family. We found it a bit tedious after a while. I only remember the loss of one ball-bearing. As he was such a safe driver it was probably the best bit of the whole trip. Sitting in the front seat I couldn't watch them for long anyway, in case I felt sick.

The precautionary pistol that Mr Fairbrass took to Spain also belonged to an old friend, for the same reason. We never actually saw it, let alone any ammunition. Of course, these days Mr Fairbrass would never have got it through Customs. There was a seven-year gap from note to book this time.

A year or so before Mother would have started writing this book, or even thinking about it, a Caravelle Airliner crashed on Blackdown Hill near Haslemere. There were no survivors. A few days later Mother and I went up to have a look. I am astonished that she made so little of that experience in this book. The nearest Tamzin got was looking 'briefly' through field glasses 'at the scar in the green forest, where the wing of an aeroplane shone white in the sun' (p209). Yet Mother and I had stood in silence for some time on Blackdown, contemplating the swathe of damage, far larger than we had expected. Debris had been scattered all along the 355 yards, but none was identifiable from our distance: no 'white wing'—that was a writerly touch.

*   *   *

I hope you have read Sally Bourne's poignant article first. She leads you so beautifully into the whole ethos of the story. For years I carried a donor card, on which I had written: 'Help yourself!' But later, alarmed by some adverse publicity, I threw it away. After reading Sally Bourne's letter I changed my mind and decided to register again, which I did with ease and equanimity through www.organdonation.nhs.uk.

Shelley Edwards, 2009

Monica Edwards on Gozo, off Malta. 1967. The neolithic temple ruins are
called Ggantija (yes, two 'g's, means 'Giantess'). She was visiting Malta with
her old friends, Pat and John Loarridge, with their daughter Ruth and her
husband Malcolm. Photo credit Malcolm Gee, who took the photograph
with Monica's camera.

A WIND BLOWN OUT
OR A CHANGE OF TACK

This brief contribution can really find little to add that isn't in the other introductions, prefaces and appendix here, or of course in Brian Parks's *Biography*.* It is just a ramble that followed its own nose, and like Topsy it just growed. Still, I hope that it adds to the position and importance of this book in the evolution of my mother's writing and life.

The coincidence recently of a call from Clarissa for new introductory material for this edition of *A Wind is Blowing*, and refinding a remarkable 6×6 cm colour slide of my mother labelled just "1967, Malta", set an idea running. I hadn't thought that the photograph would be of wider interest—it was only in the last few months that a bit of sleuthing identified the scene's location and other details.

Before my mother was writing *A Wind is Blowing* (published 1969, written in 1968), she knew that both of her children's series—the 'Romney Marsh' and the 'Farm' books—were coming to a natural completion. The children in the stories were growing up, as she had decided from the beginning that they must. The life-span of the series was therefore ordained, to end when the main characters were really no longer children. The dust jacket flap of the first edition said "for thirteen to fifteen-year-old girls" (*Children's Book News*). Tamzin was 15, but Meryon was 18 and driving. Her publishers (Collins) were asking her to introduce more adult themes, but this was something that she didn't want to do, and would surely have been tricky bearing in mind Tamzin's age.

The wind was not only blowing for Tamzin and Meryon's chance for his sight to be restored, but also blowing out both of the series. The last sentence of *A Wind is Blowing* confirmed that there was no going back on their increasingly close relationship—a theme that she first played with nine years earlier in the book of that title: *No Going Back*.

Coincidentally or not, the short poem *Wind Blown November* is her first traced published work (1931, Detroit, Michigan, in *The Bridle and Golfer*), when she was 18 years old at Rye Harbour. The similarity of the title and even her age to that of Tamzin is notable, as it opens the journey of her writings about the Marsh that is closed by *A Wind is Blowing*.

Some people sit beside a blazing fire,
　　Toes in the hearth, and elbows on their knees;
"This wind cuts to my very bones," they say,
　　And scowl upon the naked, swaying trees.

I think, perhaps, the winds are always bleak
　　To those who never understand their ways.
But as for me, I love their reckless strength,
　　I love the freshness of these wild, rough days.

No sitting over indoor fires, for me!
　　No scowling glances at the racing clouds!
I would be striding out across the marsh,
　　Far from the dust and noise of city crowds.

I would be walking where the curlews call,
　　Where seagulls wheel and shriek, in glinting flocks.
Tasting the salty tang upon my lips,
　　Watching the breakers thundering on the rocks.

Hatless, I would be letting the teasing wind
    Play with my hair, and toss it from side to side.
I would be standing where the stinging spray
    Beats on my face, as it flees from the racing tide.

I love these reckless, carefree, shouting winds,
    These scudding clouds, these swaying, windblown trees.
I want to run, and laugh and shout, and sing,
    Because I see the face of God, in these.

— Monica le Doux Newton

An untraced poem entitled *Forgotten* was published in the local press in 1929, when Monica was 16. It does contain the word 'windswept' (see Brian's *Biography*), but wind is a character of these coastal marshes anyway.

My mother had already created a new and unconnected family and location, in *Under the Rose*, the year before (published 1968, written in 1967), which freed her from the baggage of the two series. Although she considered this her best book, Romney Marsh is where her heart always lay. *A Wind is Blowing* was her last work of fiction, and her last homage to the marshes, enabling closure of the children's series. In 1967 she was a confident 54-year-old woman looking forward to a change of writing career. Both of her own children had flown the nest. Shelley had been married for ten years, and I was away at university where I had met my wife in 1967; our teenage friends that had provided such a quarry for the detail and colour for her books, had long flown too. Dad was 64 years old and farming was becoming harder, and as it happened, his tractor accident and the sale of the farm were just a year away.

Her lifelong interest in natural history had been flourishing again since 1963, particularly with the Valley badgers, resulting in *The Badgers of Punchbowl Farm* being published in 1966, a year before *A Wind is Blowing*. This was followed by two further badger books in the next ten years, before she laid her pen down, aged 63 and heralding 21 years of very active retirement.

So the photograph here shows Monica at this pivotal time of her writing life. She was visiting Gozo, on holiday with her old friends Pat and John Loarridge, and their daughter Ruth and her husband Malcolm. It hasn't been published before. The cover photograph of Brian's *Biography* was taken in 1971, and there are several other photographs of her in the *Biography* from around this time, so it doesn't really fill any great holes. But still it shows her in a way that surprised me: not the Monica in farming or country clothes, or posed as an author. No writing or farm worries whilst on Gozo, but surely wondering how the badgers were getting on …

It represents someone I never really knew, free from family and children, transcending the mother, the anchor of the farm and the farmhouse, the 'taken-for-granted', the rock, and the writer. This must apply to all her non-family holidays, about which we know so little. So little documentation. Brian Parks's *Biography* chapters include: Wife, Writer, Farmer, and Retirement—he could also have separated Naturalist and even Gardener chapters from Retirement. Not to mention writing five autobiographical books, running into 21 editions. All different people but the same person. And to understand the development of the writer and her writing, it helps to see the parallel timelines.

Another line is Travel, and *A Wind is Blowing* is her only work with any of the story set abroad. Her holidays abroad were relatively few, and none to Spain. Whilst she was writing (1947–1976), there were seven European holidays:

1960 May, aged 47—Holland, Rotterdam *Floriade* trip, with Pat Loarridge.

1965 April, aged 52—Austrian/Italian holiday with Shelley and family, by train and bus: Umhausen, Siusi/Seis (including climbing Siusi Alpe).

1967 summer, aged 54—Malta and Gozo, holiday with Loarridge family.

1970 summer, aged 57—Malta holiday, with Nick and Natalka Flemming, who were attending the *Pacem in maribus* (aka naughtily 'Pee in the Sea') conference.

1972 April, aged 59—She attended the International Camellia Society's visit (conference on 6–11 April) in Stresa, L. Maggiore, Italy, with Pat Loarridge; she also attended the Brighton ICS conference the same year. She had been a member since 1962 (ICS founded) or 1964 (first membership list). This was encouraged by her friendship with the nurseryman Michael Haworth-Booth, who would exchange shrubs for honey and other farm produce.

1973 summer, aged 60—Loire trip with Aileen Grisewood (wife of the broadcaster Freddie), seeing the chateaux, etc., including Chartreuse du Liget, Chenonceaux, Muides, Rochecotte, Valençay, Villandry, Villesavin.

1975 May, aged 62—Dordogne holiday with Sean and family (the first to Espinasse, an isolated rural cottage and grange, near Liourdres), featured in her final book, *Badger Valley*, Chapter 18 (1976). Of the six holidays to Espinasse (owned by her good friend Mariota Fuller), this first one was probably never equalled for enchantment and discovery.

After her final book, she holidayed abroad six times more to Dordogne (1977 to 1994), by which time the beloved Liourdres was changing by development and Espinasse would soon be sold. She also travelled to Sri Lanka (1991) and to the Azores (1993), all with Sean and family, hoping for and often finding wild places.

Sean Edwards, November 2022

* If you can, do read Brian Parks's *Monica Edwards—The Authorised Biography*, Girls Gone By, 2010. It is out of print but can be found second-hand. It is a beautifully readable, informative and sympathetic book.

A BITTERSWEET FAREWELL

A Wind is Blowing is the last of Monica Edwards's series of Romney Marsh novels and where we say a final goodbye to Tamzin and Meryon, Hookey Galley, Jim Decks, the Merrows and all the other characters from the fishing village of Westling and surrounding marshland.

This new Girls Gone By edition is only the third since its original publication in 1969 by Collins. During its time out of print, *A Wind is Blowing* became incredibly sought after, often unaffordable to the ordinary reader, so we are all hugely grateful to Girls Gone By for giving us the opportunity to add this title to complete a collection, re-read the story, or read for the very first time.

I had already re-collected all the other titles in the early 2000s. Reading them was like meeting old friends who haven't changed a bit, or got boring, since knowing them as a teenager in the 1970s. I was then contacted by a book dealer, herself a Monica Edwards enthusiast, with the good news that she had found me a copy of *A Wind is Blowing*. To my memory, I had never read this, so it was going to be like meeting a friend of very good old friends. The not-so-good news was the price: £90.00. But I had to have it, greatly intrigued that I knew nothing of this story.

I had loved all the other Romney Marsh books, and I bet that Monica Edwards would have pulled out all the stops to create a joyous finale to the series, complete with sparkling sea and summer sun shining down on Tamzin and friends, with all the expected elements of a Westling story: high spirits, humour, sustaining snacks at Castle Farm, eccentric but always believable characters, and maybe a party at the very end.

However, the book arrived with a little note from the bookseller: she was sure I'd like it, but with a caveat that I should not expect it to have quite the same *joie de vivre* as the other books and I should 'take it on its own terms'.

It's now—unbelievably—18 years ago that I bought and read that second-hand copy of *A Wind is Blowing*. There has been much debate on- and offline since on its merits and how it compares to the earlier titles.

The 'last of' anything is always sad and maybe this accounts for some readers finding it a 'sad read', while other comments describe it as a 'difficult book' and 'totally out of style with the other books' and even, 'the bleakest book'.

Monica Edwards had pulled out all the stops—the writing was brilliant, as ever—but the problem seems to have been that she had pulled out all the wrong ones! Rather than a vibrant storyline of Tamzin and co sorting out a Jim Decks-related issue (a nefarious one, usually), there was a shift of gear into young adult fiction territory when Meryon, within the first few pages, is blinded by ammonia in trying to prevent a bank raid (in which another innocent receives a fatal injury), provoking a seemingly uncrossable rift in his relationship with Tamzin. There is also a failed sheepdog, a tearful Mrs Merrow, and an air-crash with two further fatalities. Important characters are missing (Rissa and Roger away at Punchbowl Farm), and out of the remaining characters left to do the heavy lifting are the grim Hookey Galley and spiteful poison-pen Mrs Venus.

Peter Williams, a member of the Monica Edwards Appreciation Society, in an article he wrote for the society's magazine about Hookey Galley's character development through the series ('Hookey's Progress' *Martello* no 7), says '*A Wind is Blowing* is in some ways a strange, inconsistently plotted book, apparently trying to be as detached from the rest of the series as *No Mistaking Corker* is from the Punchbowl Farm books but hindered by the amount of baggage that survives in readers' minds from the earlier series'.

Sally Bourne, in her moving introduction, shares her experience of how the memory of reading the story thirty-five years earlier helped her through the terrible trauma of her husband's early death and led to two people having their sight restored. She is unusual in that she began at the end of the Romney Marsh series with *A Wind is Blowing* and was therefore possibly not hindered by any expectations raised by reading the earlier books.

Maybe that really is the 'problem' with this 'difficult book' that some readers have: is it too much of a leap from the uplifting *Dolphin Summer*, which takes place in a hot July just a month before the events of *A Wind is Blowing*—where Tamzin and friends once again rise to the defence of the natural world and even Hookey shows a compassionate side to his character—to the cold reality that life can change in a second?

(Before this gives the impression that all the previous stories are bathed in eternal sunlight, there are dark episodes, harsh realities and plenty of angst throughout the series: Tamzin's near-drowning in *Dolphin Summer*; the cabin boy Jonah's miserable existence on the innocent-sounding *Daisy Holman*; *Storm Ahead* with the loss of six lifeboat crew, Lindsey bitten by a possibly rabid dog, Tamzin ill with influenza; Meryon's psychological disturbance in *Hidden in a Dream*; Rissa's hidden feelings for Meryon in *No Going Back* …)

Anyone about to read *A Wind is Blowing* for the very first time or with only vague memories of it, may well be worried by the more negative criticisms that swirl around its unlikely plot points or the fact that the location switches (always risky when a book's familiar location is practically a character in its own right): how will the characters be out of context and doesn't it all sound rather depressing? However, I believe that *A Wind is Blowing* is a beautifully poignant, bittersweet story, positive and life-enhancing, thoughtful and wise, containing themes of learning to change, redemption, helping others and an overriding message of never giving up—on a situation or a person—while there is hope, while there is a wind blowing.

Peter Williams again, in his article 'Hookey's Progress', points out that '[Hookey] ends the series on his best behaviour, working with Jim to play cat and mouse with the bank robber Cutter', and 'there is some satisfaction in seeing the series end with two of Westling's strongest, most lawless personalities working in harmony to thwart a much more dangerous individual'. Mrs Venus is redeemed when Reverend Grey, in a stroke of genius, gives her a job as parish magazine reporter (with the proviso that she puts down her poison-pen forever). Meg, the failed sheepdog, finally comes into her own when she performs a heroic deed.

Monica Edwards's writing is spare and taut in the first few chapters, reflecting the bleakness of Meryon's situation ('The Man Who Has Everything', as Tamzin jokingly refers to him just before his whole future plans are destroyed in an instant); beautifully understated when describing Tamzin's reaction to Meryon finishing their relationship: 'As blind as Meryon she bumped into a chair as she crossed to the door, then shaking the blur from her eyes she ran down the hall to the sunny kitchen where Mrs. Fairbrass was making coffee. Without a word Tamzin ran to her and was held, like a little girl who has fallen down and hurt herself' (Chapter 3).

At other times her writing is as lyrically descriptive as ever: 'It was wonderful, feeling fully alive again—not alive only to her own misery, but alive to the firm sleekness and good smell of ponies, to hay scent and August heat and a robin singing his small song in the damson tree' (Chapter 4).

The irrepressible light-hearted humour is there too, throughout the whole story. There are so many funny moments to choose from, but Jim Decks's warning to Tamzin that she will catch a stutter off the tape recorder is priceless, as is the cat Billingham's 'baptism' with Jim's pint of old and mild.

For me, though, one of the best parts of Monica Edwards's writing in *A Wind is Blowing* is when Tamzin is inspired to record sounds for a Sound Newsletter. This is almost a sensory experience for the reader, as if someone has turned the volume up on things that we're used to seeing in our mind's eye in the text but not *hearing*—until we really listen along with Tamzin and Meryon: 'Now, there's a noise I never noticed—ropes slapping on a mast in the wind' (Chapter 5); 'Tamzin's tape scarcely stopped running for the next half hour as the sounds of Castle Farm went stringing onto it. Meryon's seeing hands were reminding him all the time of pigs' rough backs ... hugeness of tractor tyres and smallness of bantam eggs, of wheat running through fingers—with a hiss that Tamzin recorded' (Chapter 12).

The above scene at Castle Farm is interrupted by Mrs Fairbrass driving her car at speed to collect Meryon for the race against time to Barcelona to get Meryon's sight back. Brian Parks in his *Romney Marsh Companion* tells us that Monica Edwards never visited Barcelona, instead using the diary of her friend Betty Pullan, who had visited Spain in May 1968. It's impossible to see the joins in Monica's finely detailed depictions of the city. I especially like this simple but effective description: 'There was a golden light on the cathedral stones that was not all from the sun, but was in the stones themselves. Looking up briefly at the two great bell towers soaring into the sky, Tamzin followed Kit and Jack Fairbrass into dimness that was like walking into a forest' (Chapter 15).

I have visited Barcelona several times and I was delighted on one of our early visits to find St George's fountain just as described, in the peaceful garden with the limpid sound of the water and birds hidden in the leaves. Monica's writing enhanced my pleasure of visiting this place, which, for Tamzin, was like a kind of Mecca to which she had travelled, a pilgrim from afar. I too felt like a pilgrim, in Tamzin's footsteps, dropping a coin into the water.

On our last holiday in Spain, in 2017, in a seaside resort further down the coast, I became very ill one day and was taken by emergency ambulance to a hospital in the suburbs of Barcelona. I won't go into all the details, but it is thanks to the treatment I had there that I survived, waking up the next day in the Barcelona hospital's ICU. I was there for ten days until allowed to go home. 'Shades of Meryon', I kept thinking. I also thought about the jasmine 'trained round in a little circle', the fruit in a flat basket, and the little furry bull that Tamzin gives to Meryon: all the details in Monica's writing that shine in the mind and continue to shine. I have not returned to Barcelona, or Spain, since then, but I gladly go with Tamzin and Meryon, again and again.

Joyce Bailey, 2023

PUBLISHING HISTORY

Six years would pass from the appearance of *Dolphin Summer* before Tamzin and Meryon were once more to appear in print. In the intervening years two books featuring Rissa and Roger had appeared, *Fire in the Punchbowl* and *The Wild One*. However, those, like the earlier book, *The Outsider*, in which the main characters from both series meet, were set in and around the Devil's Punch Bowl in Surrey and fit better as part of the Punchbowl Farm series. They were published as such in 2010 in new paperback editions from Girls Gone By.

So it was in 1969 that Monica Edwards's account of the next stage in the developing story of Tamzin and Meryon was presented to readers of the Romney Marsh series with the publication of *A Wind is Blowing*. After her regular threats to end the series, which had now run for 22 years, this was the author's final book specifically written for young people.

The book sits well on the shelf with the others in the series. It is the same size—8×5½ inches (20×14cm)—and bound in dark blue cloth with title, author and publisher on the spine in silver. It was dual priced, as decimalisation was underway, at '80p 16s' and sported a full-colour painted dustwrapper by the artist Alex Jawdokimov, the picture wrapping around to include the spine.

The dustwrapper illustration (which has been reproduced on the front cover of this GGBP edition) is in many ways good, but it is one that caused me great confusion when I first read the book. Not until I had finished reading did I realise that the ruin on the cliff, high above a moored luxury yacht in a Mediterranean blue sea was actually a depiction of shingle-set Camber Castle on the Sussex marsh with the old fishing smack the *Thunderer* standing off the coast! Oh, how I wished Collins had employed Geoffrey Whittam once more. No disrespect is intended to Alex Jawdokimov. (This was one of the last commercial jobs that the artist undertook—he went freelance in 1969 and still paints, selling beautiful pictures via a number of galleries in London and elsewhere.) The guilt for this travesty lies with whoever at the publishers was responsible for briefing the artist.

At the end of the 1960s attitudes to children's books were changing, and perhaps illustrated books were seen as more suitable for the younger reader; or perhaps illustrations to accompany the text were thought to be at odds with the theme of the book. Or possibly it was simply a matter of economy. Whatever the reason, this is the only one of Monica Edwards's young people's books to have been published without internal illustrations.

The author's notes suggest that a Children's Book Club edition was planned but, if so, it was not forthcoming. Collins never reprinted the book, and so the first edition long remained the only English language version available.

There was, however, a German edition, *Solange der Wind weht*. The publisher, Engelbert, brought this out in 1973 along with *Under The Rose* and *The Wild One*, and went on to publish *Hidden in a Dream* the following year. These editions were produced with dramatic, colourful pictorial covers. In this case, shown on the next page, Tamzin and Meryon grace the cover, courtesy of the artist Eva Kausche-Kongsbak, portrayed as an attractive couple in modern dress, on the verge of adulthood. Once again there are no illustrations in the text. The translation was carried out by Reinhilde Klatte and, unlike some other translations, retains all the names of people and places unchanged. There was some editorial work: the

Monica Edwards

Solange der Wind weht

last sentence in the book was halved—removing the Emma's telltale swerve—and, sadly, I cannot find a translation for Jim's 'Jumping gin bottles!'.

Girls Gone By first published *A Wind is Blowing* in 2009. We had a number of introductory articles, all of which have been reproduced here, although in some cases updated. Since 2009, John Allsup and Joy Wotton have both died.

This time, we have two additional articles, A Bittersweet Farewell by Joyce Bailey and A Wind Blown Out or A Change of Tack by Sean Edwards.

John Allsup, 2009
Final two paragraphs by Clarissa Cridland

NOTE ON THE TEXT

For this GGBP edition of *A Wind is Blowing* we have used the text of the first edition, which contained very few typographical errors. Of these, most concern hyphenation in nouns, which was occasionally inconsistent. The majority usage has been imposed: 'sheep-dog', not 'sheepdog', 'guide dog', not 'guide-dog', 'sheep levels', not 'sheep-levels', and 'to-day', not 'today' (but 'tomorrow', not 'to-morrow').

The book generally uses '-ize' spellings ('memorize', 'symbolize', etc), and 'realize' also appeared once, but there were two instances of 'realisation' and three of 'realise'. We have changed these to 'realization' and 'realize' for consistency.

The usual style in this book for the titles of doctors is 'Dr.' in narration but 'Doctor' in direct speech. We have corrected two instances of 'Dr.' that appeared in speeches, to match this general rule.

'Lippizaner' (for the breed of horse) has been corrected to 'Lipizzaner' (p103), 'anihilation' to 'annihilation' (p191), 'french window' to 'French window' (p197), 'it's' to 'its' in 'its sliding oblique descent' (p200), 'venetian blinds' to 'Venetian blinds' (p203) and 'Coca Cola' to 'Coca-Cola' (which is the correct spelling for the trade mark, p208).

We have amended two strange wordings that we believe to have been typographical errors, changing 'dogged qual-that' to 'dogged quality that' on (p177) and 'has' to 'had' in 'the cows the young woman had spoken of' on (p209). We have added one pair of opening quotes that were missing at the start of a speech, and deleted a pair of closing ones that appeared at the end of a paragraph of narration. In one place we have corrected a reversed apostrophe, at the start of ""'Course I know"", and in another place we have changed a comma to a full stop where it was clear that what followed it was the start of a new sentence.

We have inserted three commas where it seemed obvious that they had simply been omitted: (pp.193, 217, 224). We have also moved one comma (p192) (it was after the 'and' in the first edition).

On (p103) the repeated word in "'I was not sure if you arrive in in time'" might be a typographical error, but we have not changed it because might be deliberate—the speaker's English is not meant to be perfect.

Monica Edwards often uses a semi-colon where a comma or a colon would generally be thought more correct: we have not altered this punctuation, considering it to be a part of her style.

The publisher's blurb from the first edition dustwrapper is reproduced on the back cover of this GGBP edition. It contained two punctuation errors, which we have corrected by inserting the commas on lines 19 and 27.

We hope that we have not introduced any new errors.

Rich Cutler and Sarah Woodall, 2009

For this 2023 edition, a contents page and running heads have been added for ease of use, but please note that owing to the lack of chapter titles in the original, neither featured in the first edition.

A few further corrections have been made to the text. The spelling mistake 'mazagine' has been corrected. We have hyphenated 'waiting-room' once to match the majority usage.

In the phrase 'The man who has has everything' (p99), the repeated word has been deleted, and we have changed 'the things had had become' to 'the things that had become' (p158). In 'she him told about' (p157), we have switched the middle two words. On one occasion Tamzin is described as giggling, 'imaging it' (p157). This should almost certainly be 'imagining it', so we have made this adjustment.

Finally, all spaced en-rules in the original text have been changed to unspaced em-rules to match GGBP style.

Alison Neale, 2023

A Wind is Blowing was originally published without a map. The map by Geoffrey Whittam which appears overleaf was printed on the endpapers of several other books in the Romney Marsh series.

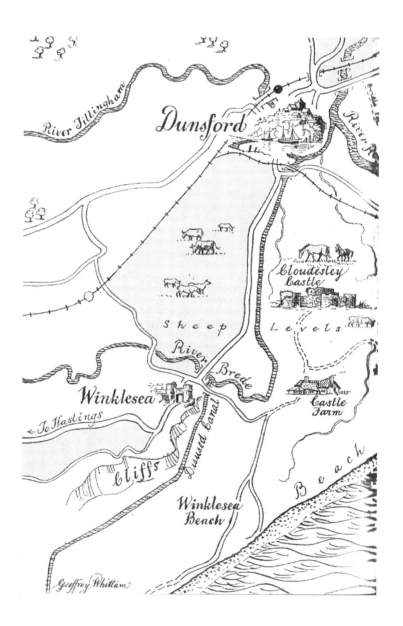

Geoffrey Whittam

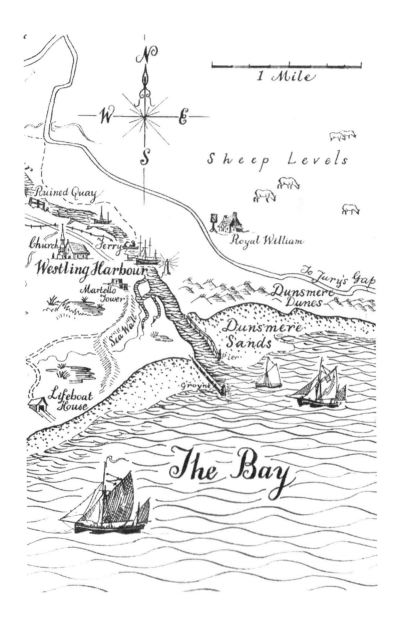

N W E S

1 Mile

Sheep Levels

Ruined Quay

Church Ferry

Westling Harbour

Royal William

Martello Tower

To Jury's Gap

Dunsmere Dunes

Sea Wall

Dunsmere Sands

Pier

Lifeboat House

Groyne

The Bay

85

MONICA EDWARDS

A WIND IS BLOWING

For
Arthur William Ashman
and his guide dogs
Booboo and Sally,
trained by himself
who were the inspiration for this book.

CONTENTS

Page

Chapter One

In Dunsford's picturesque High Street several people turned to look at the girl with long fair hair and long brown legs, lugging her load of shopping through the August afternoon crowd.

In her own small fishing village, two miles down the river, no one noticed how good-looking the vicar's daughter was becoming in her fifteenth year; she was just Tamzin Grey whom they had known since she was three; a little wild, a little serious, blazingly honest, but otherwise no different from anyone else.

Summer visitors swarmed like bees in Dunsford, sketching, snapping, shopping and just looking. They brought prosperity, Tamzin understood that, but she liked the old town best when the summer people left it to dream on its stranded cliff-top as it had done for all the years since the sea had deserted the town and the whole of Romney Marsh below it. She was making for the cliff-edge, now. It appeared quite suddenly, as if the High Street had toppled over it in the thick of all its busyness. The right-angled bend could hardly expect to be noticed, except by drivers, in the face of such a breath-taking view—on a clear day, across a hundred square miles without a noticeable shadow, and the sea beyond.

With a brief glance at the familiar distances Tamzin thankfully lowered her basket and parcels beside a large parked vehicle with faint station-wagon lines. This was the converted hearse, Emma, belonging to her friend Meryon Fairbrass. It had seen a long, useful and variegated life, carrying more and stranger things than coffins in its time. Just now it had a cargo of Fairbrass shopping; a sack of chicken-meal in the middle where the coffins used to rest, a roll of wire-netting down each side and heaps of various groceries and vegetables wherever they would go, together with a plastic rubbish-bin and two buckets.

Meryon couldn't have heard her feet in their old white tennis shoes but he turned from leaning on the cliff fence and came across to open the double rear doors. He had a gipsy look, except for quite brilliant blue eyes, like those of a Siamese cat. With an easy movement he swung her stuff into the hearse. She reached in and plonked a bunch of yellow chrysanthemums on the meal sack.

"The final touch! Funeral tribute. I never did like chrysanthemums before the autumn so it doesn't matter being disrespectful to them."

"No reason why you should be disrespectful to hen-meal, a worthy substance. That the lot? I should hate to lock your hair in. And why do you buy chrysanthemums in August if you feel that way about them?"

"If your mother's going to put up with me for a few days I think she deserves the nicest flowers in Dunsford; and all the nicer ones than these were fainting from heat; so what would you have done?"

"Come and lean over the fence and look at the view, like a well instructed tripper, and I'll tell you."

"Well?" she said, gazing out, her hands on the rail.

"They looked stunning next to your palomino mane and that faded blue dress. Give them that."

"You were going to tell me what you'd have done."

"Bought them; because etcetera, as aforesaid."

"But not if you were me."

He grinned at her. "Isn't it lucky that I'm not? Because if I were you, and you were me, you mightn't like you as much as I do now I'm me, if you follow."

"I'd make a bad doctor," she said, "and you'd never be able to ride Cascade. We'd better stay us."

He turned his back on the view to lean against the fence and study the colourful shoppers. "Has it ever struck you how lucky we are, just to be us?"

"Yes, it frightens me sometimes. It doesn't seem fair. Knowing what we want to do, who we want to be with, and living where we do." She looked down across the bright river with its little yachts and fishing boats, over the wide grazings flecked with sheep, to her own village of Westling, a huddle of masts and cottages behind the spire of a boat-shaped church; then south-westwards beyond the lonely ruins of Cloudesley Castle, to where Meryon's home was hidden in the trees some two miles along the stranded cliff.

Meryon was still looking at the holiday people. "For a week or two they have it all, just the same as us. But they must go back—to deadly places, sometimes."

"Perhaps they want to go back. Perhaps what we'd think deadly is alive for them. And even if you are The Man Who Has Everything, is there anything wrong with enjoying it?"

He turned to look seawards. "Supposing my 'A' Level results aren't good enough?"

"Men who have everything have what exams take."

"Honest, it's too serious for teasing. Sometimes I wake up remembering questions I could have answered better." She was silent, and he went on, "If I fail on this, there's nothing else I want to do. There never was. You know that."

After a moment she said, "I've known you for years and never heard you even admit the possibility before."

"Told you it was serious." Suddenly he grinned at her. "A touch of examinosis—forget it! Let's go on board the Emma and weigh anchor, unseaworthy as she is. This evening you're going to see my new dinghy, whether you want to or not. And sail her."

"That sounds more like a pirate's descendant! What your ancestor would have thought of such faint-heartedness—look, the Emma has admirers peering inside."

"She's used to it; it's her shady past. Fascinates them."

"Flowers, too," said a girl whose back view bent towards them. "What a giggle! D'you think there might be a body in that sack?"

Her friend, an anxious girl, urged her with an audible whisper. "Come along, Peg, the young man's going to get in. I'm not sure," she added as she hurried the thin one away, "it isn't sacrilegious."

"The dinghy's fibreglass," Meryon was saying, too used to the Emma's being a side-show to take much notice. "Dark blue. White sails." He slipped in the ignition key. "Different as could be from the old crates we were brought up with."

"I like the crates—tar and fish-scales and old rope—"

A sudden scream from the High Street cut her off, slicing the air. His hand still on the key Meryon turned to look through the side window. It was as if the street had been switched off, like a clockwork toy. People who had been moving had stopped where they stood, all looking towards a place where stone steps led up to an open door.

"The Bank," Meryon said, his fingers going to the door handle. "Couldn't possibly be a raid, would you think? In Dunsford?"

"Dark-green car along there has a door half open—"

"I'm going to see."

"Meryon—don't!"

He was already out. "Stay where you are. Back in a moment!"

Watching him, Tamzin didn't see the two men appear in the Bank doorway. Then everything was in her view at once; a swaying struggle at the top of the steps, one of the two men falling—she heard the crack as his head hit the stone—and Meryon throwing himself at the second man where the steps came on to the pavement.

A surging noise, like the sea, went up from the holiday people. Tamzin saw the man fling out his arm in a throwing motion, then turn and run to the dark-green car. Hands reached from inside and he was hauled in and driven away, the low car parting the shoppers as a boat parts water. Meryon was just standing there, like anyone else. His tiger-leap had fizzled out as he had launched it. Before most of the crowd had stopped gaping after the car Tamzin had jumped from the Emma and was running. There were people attending to the man who had fallen. Someone had a hand on Meryon's shoulder, but stood aside as she came.

"Fellow squirted something into his face—from a bottle—acid, or something. You know him?"

She nodded, gazing at Meryon; he was drying his face on a handkerchief.

"Meryon!"

He turned, a look of intense agony crossing his face. "One thing I didn't think of—ammonia. Stopped me in my tracks. Has he got away?" He was looking past her ear, towards the bare brick wall of the Bank. The bright blue of his eyes had blurred over. His hands went over them and she saw that he was in very great pain. Horror and disbelief surged in her.

"Meryon! Can you see?"

"No, blast. Eyes got it—be all right when I get them washed—"

Suddenly she swung round. "Quick—somebody—help me get him to a doctor—or to the hospital."

"They're phoning in the bank for a doctor, for the other chap," a man told her. "And police."

"It won't do! We've got to get him somewhere for treatment—quickly!"

A woman with short white hair and a pretty face thrust through the staring people. "My car's just along here."

"Oh, thank you!" Tamzin was struggling against panic.

"Better go and lock Emma," Meryon said, fishing the keys from his pocket.

"Oh, no! Even a minute might count." Her fingers were on his arm.

A familiar voice came from the crowd. "I'll do it! Give the keys to me; they'll be in my shop when they're wanted. Don't worry!"

Meryon recognized the voice as that of a local shop-keeper. "Thanks, Alec!"

He came with Tamzin, his steps uncertain, the spring gone out of them. His eyes were streaming, now. It was terrible having to help him into the stranger's car—a fast car, Tamzin noticed with gratitude; at any other time Meryon would have considered all its details with loving interest.

"Hospital would be best, wouldn't it, to be sure of finding a doctor." The pretty woman was practical too. "You know the way?"

"Yes, yes—straight down through the Land Gate …"

Chapter Two

Worse than the first shock, worse than the traffic hold-ups before the fast clear run, worse than anything yet was the waiting. She was alone in the hospital waiting-room, the kindly stranger gone on her way when Meryon's parents arrived. They were with the doctor now before seeing Meryon.

There were other people in the waiting-room but she stood looking out of the window. A far distant glimmer of the sea through trees was more comforting than talking to strangers; it was where they had sailed so often, where they had planned to take the new dinghy this weekend.

A young nurse came in once, smiling at Tamzin. "All right?"

"Yes, thank you. Will they let him go home?"

"You'll soon know. Parents have just gone in to see him. His mother's just like him, isn't she? Small edition."

Tamzin nodded.

"He must be awfully brave, tackling a bandit like that. He's your boy-friend, I know; I sometimes go sailing myself and I've seen you. Don't worry, now! The doctors here are wonderful."

"With eye damage, too?"

"With everything. And when it's a specialist's job they know just where to turn up the right one."

The Fairbrass red Rover was on the forecourt. Tamzin would go back in it with Meryon and his mother while Mr. Fairbrass drove home the Emma with her load of shopping. The only thing about his father that was like Meryon was his height and breadth, and a rugged independence that made it no use trying to influence either of them. Everything else about Mr. Fairbrass put Tamzin in mind of eagles. She swung round as the door opened again. The eagle was smiling at her.

"He wants to see you." There was no telling anything from his face. "I mean see figuratively—he's got a bandage on, of course, just for the night, while the treatment works."

"Not coming home?"

"Tomorrow, perhaps. We're to come in the morning, after the doctor's seen him again."

Mrs. Fairbrass had a look of strain, but she was quiet and self-possessed. "We'll be in the car, love. Don't stay long."

"Ten minutes," said the nurse in the corridor. "I'll show you where he is."

He was in a small room by himself and in bed—how he would hate that in broad daylight, was Tamzin's first thought. She was prepared for the bandage, but not for the extent of it—the ammonia must have affected the skin around the eyes.

"It's me," she said.

"A right Charlie, I feel."

She sat down by the bed, hauling up cheerfulness from some cellar of her mind where it had sunk. "Apart from a Charlie, how else do you feel? Hurt at all?"

"No. Given me some beastly dope. Reminds me of when I swigged a bottle of Mrs. Merrow's dandelion wine. Hospital pyjamas, too."

"Never mind; it might be only for a night."

There was a moment's uneasy silence before she tried, "What did he say—the doctor?"

"As much of nothing as they usually do when they're easing a bump. Face will be all right, he says—we got here quickly enough for that. As if I cared."

"Of course you care! Think of going through life with a marked face."

"You don't need a decent face to qualify in medicine."

She looked at him, but the white bandage and black hair thrusting over it were no guide to what was going on in his mind. He went on after a moment, "When I asked if vision would soon be O.K. he said, 'Well, you can't expect one hundred per cent straight away, after that packet, can you?'"

"At least 'A' Levels are over," she said, hating herself for persisting in looking on the bright side but not daring to look anywhere else.

He ignored this. "So no sailing the new dinghy this weekend, anyway. Now tell me we can go out for a nice walk in the country with you leading me."

"Do you think I *want* to cry?" she said, her voice wavering.

"Sorry!" His hand came out, groping for hers. "I'm a great clod-hopping oaf."

"You can show me the boat, anyway, can't you? You'll be able to see well enough for that." Since he made no answer she went on, "The bank clerk—have you heard how he is?"

"Yes. Died on the way here. Fractured skull. I couldn't even save that. Blokes got away with all their loot. Proper muck I made of it all." His fingers drew away from her hand. "Remember how splendid our world was, five minutes before? What did you call me? The man who has everything."

She burst out, "You're talking as if it were your *fault*, when nobody else in the street stopped any of it, either; as if you were blind already, when perhaps in a week or two you'll see as well as ever in your life!"

"And perhaps not." His voice had a bitterness she had never heard before. "I have some dim idea of what ammonia can do to eye tissue, after years of swotting chemistry, biology and physics."

He couldn't see her, but she wouldn't let her face show what she felt. "You don't know there's any real damage—and you're alive! Not like the bank clerk, losing everything."

"He may be the lucky one."

This was a Meryon she did not know at all. Always he had been the optimistic one, the rock people leaned on, reasonable and unshakable.

Putting her head round the door the sailing nurse saved her from trying to find the unfindable answer. "Ten minutes!"

"I'm coming in the morning," Tamzin said to him.

"I shouldn't bother. Pity to muck up a good weekend. Why not spend it riding?"

"Lots of reasons," she told him lightly, "that I'm not going to tell you."

In the car Tamzin knew that she couldn't bear now the long summer evening at Meryon's house, the slow morning hours there until they could return to the hospital. She wanted to fill up every moment with so much activity that there was no time left for thinking. Mrs. Fairbrass understood her enough to guess the way she would be feeling.

"It's just as easy to drop you at the vicarage and pick you up in the morning, if you like—we've got to go to the Emma for Jack to drive her home, so you could collect your case. Sad not to be taking the new dinghy out, till his eyes are better anyway, but you could ride and I know you love that."

"I think I'd like to, until we can go back for him. He didn't want me to go back to the hospital but I will, unless you say I can't."

Too numb to take much notice of Meryon's Emma at the high viewpoint where, so short a time ago, they had been so happy, she sat silent while her case was handed in to her. The chrysanthemums would still be lying on the hen-meal sack … it didn't seem possible … she couldn't look.

The Rover was sliding up the High Street now, past the place where it had all happened. Tamzin shut her eyes.

Presently Mrs. Fairbrass turned the car into the Westling road. "We have to try to understand. He always hated being ill, all his life. Hated failing, too."

"I don't think I've ever known him fail at anything. Nor be ill."

"Well, now he's got both together. He's not going to want people looking on, especially his girl-friend."

Tamzin stared out over the Marsh to where masts outlined the stretch of river where the small harbour was. "It isn't much good being a best friend if you're no use in trouble, is it?"

Mrs. Fairbrass slowed for a party of Romney Marsh sheep leisurely crossing the road. "I don't think that's his idea of what friends are for, somehow—not his friends, anyway. I never knew anyone less willing to be helped." The sheep panted in the hot sun, turning amber eyes to watch the car slide past them.

"How he'll hate having things done for him in hospital," Tamzin said. "He'll be so glad to get away, perhaps he won't mind not seeing too well at first—so long as they give him a clear bill of health for seeing better later." She turned sharply, not getting an immediate answer. "They will, won't they? You do think they will?"

"I think they'll let him go home tomorrow. It's early after such a shock, but his doctor can keep an eye on him, and we can run him back there if necessary."

"But his sight? His eyes will be all right? When they've done what they can?"

Mrs. Fairbrass changed down for the twisting corner where the old single-line railway crossed the road on its way to the harbour.

"I wish I knew," she said. "I wish I knew."

Full of her own anxiety Tamzin had not thought much until that moment of Meryon's parents. Quiet though the answer had been, she understood it as a cry of distress. There were only these three in the Fairbrass family, but the understanding between them surprised even Meryon at times, in view of the family warfare that seemed normal among many of his friends.

Wanting reassurance herself, she tried to reassure them both. "They will, I'm sure! Doctors and surgeons can do incredible things, now, can't they? Giving people new hearts, even. Ammonia burns can't be anything to them—and we got him there so quickly."

Mrs. Fairbrass patted her knee. They were going down through the village, now, past the Post Office, the Coastguards and the tinned fruit window display of Smiling Morn the grocer—now there was a miserable character for you, and nothing on earth to be miserable about.

The Rover drew up at the vicarage gate and Tamzin opened the door. She could hear her mind shouting out, "Oh, why did he have to do it?" but her voice was saying steadily, "It's awfully good of you. What time shall I be ready in the morning?"

Tamzin's parents knew how shattered she was because of the bursting energy that came into the house with her. There was a kind of theatrical cheerfulness, too, that was quite uncharacteristic and deceived no one, not even Tamzin's eight year old brother Diccon.

"What's the matter?" he inquired.

"You missed a real adventure, Dicky! Meryon tackled a bank robber, on Dunsford High Street. Pitched straight into him."

"Who won?" Diccon asked, his interest roused.

"Was Meryon hurt?" Mrs. Grey saw a reason for Tamzin's return and unnatural cheerfulness.

"The man threw ammonia at him. They're keeping him in hospital for the night, so I thought I'd come home and exercise Cascade. But I'll be going back tomorrow. The man got away, Dicky, and I don't really want to talk about it at the moment. Mother, darling, you've put the new curtains up! Don't they look nice? Mrs. Fairbrass didn't come in because she has to get back and feed their hens, but she will in the morning when they come for me. And Daddy, Mr. F. is bringing you his electric drill for your bathroom cabinet." She had thrown down her overnight case on to a kitchen chair and picked up the ginger cat Schnooky.

"Have you had tea, love?" Her mother was groping for safe talking ground, until the picture was clearer.

"There was tea at the hospital," said Tamzin, who had refused it. "They're awfully kind but they keep you waiting and don't tell you anything. Not Meryon's style. He hates people being kind and not telling him the facts."

"Perhaps they don't know them, yet," the vicar said. He was mending a broken toaster with a kind of helpless concentration. "They'll tell him when they do. Doctor Hargreaves would see to that. Ammonia got him in the face?"

"Yes. I think I'll ride straight away, while the tide's low. Coming, Dicky? I bet Banner needs a gallop, too."

Cascade was whiter than the wave-crests that shattered round his hoofs. Like a small Lipizzaner horse he was all arching lines and sprung movement, carrying his head proudly. Banner was a moorland pony rescued from gipsies; honest and plodding and endearing he was a foil to Cascade's showiness, but he slowed a ride down. Tamzin wanted to gallop wildly, to plunge right into the sea with splashes shooting to the sky, to jump the breakwaters and race another rider, the way she used to when her friend Rissa came on her chestnut pony. But Rissa and her cousin Roger were away at a Surrey farm and the pony was with them. Tamzin had never missed her more. It was not that she could have told her—or anyone—much of her anxiety about Meryon, but she was so reasonable and clear-thinking that just being with her was a source of strength.

"We'll go to Castle Farm," she called down the wind to Diccon, and swung up from the long lonely shore towards the grazings where once the sea had been. This was the land they had looked across from the end of Dunsford High Street, all that time ago that was only the afternoon just gone—the land of sheep and winds and tide-creeks, of curlews and wild swans, of long green gallops and old sea-battles and strange things dug out of ditches.

The farmhouse had been built of stones from the ruined castle, so had its barn and cowsheds; but still the castle stood there in the middle of the Marsh, big and brooding. It had stones enough to spare. Tamzin and Diccon knew all its stones, and its vaults and stairs and high viewpoints, but they left it to the sheep and the jackdaws, away to the east, and galloped to the gates of Castle Farm. There was a great joyful barking from the yard and a flurry of black and white as a young collie dog rushed to the gate in a swirling of plumed tail.

"Meg!" a voice roared from the open kitchen door, and the farmer Mr. Merrow was there. The young dog's tail and ears drooped as she slewed a look backwards, but lifted again as she looked hopefully at the riders.

"Don't encourage her! Never had one so bad to learn—and a daughter of Turk. *Meg!*"

"We didn't," Tamzin said across the gate. "But she's young, isn't she?"

"Old enough to shape on better nor she is. Too friendly by half to be a sheep-dog." He suddenly smiled. "Now—you're coming in to see the missus and Mike and Joseph?" William Merrow was a friendly man but, like all the sheep men, he required a reserved single-mindedness from his working dogs. "Pet 'em and you spoil 'em for sheep," was the rule; "then you can only get shot of 'em."

"We just rode over to say hullo," Tamzin said. "We ought to get back." She wanted to keep going, to keep on running away from something, or running to something, she hardly knew which.

"It's an awful thing," Diccon said when they were trotting towards the castle, "for a sheep-dog to fail and be made somebody's pet. Do you remember the one the Deeproses gave to Mrs. Gudgeon?"

"It died, didn't it?"

"Yes. Mrs. Merrow said she thought it died of shame."

"Oh, I shouldn't think so," Tamzin said, automatically reassuring to the younger brother.

They rode right round the castle, circling its thick bastions. She slid to the ground and thrust Cascade's reins at Diccon. "Jump down and hold him a minute, I want to go on to the wall." Running through the crumbled doorway she crossed the grassy floor between invading elderberry bushes hung with green clusters, and scrambled up the rubble of centuries to the outer wall-top. Always there had been a kind of reassurance in the sea and the Marsh from this high place; but not now. Now there was no comfort anywhere—just a skyful of plaintive peewits and below them the snake-lines of reeds and wind-raked willows where the dykes ran, and a haze hanging over the sea. The heart-aching call of a curlew came crying down the wind. She climbed down and went leaping through the ruins to Diccon and the grazing ponies.

"You're like a grasshopper," he complained, "jumping about all the time. Whatever's the matter?"

"I don't know," she said, her foot in the stirrup. "I wish I did."

When the ponies were back in the vicarage paddock and supper had been enjoyed in spite of herself—it was dabs and runner beans and a cold lemon soufflé—she was away again while the light lasted; round to the Point this time, to find Jim Decks at his ferry hut. He was sitting on the bench outside it in the low sun, knitting at his sea-boot stockings as had been his custom for all of fifty years.

"Jim."

"Ar, gal, I heard about it."

She sat down, holding his wool-ball.

"Told me in the Conk," he said, nodding backwards at the William the Conqueror Inn across the shingle road. "They guv it out with the beer."

"Jim, I think he's blind."

The old man put down his stocking and looked at her straight. "You don't know it, do yer? Well, don't say it, then, see? Jumping gin bottles, gal, don't run yer sails down while there's a wind blowin', or you're no shipmate of mine."

She grinned at him, a shaky grin.

"Nor of hissen," said Jim, taking up his knitting and fiercely stabbing a needle into it. The setting sun flashed on the steel of the needles and on the gold of his small round ear-rings. "Pity the feller got away. I lay that hurt him as much as anything, and him of a good pirate fambly."

"But what can you do if you can't see?" Tamzin said bleakly. After a minute she added, her voice falling away, "Do you know what Diccon once said to me? It was when we had a church collection for St. Dunstan's and I was explaining it. He said, 'It would be awful to be blind. It would be just a picture of your eyes without the magic miracle that makes them see.' I keep remembering."

Old Jim shot his white beard out towards her. "Then try disremembering."

She looked at him sadly. "I only told you because I thought you'd understand."

The old man's face softened a little. It was like sun on granite. "You gotter live with yerself, ole young un; and other folks has, too." His gaze lifted across the sliding river to the ferry-steps at the other side. "Dang me if that ent Hookey Galley waiting, the ole snitcher, and neither of us doing nothing. Git and fetch him, gal. Nuthen like work—thass bettern beer fer drowning worry in."

Chapter Three

Tamzin began to hate that hospital waiting-room. The ordeal seemed longer than before. This time there was cloud over her distant view and no one else in the room. The sailing nurse did not come in to encourage her; she was busy somewhere, perhaps, with someone more desperately ill than Meryon. Not old enough or close enough to the patient for the doctor to include her in his interview, Tamzin could only wait. In the end Jack Fairbrass came in alone.

"Well, he's got his discharge, as long as his doctor sees him at home. Just getting into the car."

"You mean—he's all right?" Incredulous hope surged.

"No. Not yet." She knew that he was trying to find words. "He can't see at all. But there's a real chance that he will do, after further treatment. We're to take him up to London to see Sir John Weymouth—he's one of the really top-notch eye surgeons."

She took a deep breath and frowned down at her hands, not knowing how good or not this news might be. "When? When will you know?"

"In a few days. We go up on Tuesday morning." He put a hand on her shoulder. "Doctor Hargreaves thinks there is a really good chance."

"That's great, isn't it? … Can we go, now?"

"There is one other thing."

She looked up quickly.

"He's taking the blindness part rather badly."

"Yes?"

"Tamzin. He doesn't want you to come back with us."

She knew again that he was searching for words, that he didn't want to hurt her. "I know. He pretty well said so yesterday. I think I understand. But I'd still like to come."

"All right, if you're sure …" He was silent for a brief second. "I nearly began to give you some advice, but you know him as well as anyone."

"I shan't be tearful, if that's what you're thinking of."

"Nor the opposite—too cheerful?"

"I was never any good at acting. I'll just be the same as usual."

"And if he still says no?"

She hesitated, too bewildered to think very clearly. "I suppose I'll go. But we always did like being together, and I haven't changed, have I?"

"*He* has, though," said Mr. Fairbrass; "in more ways than losing his sight."

The bandages were off. After the renewed shock of seeing again the brilliant eyes dulled and useless, Tamzin found that she could control her underlying horror and distress, just as she could control Cascade's horror of the disturbingly unfamiliar. It was, after all, only the eyes, she told herself. There was little sign of burning on the tanned skin of the face. The dressings had done good work. There was a difference to the face, though. She knew it as soon as she bent to slide herself into the Rover. It was older and harder; the liveliness gone from it.

She said, "Hullo," in her ordinary voice, but he did not turn. "Can't get rid of me, can you?" she added. "I'd hate to miss my weekend."

"Well, you can always take the dinghy out," he said as his father backed out of their parking space.

On the two mile run home she might have been a stranger; he

was polite and reserved, as he used to be with strangers. Much of the time they sat in silence, she found it so difficult to keep up anything like their usual easy conversation. She was glad when the Rover turned into the shady drive and the old house showed through the trees. The orange-red tiles of the roof came halfway down the walls as well, in the Sussex tradition. The woodwork was all white, and an evergreen magnolia climbed round the south windows, holding up its white globes among polished leaves.

Because she felt sensitively that Meryon would not want her to see him being led into the house, she ran over the lawn calling to Burma, his young brown Burmese cat, who came to greet her with his tail in the air. She played with him for a minute and then carried him indoors.

Meryon was standing alone in the sitting room near a window, his back to the room.

"Burma was watching a chaffinch; he could easily have caught it," she said. "I wonder if he'll ever grow out of gazing at the wonders of nature and start hunting, like other cats?"

He made a slight movement but said nothing and did not turn round. She went on, "You said you'd play me your new record. Part of the plan to educate me in jazz!"

"Bull's eye," he said. "Dead safe topic. Ears are O.K. Another thing's handicrafts, in case you get stuck."

"All right!" she flashed. "You asked for it—you're going to find your wood-carving pretty tricky for the next week or two, until they've mended your eyes. Much better teach me about jazz."

"It's an idea, all the same. I could whittle myself a white stick," he said drily.

Burma slipped down from her arms with an elusive feline twist and brushed his length past Meryon's ankle. "He prefers you," she said, ignoring the white stick. "He always did. Oh, well, I'll put the record on, then. May I?"

"I can put my own records on."

She said, "Why do you have to be so blazing independent? It isn't even reasonable."

He was venturing round the furniture. "Because I am blazing independent. And—if you must have it—because I know they can't do anything about my eyes. You don't think I haven't found all that out? Knowing Doctor Hargreaves as I do. Don't forget I worked with him through quite a few weekends as theatre orderly and all that." He had reached the record player and was feeling for its lid fastening.

She stood watching him, on edge to help but making herself stay still. "But what about Sir John Weymouth? Doctor Hargreaves wouldn't send you to see him if he didn't think he could do anything! The—the record's on the table next to the player."

He turned and began making his way back. "I don't think I want to play it. And you don't want to hear it. Let's at least be as honest as we've always been."

"What did Doctor Hargreaves tell you?" She gathered up the Burmese cat and braced herself to hear when she wanted to run. Meryon found the sofa arm and sat on it.

"Corneas have gone. The centres, that is. He thinks they're graftable. That's what he wants Sir John to confirm."

"*Well*—" There was hope and excitement and query in the word.

"Listen, Tamzin. I want you to try to understand me—over this more than over anything you have before. It's asking a lot, because I don't properly understand myself."

Her heart ached for him. "Go on."

"I can't accept a graft. Even if Sir John says it's possible and offers one."

"But, Meryon—"

"Listen. There are never enough corneas to go round. There's a waiting list. Well, I'm not going on to it. Call me what you like—silly, quixotic, self-made martyr, crazy. You'll probably be right. But I'm not going on it."

"You've every bit as much right as everyone else! More, because throwing away your chance to see means throwing away a doctor—and the country needs doctors. You must see that! It's just lunatic to give up your chance to every other person waiting, when what they probably need just as much is more doctors."

He laughed shortly. "That's one thing you can't kid me about, now—that anyone could need anything more than two good eyes."

"But when it comes to your turn?"

"There will be another string of helpless people waiting."

"And what about you, for heaven's sake? Aren't you a helpless person waiting? You don't have to destroy yourself for their sake!"

Again the short laugh. "I don't think that's the whole, or even part, of the reason—doing it for their sake. What did you say about being blazing independent? I agreed it was true and it is—so cussed independent and self-opinionated I think I'm not as helpless as others waiting."

Gazing at him over the golden-brown cat, who played with her fingers, she tried to take in and understand the meaning of what he said. Suddenly she burst out, "You're wrong! You must see you're wrong!"

He said sadly, "I shouldn't have expected you to understand. You won't understand this, either—I want you to go home, just as I said at the hospital. I've got to work this out for myself. And, for a long time, by myself—until I get the hang of this different world. We had a better friendship than most boy-and-girl friendships, and we meant it to last. It's finished, now. I want you to accept that, because I mean it. I'm finished with it, anyway; I won't be anybody's damaged article. If you don't see the right of it now you will one day when you're older, and find yourself a whole man."

She tried to fight them back but tears ran down her face and on to Burma. He twitched his fur at their fall and wriggled down to lick them off. As blind as Meryon she bumped into a chair as she crossed to the door, then shaking the blur from her eyes she ran down the hall to the sunny kitchen where Mrs. Fairbrass was making coffee. Without a word Tamzin ran to her and was held, like a little girl who has fallen down and hurt herself.

Chapter Four

For Tamzin there was a kind of twilight period of shock and grief that no one else could penetrate; perhaps least of all her own loving and understanding family, who—even Diccon—had the wisdom to see that this was a darkness which must lift in its own good time and of its own accord. For a few days like a boat without a helmsman she drifted, riding about the Marsh questioning herself and God, or the seagulls and the sea, or the wind and sun—why, why, why?

With Diccon she rode to Castle Farm again, inquiring about Meg the sheep-dog and hearing no good. She sat with Old Jim on the bench outside the ferry hut, holding his wool, playing with his piebald cat, saying nothing, except a word here and there about the weather or the ferry or the fishing. Jim said nothing, either, although he knew about Tamzin's tragedy. He usually knew about everything on the river side of the Marsh, by reason of his business as ferryman. He let her work out her grief by herself, as she had to do, although he wouldn't have understood how much just his imperturbable presence helped her.

Only once did she burst out to any other person. It was on the day that Meryon went to see Sir John Weymouth; she had come on her father in the garden and suddenly cried out, "Daddy, I can't bear it!" He comforted her for a while as he had when she was small, and when she would listen he said gently, "If you'll think about *other* blind people, and try to help them, you will feel better, and bear it." It was all that he said, and it seemed to her to come out of a deep well of wisdom, but she rejected it as a wonderful impossible ideal, typical of him, and slid back into her twilight.

On the Thursday morning she had a letter from Mrs. Fairbrass, written on their return from London. Sir John had confirmed Doctor Hargreaves' diagnosis, that both the eyes were suitable for grafting, and he was prepared to arrange for this and carry out the operation when corneas became available. Meryon had refused to have anything to do with it, and nothing that anyone said made any difference. "But Sir John told us afterwards," she wrote, "that this was probably still a result of shock; he thought that Meryon would come round to the idea soon because, he said, he is an exceptionally intelligent young man. Seems to have been right about that, anyway; 'A' Level results came in this morning's post—four passes, three with A grading. I suppose this means his provisional acceptance at Cambridge is confirmed."

Tamzin went as usual to fetch up the ponies and put them in the stable away from the flies that swarmed as soon as the sun was up. To Smiling Morn the grocer, passing along the paddock wall, there was no noticeable difference in the Tamzin he had known and often disapproved of for so long.

"It's a nice day," she said to him over the wall, and he looked back at her with his severe debunking eyes.

"Maybe. But it'll rain by midday, you'll see."

Sliding a rope round Cascade's neck and grasping Banner's forelock she led them over the summer-dried pasture to the cool darkness of the stable where hay was waiting in the racks. Diccon found her there twenty minutes later, crying into Cascade's mane; and because he felt helpless in the face of such grief he went out again, silent in his plimsolls, and looked abstractedly for caterpillars.

But it was here that Tamzin came to terms with herself. Crying bitterly and desolately for a long time it seemed as if grief and hopelessness began to go out of her with the tears, until there was only a clear calm like the sea after storm. She had been drifting in that storm, but now her boat was answering to the helm again, and there was a star to steer by.

With a wisp of hay in his teeth Cascade turned to look at her as she leaned against him to re-read her letter. She slid a hand down his muzzle and turned the page to read on from where she had abruptly stopped.

"You mustn't mind that he hasn't asked for you; he doesn't, yet, want anyone at all, while he's getting to grips with a different world. He's still being quite fiercely independent, no help accepted over anything; we're gradually learning not to offer any. It really is astonishing how he gets about and manages alone. We got him a little tape recorder while we were in London—he's always wanted one. This one has cassettes—easier to handle than reels. At first he just left it in its box, but presently he got it out and began experimenting, and had the hang of it long before I could have done, even using my eyes. Love as ever, Kit Fairbrass."

Tamzin put the letter in her jeans pocket and looked around her. The stable had a neglected air of hastily swept floor and uncleaned tack hanging crookedly on the pegs. Even the ponies looked somehow dusty and unkempt. Rolling her sleeves up, she took the dandy brush down from its shelf above the corn-bin and looked at it for a moment. Then she began. It was wonderful, feeling fully alive again—not alive only to her own misery, but alive to the firm sleekness and good smell of ponies, to hay scent and August heat and a robin singing his small song in the damson tree. Alive to thinking, as well, after days of muddled no-thought. As she worked, she was thinking quite a lot.

Later in the morning she wrote two letters. The first was in answer to Mrs. Fairbrass, and one of the things in it was, "The tape recorder was a marvellous idea; the more you think about it the more you see what he can do with it. What make is it?"

The second letter was to The Royal National Institute for the Blind. It said; "Dear Sirs, I know that people sometimes send letters by 'Tape', and this must be especially useful for blind people. I wonder if you know of one—or two, perhaps—who would like to have these kind of letters? I should be glad to hear, as I am thinking of getting a tape recorder. Yours sincerely, Tamzin Grey (aged nearly 15)."

After this she got her Post Office Savings Book out of its drawer and had a careful look into it.

"The tide's right up," Diccon said wistfully in the doorway of her room. "You wouldn't like to come for a swim, I suppose?"

She swung round, then looked to the open window. It was full of blue air and seagulls and sunlight on water. A trawler was coming up the river with the tide. "Yes, I think I would—I really would!"

Suddenly there was a strange newness about everything. It was like finding the old things and places and people again after a long illness. She couldn't believe that she had drifted so far away from it all as almost to have forgotten what the normal world was like—the water so dark and silky, the river mud so cool between the toes, the boats so coloured, and all under a sun more bright and burning than it could ever have been before.

Mrs. Fairbrass wrote again in a day or two with news of Meryon's progress. "Much more cheerful now that we've really learned to leave him to work things out for himself. It's very difficult, of course, not to rush in when he's heading for trouble—and he's had some bangs and bashings as you can imagine—but that's how he wants it. At present he's mentally mapping his way all over the house and garden. Our part in it, I see, is never to move any furniture. He's taped three different voices of Burma, Jack playing the flute, and three bird-songs—one a sparrow's, I admit. The recorder is portable so he can carry it about anywhere he likes. Jack and I know he's champing to go beyond the house and garden, but he's still much too independent to allow himself to be taken. Perhaps when he's exhausted the possibilities here, it will be different." And there was a P.S. giving the name of the tape recorder. Tamzin noted it down and found out its price from a Dunsford shop by telephone. She could just make it, with seven and six left in her savings after the recorder and four cassettes were paid for.

"Dad, would it be all right for me to buy a tape recorder, out of my Post Office savings?"

As it was a Saturday morning Mr. Grey had begun on the composition of three sermons, for his two churches, while digging potatoes in his kitchen garden. He was a man who seldom enjoyed the luxury of doing one thing at a time.

"How much?"

The digging made satisfying cracking and crumbling noises as the white potatoes emerged through rich transported river-mud. Tamzin suddenly thought how much she would enjoy recording it for Meryon and the two others whose addresses she was hoping for by every post—"Potato-digging in our garden, with seagulls in the background"—"How much?" she said as off-handedly as she could. "Oh, about all, more or less, I think."

"What does Mother say?"

Tamzin was helping to gather the potatoes; they were like beautiful white earth-eggs. "I *think* she would say yes. I asked you first because it was your idea."

"*My* idea?" The vicar sat on his fork-handle and looked at her.

"About thinking of blind people and trying to help. And, you know, you were right."

"Was I, now?"

"That it's the answer, I mean—makes everything come right. How did you know?"

117

"Well—" The vicar considered. "I wasn't exactly the *originator* of the idea of losing yourself to find yourself, you know. You might say my personal experiences have confirmed it, for me at least. Parsons are usually up to the ears in other people's predicaments; I just found there's nothing so effective for squashing your own. So even from a downright selfish angle I thoroughly recommend it."

"Dad, you're marvellous!" she said, grinning at him.

"I know," he said modestly. "I can't think why more people don't notice it!"

"So it's all right about the tape recorder?" The grin widened. "I'd thought of a kind of Sound News-Letter service—no, it would be more of a magazine. I never knew how many sounds there are until I started thinking about them."

"I haven't said it's all right. You rushed on before I could."

"Yes, I know. I was afraid if I didn't you mightn't."

"Meryon's got one, I hear."

"Yes," she said. "I was just thinking he'd like the sound of potatoes. Who'd ever have thought they made a noise at all?"

The vicar picked up the basket and fork and turned towards the house. "There are peas; that's a good noise—the pod popping and the rattle into the bowl. With a running commentary, of course. And a horse eating hay—very nice, that, one of my favourite sounds; I sometimes stop and listen when I pass the stable …"

Chapter Five

When Tamzin had the hang of her tape recorder the first thing she did with it was to imagine Meryon in the garden with her and talk to him. It was terrible at first. Although she had been careful to make sure that no one was in view or earshot of this first attempt she felt so silly, sitting talking to a stick of a microphone; the sentences came out short and jerky.

"Hullo! It's so hot this afternoon, I'm not riding. I'll go to the farm this evening. What were the other two birds you recorded, beside the sparrow? There's something twittering in the tree behind me—listen ... Do you know what that bird is? I'm not much good at them, but I'd like to be—I'm willing to learn if I can't have my lesson on jazz!"

The grey cat, Willow, was on her knee—she had been named after silver-grey scuts of pussy-willow—and was purring. Tamzin held the microphone very close and tickled her throat to encourage her. "I hope that sounds like pumas at the zoo, but it's Willow. Play it to Burma and see what he does! Perhaps he'll send a message back to Willow and Schnooky."

She couldn't resist stopping and playing it back to herself at this point, just to see how it all came out. "That can't be my voice!" was her first reaction, until she remembered being told in the shop that everyone usually thought this. The purring was magnificent, much louder than life because she had held the microphone so close.

"Jim is being very secretive again, all of a sudden, and doing repairs to the old *Thunderer*—both ominous signs." She was beginning really to get the hang of talking into the thing, now. "No other symptoms yet, but I'd say those are enough to guess he's up to something, and it's fairly certain to be unlawful. Anyway, as long as Hookey isn't involved it can't be too awful. Have you any ideas? Smuggling's always the obvious thing to think of, with Jim—he's the one who said it's in his blood—but he's never been terribly secretive with *us* about that, has he?"

The arrival of the afternoon post, with its possibilities of addresses from the R.N.I.B., caused her to switch off and go to investigate. There was no letter for her in the hall where, on a summer's day, the postman walked in to leave the mail, but there was a small padded packet, such as she hadn't seen before. Curious but a little disappointed she sat on the front steps to open it, while Willow and Schnooky pounced out at each other and Tamzin's feet from the summer jasmine that jungled over the porch. Before it was properly unpacked she had guessed what it was, and she was right—a cassette for a tape recorder. Unreasonably, because the handwriting was strange, she had a sudden wild hope that it was from Meryon. There was no written message with it. Her fingers smoothed the wrapper to reveal what was visible of the postmark; ONDON—that must be London. Oh, well, she said to herself; but she put the cassette into the recorder in place of her own partly filled tape and switched on.

"Hullo, Tamzin," said a boy's voice, oddly gruff. "I hear you are looking for a tapespondent."

She had a sudden impulse to look round into the hall; it was so strange to be listening to someone who wasn't there—but no stranger than the telephone, she told herself reprovingly. The gruff voice went on after a fractional pause, "I'm Simon. Eighteen, five foot eleven and ginger. I hope I'll do. Willing to answer anything else you want to know. I imagine you as rather tall and very dark—

probably frighteningly efficient." Tamzin laughed aloud. "It would be nice to be wrong about that, but I'll stick to the tall dark part. From your address I know you live in a Sussex fishing village. I like the idea of that, too, because it must be about as different from London as could be.

"It's funny not knowing anything about you. Do you like animals? Dogs? If so, you'd like Jan. She's my guide dog, a black labrador. I can send you a photo of her, if you like. We've got lots. People are always photographing her, partly because she's very photogenic but mostly because she enjoys it so much. She really does. You can't help thinking she knows all about it. The moment a camera appears she sits and looks beautiful, keeping still and posing like a professional. As soon as the shutter clicks she rushes up with her tail swirling round and round—she doesn't wag like ordinary dogs—and bounces round the camera, barking. But the minute anyone looks in the viewfinder again, she's sitting still and looking beautiful. It's classic!

"How do I know? Well, I think all your other senses—especially hearing—are so much sharper when you aren't distracted by sight."

Tamzin found that she had to switch off for a moment to think about this extraordinary remark, "distracted by sight." Was she? Was there some kind of unknown world that she was blind to, because she could see?

There was not much more on this short tape.

"It'll be great if you decide to take me on for tape exchange. London is hot and noisy, and I try to think of what your village sounds like. All I can think of is seagulls. Good-bye from Simon."

Seagulls! she said to herself. Gosh, this is going to be fun—all *I* can think of is seagulls! That's because I'm distracted by sight. Now I'm going straight round to the Point to find out what it does sound like.

She changed the cassettes again, slipping in a new one, and swung off round Smiling Morn's corner, feeling wonderful.

After the first self-conscious moments of looking around to see that no one was listening, she started, feeling quite experienced.

"Hullo, Simon, this is me, Tamzin. Yes, of course you'll do. And if it's village sounds you want—well, here goes. I'm sitting on the jetty looking down at the river. I couldn't for the life of me think what Westling sounded like, so now we're both going to find out. Listen …" She let the tape run on for a minute, and then joined in. "Can you hear the water slapping on the side of the *Alice*?—I'm holding the microphone over the edge as far as I can— She's an old wooden fishing smack, tied up to the jetty. There are your seagulls! Oh, larks, too—are they too far away across the river? A motor trawler going out—she comes down from Dunsford … Now, there's a noise I never noticed—ropes slapping on a mast in the wind. They're the *Alice*'s halyards. I can hear the sea in the distance, but I'm sure that's too far … How funny you thinking I was tall and dark—and efficient. Reverse all that and it's me. Yes, I'd love to have a photograph of Jan; and one of you if you've got one to spare, so that I can know who I'm talking to."

Down at the ferry she found Jim Decks pushing off to fetch a holiday family from the other side, and went across with him to record the oars in the rowlocks and the dipping and dripping of their blades. She tried unsuccessfully to get Jim to say hullo into the microphone for Simon, but anyway Simon was going to have fun distantly hearing him warning Tamzin about the hazards of monkeying with Nature—"Thass a mortacious bad thing, boxing yer voice up fer any snitcher to meddle with, stands to reason. Blow that fer a caper. I tellee, gal, likely as not you'll catch a stutter off of it—same as a chap I knew once what spoke along the telephone, spite of me and my mates warned him." Thinking himself safe at half a dinghy's distance the ferryman went on for the rest of the crossing about the price of rope, and how porridge wasn't what porridge used to be, and nothing in the smuggling business with all this home wine-making, and the unreasonableness of women, in particular over taking boots off in bed and suchlike matters. Tamzin listened sympathetically, but her mind's eye gleamed at the thought of Simon's windfall.

It was only later, in the early evening, when she was riding out of the vicarage gate with Diccon on the way to Castle Farm, the tape recorder over her shoulder, that sudden doubts assailed her. Was it right to pass on someone's remarks without their knowing? He hadn't *said* they were private. Still …

Jim was in the William the Conqueror with a mug on one knee and his cat—which usually followed him—on the other. He was near the door to keep an eye on the ferry, so Tamzin didn't have to dismount.

"Hey, gal!" The mug waved above the piebald cat, and the cat and pony snorted at each other with necks outstretched. Tamzin shortened rein. "Jim, what you were saying, about rope and porridge and wine-making and women—can I put it in a letter to someone—it wasn't private?"

The ferryman thrust out his small beard at her. "Rope and porridge and wine and women?" He glared across the sloshing beer. "I never! Thass that grocer been at you, I lay, grocing around everyone's back doors, the ole scorpion, do anything to tar a man's face behind his back. Jumping gin bottles and sink me fer a coghead—"

"It's all right, Jim, no one's been saying anything about you. I wouldn't believe them if they did, anyway, and you know that. But supposing you had been talking to me about the price of rope and things—it wouldn't matter my putting it in a letter to a friend?"

"We-ell, a-course not, stands to reason, don' it, gal? Might even help fetch the price down a bit, hey? If you was to be writting to the proper quarters. And porridge, you was saying? That ent no good no more. Now you might writ to them as mills it and tellem from me—there ent no body in it same as there used to was. You tellem that, ole young un! I lay they bash the oats too heavy." The beer mug went up and came down, symbolizing bashing, and Billingham the cat received a baptism of old and mild. Her outraged rush through Cascade's legs took him so much by surprise that he switched right round before he knew what had happened.

"Swapped ends, he did," Jim said sympathetically, helping Tamzin to remount. "Never did trust 'em, horses—now thass an unseamanlike animal, not like my ole cat what been to sea a dunnamany times and know her stuff. An' if you see that grocer—" he called as Tamzin turned Cascade to join Diccon, riding up from the river's edge.

"All right, Jim! I'll remember."

"He's doing up the *Thunderer*," Diccon said as they rode below the harbour mast, headed for the Martello Tower and the grazings. "I was watching. D'you think he's going to start fishing again?"

"I shouldn't think so," she said; then added, "How d'you mean, watching? He isn't working on it now."

"But Hookey Galley is." Diccon turned Banner under the Tower wall, the ponies' hoofs crunching on the dry shingle path. "I heard hammering in the cabin, and then his face looked out. But it bobbed back again. You can't mistake it, can you? It makes me think of those corpse-eating birds."

"He can't help the shape of his nose," Tamzin said.

"It isn't so much the nose as the eyes," said Diccon. "They make me think of vultures *looking* for something."

"The only thing I think is, I'm sorry he's doing a job for Jim." She touched Cascade with her heels as they came down from the shingle to the springy turf of the sheep levels. With a single stride the white pony was into a canter, more like something released than something told to go. Tamzin never lost the thrill of it—the smoothness and power, the mane blowing back, and the wind suddenly into her face. She pulled firmly on the recorder strap to stop it bumping on her back. Diccon was making Indian noises, pounding level with her, and sheep watched, amazed, in bunches along the sea wall as the ponies flew by towards the farm. Five swans went up from the Redshanks' Pool as they passed, leaving only two feathers floating, curled like wood-shavings, bright on the dark water.

The farmyard seemed quiet in the evening sun; a few ducks preening, oiling their feathers against the wet of pond life, a few brown hens walking about examining the ground, first with one eye and then the other. At the open door Tamzin looked in, calling, "Anyone there?" the reins over her arm. A hasty snuffle came to her ears, and then a sniff and the firm blowing of a nose. A chair was scraped back on the stone floor and Mrs. Merrow appeared from the shadows. She was like a warm pink quilt, soft and comforting, Tamzin often thought; a kind of universal mother to anything in need—people, animals and plants. A year or two ago she had adopted, without a second's hesitation, a rough wild boy of unknown parentage who had been living and working in cattle-ships. Called by the seamen Jonah so that misfortune could be blamed on him, he had been re-christened by Mrs. Merrow, Joseph, and was now as much a Merrow as her own son Mike.

The pink quilt was pinker than usual. Diccon, too, knew that Mrs. Merrow had been crying. This was not unheard of, as her warm heart would ache to tears over any creature in distress; a honey-bee drowned in the horse-trough was not too small, nor a cow crying for her calf too ordinary a farm event. She knew her weakness and was always apologetic for it, as if it were a bad habit.

"Now, tie up and come right in, loves! You mustn't mind me—sniff—you know the way I carry on, by now. That's what William always says to me—'You do carry on so, gal'." She found a clean corner of her handkerchief and dabbed her nose. "I've got some lovely Victorias in for jam. If you look you'll find some real tender eating. Wash your hands and you can help me stone them while you tell me all your news."

It was usually better to follow this kind of lead and not to dig into the grief of the day with inquiries. Diccon was already examining the bowl of plums and Tamzin found herself a stoning-knife from the table drawer.

"I've got a tape recorder, Mrs. Merrow—this is it—I was going to do the sounds of Castle Farm, to send to Meryon and another blind friend. The grandfather clock and the ducks and the milking and everything; and I told Meryon Meg would be sure to send him a message." Tamzin was looking round the stone-floored kitchen with its dresser and scrubbed table and old black cooking range that Mrs. Merrow still preferred to her modern electric one. "Where is she?"

A fresh outbreak of blowing and dabbing told at once the way things were. Tamzin paused with a plum half cut open. "He hasn't said she won't do?"

A silent nodding accompanied the sniffs, and the pinkness was very evident again.

"He'll change his mind, you'll see," Tamzin said comfortingly; "or even if he doesn't, perhaps he'd let you keep her as a pet. You haven't got one, have you?"

"Well, only my hens and that, and the farm cats, and the calves and my tame robin, and the cow that lost its tail, poor thing. He don't hold with pets on a farm—and rightly, too," she added staunchly, defending her man. "Farm creatures must earn their living, same as farm people. And Meg she just fooled and frolicked and enjoyed herself—you couldn't help getting fond of her, though! I miss her now she's gone, and you must excuse me." The handkerchief was opened but now offered no dry place.

Tamzin dropped her knife on the table and swung round holding the plum. "Gone?"

"What—you mean away?" Diccon didn't believe it. Castle Farm

dogs were never failed. They won prizes in sheep-dog trials or—according to William Merrow—they were shot: never given away.

Mrs. Merrow dried her face on her apron-corners. "He was going to shoot her, but when it came to it he gave her to the holiday people from the Watch Houses—the Maxwells. It wasn't even that they were set on having her, but when they heard she was to be shot—he always said that were kinder to a sheep-dog than being a living failure—they took her."

Tamzin and Diccon gazed, speechless, at the sad kind face. Mrs. Merrow took up Tamzin's stoning job as one who realizes that sorrow must not interfere with work. "The pity is they live in London. That's no place for a born and bred sheep-dog. Rightly, I think, William knew what he was talking about. Eat her heart out in the streets, with never a sight of green grazings."

"When?" Tamzin asked. "When did they take her?"

"When they came for their milk. This morning. Because they said they were going, to-day."

Tamzin went to the window and looked out across the grazings and the tide-creeks to the pair of low black Watch Houses, once used by coastguards but now by holiday families. There was a blue car parked outside, just visible through gorse clumps, but it was too far to see anything else. They might still be there, the holiday family. The seed of an idea blew from somewhere into her mind; it took root and began growing beanstalk fashion. She was afraid to mention it, to delay it with talking, even perhaps to start up discussion or opposition. She swung to look at the grandfather clock.

"Is that the time? My heavens! We've got to call somewhere on the way back. Come on, Dicky! Sorry about the plums, Mrs. Merrow—we'll come earlier next time—and don't worry about Meg; she might have a lovely life, you never know!"

"Useful is what sheep-dogs need to be." This was the creed on sheep-farms, and all the Merrows had been brought up in it.

"Perhaps that, too." Tamzin was snatching Cascade's reins, her foot in the stirrup. But Mrs. Merrow knew about London life from the papers; once she had even been there and seen the streets for herself—not a field or a cow; so she watched sadly as the ponies galloped away with their long tails streaming.

Chapter Six

"What—" Diccon began, shouting after Tamzin as they galloped—"Wherever are we going?"

Her answer came back down the wind, "To rescue Meg!"

Cascade had the wind in his head and suddenly began shying—a thing he seldom did. Tamzin was taken by surprise and failed to notice the blue car pulling away on to the rough Marsh track that led to the road and civilization; but Diccon saw. "It's too late—look!"

She swung Cascade, pulling him up on his hocks, screwing her eyes into the sun. She couldn't believe it. But as she gazed her dashed hopes rose inside her. The little car heaved and dipped along the sheep track, like a dinghy rocking through breakers. She knew that track. "Dicky! There might still be time. Keep on the path and I'll wait for you at the end—I'm going to try to cut across, over the tide-creeks."

Diccon gazed at her, clutching his reins. "He'll never jump them."

"He'll have to—" She was already away, her voice snatched on the wind, like the castle jackdaws that tumbled in the sky.

The race was on. Now Cascade was gaining, flying along the short-bitten turf while the car rolled, pitching heavily in the pot-holes; then it was the pony floundering with his hind-legs in the creek that was just too wide a jump for him, and the car bowling along a smooth stretch. Despair came as she threw herself off to help the struggling pony. Hope returned as the car hit a shingle patch and wallowed in it while Cascade flew again, his small hoofs clipping the yellow hawkbit in the grass.

She didn't know quite how the urgency had developed, why suddenly she felt that Meg must be rescued, except that now she had set out to do it she would not give up until hope was all gone.

Now she and the car were both speeding, drawing closer as they neared the gate to the road; but the last creek lay ahead. It was dark, reed-fringed and impossibly wide. For the car there was a gate to open—blessed delay, she hoped it would jam. Cascade was gathering himself, the strong jumping-muscles tightening, when a skein of wild duck went up from the creek. In a moment he had spun a half-circle and flung Tamzin to the ground. He was snorting at the end of the reins which she had desperately kept clutched—Meg's life-line—as she scrambled to her feet and to the saddle again. Her hand went round to the tape recorder on her back—it felt all right, but there was no time now to investigate. The car was moving through the gate, a woman—Mrs. Maxwell?—standing ready to close it. There was nothing now but the firm road all the way to London; impossible, quite impossible, for a pony to catch up—but, doggedly, Tamzin turned Cascade and rode him in again to the jump. It seemed a kind of bitter joke of fate that this time he flew it like a sea-swallow, his hoofs falling silent in the turf and flicking on towards the gate; his supreme jump, that was too late to matter any more. Already the blue car was a hundred yards down the sea road, between a lorry and a van.

Incredulously, Tamzin saw it begin to slow down and draw to a standstill, just beside a little garage at the roadside. Petrol, of course! They were stopping for petrol.

She was through the gate in a second, swerving Cascade up on the grass verge and flying down the lane, two campers staring from their tent beyond the fence.

Meg was in the back of the car with Mrs. Maxwell. Tamzin looked in, holding Cascade. "Excuse me—"

"Aren't you the girl who goes to the farm?"

"Yes. I've just heard about Meg. I—Mrs. Merrow said perhaps you didn't really want her. It sounds awful, but—" The garage man was hanging up the petrol-pump. Cascade didn't like the smell and was snorting. Banner was near the gate, slowed to a trot. Mr. Maxwell counted out money and Tamzin wished she were submerging under kindly waves.

"You mean, you want her?" Mrs. Maxwell prompted. She was elderly, gentle and worried-looking. Meg was exuberant and gay, beating the car with her plumy black tail, treading in a box of runner beans and knocking a handbag off the seat.

"I—well—she isn't really a town dog. I just thought—"

Meg reached out her nose and licked indiscriminately Cascade's muzzle and Tamzin's hand on the rein.

"If you're trying to say you'd take her off our hands," said Mr. Maxwell, finishing the petrol business, "I tell you, we'd be glad. Wouldn't we, Freda?"

"We've both rather regretted being so impulsive," she admitted with a harassed smile. "But it seemed such a shame, a nice dog being shot. So young, too. She *is* rather rough, though, and we aren't used to dogs. If you'd really like to have her ..."

When Diccon came trotting up to the garage he found Tamzin standing between Meg and Cascade, the blue car disappearing down the lane. The collie, like most of her kind, wore no collar; Tamzin held her on a piece of string provided by Mr. Maxwell.

"You've got her! I never thought ... What are you going to do with her now?" Banner was blowing, his brown sides heaving.

The garage man looked on, wiping the oil off his hands. "A bit late to start asking that, if she doesn't know, isn't it?"

Tamzin looked at Meg, who whirled herself into a cheerful flourish and wasn't worried. Cascade took a long sighing breath and rubbed his muzzle on a delicately extended foreleg. "I thought at first," Tamzin said, "we'd take her home."

"She doesn't know," the man said, like someone giving a running commentary, and he tossed aside his oily rag.

"Then I thought about Schnooky and Willow, and that it wouldn't really be fair to bring a grown dog home when you have two established cats. A little puppy would be different." Meg jumped round in a circle and got a leg over her string.

"She'll have to think again, then, won't she?" the man asked of anyone and everything, and he took a spanner to a lawn-mower that was in for repairing.

"Then suddenly—only this minute, really—I thought what good company she'd be for Meryon. She knows him, too. Not like a strange dog. And Burma's only a kitten, really, and wouldn't mind so much."

"Well, if she's thought all that," said the man, "she can get off my concrete, can't she? And let people reach their petrol if they want some, which I hope they will soon, seeing as that's what it's there for."

"I only wanted to think things out a bit," Tamzin said to him, "and let the ponies have a blow. There's no one waiting for petrol. And I oughtn't really to take a dog straight to someone's house without warning, ought I? Meryon won't see us, of course. Still, if Mrs. Fairbrass will take her in, I can explain to him about it on tape—it'll be a good chance to see if the tape recorder's all right after that fall."

"Act first, think after, that's teenagers all over." The man hit the mower with the spanner. "No sense of responsibility. And that's what we pay our rates for."

Tamzin put a foot in the stirrup; she had the reins and Cascade's mane and Meg's string in her hands. "Come on, Dicky. We'll chance it."

Mrs. Fairbrass opened the door of Meryon's room; he was standing at the window where once he had looked out from this high green cliff across the sheep levels to the far sea. Until he heard steps on the landing he had been furiously hunting for a comb which he had dropped on the floor. He didn't ask his mother to find it but stood burning with frustration over the magnified irritation of it, waiting for her to speak.

"Tamzin's here. With Diccon. They were at the farm and rode across."

"I asked her not to come."

"I know. And she knows. They just brought something for you—two things. I thought you might like to say hullo."

"I'd rather not. And I don't really want anyone to bring me things."

"She says you can send both back if you want to; but they might entertain you a bit, I think, and they aren't really presents. I'll go and get them, shall I? And tell her—what?"

"You needn't tell her anything, need you?" There was a kind of bruised resentment in the otherwise dull voice that held none of its usual liveliness. He heard the door close and bent to feel around for the infuriating comb again, not that it mattered if he combed his hair …

When his mother came back there was an exuberant patter and scuffle coming with her; he could hear it down the landing, claws sliding off the carpet to the polished wood. His ruffled mind stilled itself to listen questioningly. His family—and Tamzin's—had no dog. There was the door noise, and then a loud and cheerful sneezy snuffling.

"This is Meg. She's been in awful trouble. Tamzin says you're old friends; and there's a tape here that tells you about it; it's on your table."

"She hasn't got a tape recorder," Meryon said uncertainly.

Mrs. Fairbrass was coming across the room. "She has, though. She's afraid you'll be wild about it but she says it's as much for her own fun as anybody's, and that she's sending cassettes to other people. She says one is called Simon."

"Did she, now?"

"I'll be back in a few minutes, but I've got a pie in the oven I must see to."

As the door closed again Meg, freed from her string, came across in a bound of delighted recognizing greeting. Meryon put out a hand to the silky head and ears. "Hey, girl! You in trouble, too?" It didn't sound much like it. Clearly in the full enjoyment of life the collie whirled round exploring the room, with frequent rushes back to push her muzzle into Meryon's hands. He heard her pounce playfully on something and scrape it with her paw, a rough sound, of something hard and ribbed. He went across to her, his hands seeing for him, and reached down to her paws. His fingers found and slid into his pocket the lost comb.

Mrs. Fairbrass didn't come back for half an hour or so, by which time Meryon had played Tamzin's cassette twice. He was sitting in his old easy chair that had a broken spring from the time years ago when he used to take running leaps into it. Meg was leaning against it, thumping the carpet with her tail.

"She's gone, I suppose," he said.

"Yes." Mrs. Fairbrass sat down on the window seat. "She rang up the vicarage to say they had come on here and were on their way back, and she sent you her love."

"Oh. What was she wearing?"

"Let me see—some kind of slacks, jeans perhaps, navy I think; and a red pullover."

"You mean, you aren't sure?" It was incredible how blind anyone could be when they actually had eyes.

"They *were* red and blue. I remember now."

"That chap Simon—did she say any more about him?"

"No, I don't think so. Perhaps there's something on the tape.

She'd be awfully pleased for you to answer it, I know." Meg had come over to greet her, all sparkle and grin and swirl. "She's rather beautiful, really, isn't she?" Mrs. Fairbrass said.

"A good collie type. Bred along the right lines," Meryon told her. "Pity she didn't make it. I expect you've heard her history." He paused a moment and added casually, "O.K. if we keep her?"

Chapter Seven

Tamzin couldn't remember ever being so busy in school holidays as she was now with the tape recorder, nor so absorbed and fascinated by what she was doing.

Simon sent her a tape as full of interesting things about London life as her village recordings were to him. "Your ferryman is great. The sort of bloke everyone would like to know but never does. I laughed and laughed about the porridge and the chaps who caught a stutter off the phone; and I can't wait to know what really is going on in the *Thunderer*. Do watch out for yourself, though; that Hookey sounds something of a danger man.

"Jan excelled herself last week. Mum had to go into hospital for a few days for an ear op.—quite a minor one—and as Dad was at work Jan and I took her. Dad saw her that evening and Jan and I went along the next day; but blow me if I could remember where Mum was when we got there—a whacking great building with several blocks and floors—and there seemed no one handy to ask. But Jan seemed to know where she wanted to go, so I went with her—up several lots of stairs and round corners and along passages, thought we were never stopping, until she fetched up at a door somewhere and a nurse said, 'Can I help you?' Turned out we were plumb outside the Margaret Ward, where Mum was! Jan had never been anywhere near the building except for the once when we took Mum in there."

Tamzin had a new tapespondent, a boy of ten called Thomas

who had lost his sight because of an illness three years before. First she recorded the sounds of Diccon's clockwork railway for him, the winding-up and the running round the track, and Diccon shunting the wagons and saying when the trains went in and came out of tunnels. Then for both Simon and Thomas she did a tour of the house with the sounds and description of each room. The kitchen came out best, she thought, with its cheerful noises of cooking; Mrs. Grey giving a commentary on it all—"beautiful bluey-green mackerel; Tamzin and Diccon bought them off a boat called *Nancybell* early this morning. These peas I'm podding grew in our garden."

The vicar obligingly banged on his old typewriter in the study, and Diccon played *Chopsticks* on the drawing room piano, and Mrs. Briggs, who cleaned for them, washed up loudly in the scullery while singing a hymn and slapping down her plimsolled foot in time. The bathroom was so good, sounding like a concert hall, that Tamzin and Diccon couldn't resist singing *Frère Jacques* in it.

She told Simon about Smiling Morn and how gloomy he always was, and then took the tape recorder with her to his shop when she went with the vicarage shopping list, but he wouldn't co-operate. When she told him about Simon being blind he said that was no bad thing, in a world was wicked as this, and it might be better to be deaf as well, besides—in the case of some people—dumb into the bargain, considering the scandals that went around. Since the grocer didn't seem to realize that he was being recorded willy nilly, Tamzin just hoped that Simon would find it entertaining; and then Mrs. Venus came in for her packet of Sugar Snazzles, and she was so fascinating that Tamzin stifled her conscience and didn't tell her that all she said was being taken down, as it were, in evidence.

Although she looked so kind and comfortable Mrs. Venus was so scurrilous that it could scarcely be believed. Her favourite occupation in the scandal field was sending poison-pen letters about other people in the village, mostly to Tamzin's father. It was to get the "free ball-pen with every packet" for writing them that she bought her Sugar Snazzles.

"Changed their offer again," Smiling Morn told her with miserable pleasure. "No more ball-pens. Have to do 'em in pencil, or go over to arsenic." Everyone knew about the letters; she made no secret of them; and although they were always signed *One Who Knows*, she usually asked the vicar if he had received and read them. "Poison the lot," said the grocer, "and you'll be shut of having to write about 'em."

Ignoring him, Mrs. Venus delicately lifted the packet from the worn wooden counter and examined it, reading slowly aloud. "'Send only nineteen shillings and elevenpence and four coupons and you too can take Happisnaps with this super-plastic easy-work Snap-o-Matic colour camera.' Think of that."

The grocer, whose proper name was Mr. Goldeye, spread his large hands on the counter and sent her a sideways look. "Do some right snooping with that, you could." He picked up Tamzin's list and peered at it before stumping off, flat-footed, for a packet of soap powder and a tin of wax polish.

"'No skill needed, a child could use it'," read Mrs. Venus, marvelling. "I'll take four packets."

"Making a path with them?" Mr. Goldeye cynically inquired from behind a partition.

"Pay you sometime." Mrs. Venus swept up the packets and flounced out with a jangle of doorbell.

"Live to see the day," the grocer said joylessly to Tamzin, slapping down the polish and soap powder. "Happy snaps! Tell yer pa to look out, is all I can say. And tell yer ma we're out of sardines, had a run on 'em from the Survival Camp. They'll survive all right."

Mrs. Venus must have received her camera almost by return of post. Tamzin first noticed her peering into the viewfinder at Smiling Morn's corner one morning soon after the shop encounter, but she didn't pay much attention because she was playing for the third time, at her attic window, a tape from Meryon. It was not much really, as letters from boy-friends went, but the mere fact of his having recorded and sent one to her was a great thing in her shattered world.

The first part was so stilted and polite, with comments on local and world news and even sport, it might have come from a stranger—no, worse than that, because Simon and Thomas were far friendlier. Then a sudden snuffle intervened. A short pause was followed by Meryon saying in his ordinary voice, "Meg, of course! You did a good thing there. Made quite a difference. The Merrows can't know how intelligent she really is, or they'd kick themselves. Not as sloppy as they thought, either. A bit of friendly attention and she settles down quite sensibly, for her. That's what her temperament needed; just didn't take to the strict life of a sheep-dog.

"You know, I think she knows I'm blind." Tamzin could hardly bear this in that ordinary Meryonish voice. "When I put a lead on her she sobers down and goes carefully, almost like a pukka guide dog. It's surprising, actually, how much quicker I can get about with her. Been a few croppers, of course, but I think if I had a stiff lead, something like a guide dog harness, I'd keep more vertical. Must see what I can rig up."

There was more about Meg and about Burma—"He had the upper hand from the start; poor Meg never knows when she's going to be bounced from where."—and some speculations on Jim Decks's repairing of his old smack. There was also a brief, curt query which made Tamzin smile; "Who's this Simon bloke?"

Simon had quickly responded to her tape of village and vicarage sounds, and he had sent her the two photographs. Jan was a wise and humorous dog, you could see at a glance, and Simon had that kind of nice-ugly face that you took to at once. She would put them both up in her room.

"I really did enjoy that," Simon said. "All the rooms have a different kind of sound—I wonder if you noticed? The kitchen very lived-in and warm, somehow; drawing room gave a comfortable impression, as if the sound was absorbed in cushions and curtains and easy chairs; hall empty and echoey; spare room nearly as echoey; but not yours and Diccon's—I guessed you'd both left clothes and things lying about."

Well, he was right there, Tamzin said to herself, as she sat on her bed with the recorder on her knee.

"Outdoor recordings were awfully noisy—wind in the mike. It's an old trouble. A little breeze comes out like half a gale. You could try with your back to it; but do go on doing them, the outdoor ones—it's a new world to a townee.

"You ask do I know night from day and the answer is yes! Mainly by birds. Seems funny in the big city, but even we have sparrows; millions, I should think. Listen for a minute and if you hear them it's day. Other sounds are different, too. No, I don't bother to switch lights on, but some blind people do; I think mainly to let other people know there's someone at home.

"What can anyone say about Smiling Morn and Mrs. Venus? I laughed so much Mum came up to see what was the matter! But really I think they're tragic—Mrs. V. anyway. Don't you? I reckon that grocer *enjoys* his miseries. Well, if he doesn't, I did! Tell me more."

At once Tamzin wanted to rush out and begin her reply. It was a soft day, unusual for August: under a high cloud-film there was a haze over the quiet sea, and hardly any wind. But first she had to thank Simon for the photographs, and then tell him about Meg: and that meant telling him something, at least, about Meryon. There wasn't very much tape left when she went round to the Point and up to her old place on a bollard at the edge of the jetty.

"I'm here again, at the harbour, and this time there's no wind. It's nearly high tide and some children are splashing about near the ferry boat. Old Jim's shouting terrible threats at them—can you hear?—

because they've splashed inside the boat, and they're shouting back at him. The fishing boats are all out, except *Thunderer*, across the river. Hookey is still doing his repairs—you can hear the hammering, I expect. His ancestor had an arm eaten by a shark and wore a hook, and the name passed down in the family. Whatever he does is fishy, you were right about that—either fishy-fishy or sinister-fishy ..."

She suddenly stopped, letting the tape recorder run on unheeded for a moment as she stared, before switching it off; someone's head and shoulders had appeared in the companion-way from the cabin. Hookey, perhaps, had slipped off down there without her noticing. Her eyes raked over the little ship and presently discovered Hookey's hammer-arm swinging up again behind the heavy boom, and then his clear profile as he raised himself to look over his shoulder. The head in the companion-way went down and disappeared. Tamzin sat gazing for a minute or two, wondering, and remembering other times, and forgetting about recording; and then she walked along the wooden jetty and down to the ferry hut.

Jim had an oil-stove burning inside and was boiling a bucket of shrimps. The steam misted through the doorway smelling wonderful; it gave the old man a mysterious look, drifting round him as he bent to stir and test and taste like a sorcerer brewing a spell. Tamzin sat on an empty fish-box.

"To a turn," Jim told her. "You come in at the crucial moment." He turned out the stove. "Fetch us the plate."

She reached for the chipped enamel dish that he always kept polished with newspaper and propped on a ledge for ferry hut use, and held it while he scooped out, with his long-handled sieve, a good plateful. The rest were quickly ladled into a large trug-basket to finish draining as they cooled.

"You got that machine with you," he observed disapprovingly as he sat opposite her and put the plate between them.

Tamzin took a shrimp. "But it isn't switched on."

"I lay that Simon woulder liked hearing a shrimp-boiling, I lay he never have."

Tamzin looked up over her de-legging, de-heading and de-tailing. "But you said—"

"An' another thing, you don't wanter multilate the little perishers, you wanter ate 'em whole, same as like this ..." He popped a collection through his beard.

"Hookey's still busy on *Thunderer*, I see," she said, continuing to dismember her shrimps. "Is there anyone else on board with him?"

"Wodjer ask that for, hey?"

"Oh, I just wondered. Is there?"

The ferryman glared at her over a sprouting of shrimp legs and whiskers. "Why for should there be anyone else on board? Hookey ent got no workmate. An' I'd tellee fer why he hasn't, gal, 'cept you know as well as me—no one won't work with that codger. As uncivil a bloke as God ever made."

"Are you going fishing again, Jim?" The question seemed innocent enough but it drew another glare from Jim.

"If a feller has a boat what's dilapidating, an' he up and mends it, thass his affair, ent it?"

There was no answer from Tamzin, who frowned at her shrimps as she sat thinking. The old man suddenly flashed at her, "Bad enough that ole Venus basket snooping into folks's business, without you starting! Jumping gin bottles, gal—" He slid a sideways look at her, and his anger fizzled out. "Take another handful, while they're hot!" But he wouldn't smile.

After a while Tamzin wandered back to the jetty, and up and down the river, stopping whenever she felt solitary enough to finish her Simon recording. Once she caught a fleeting view of Mrs. Venus picking her way between the dinghies pulled up at the edge of the river, and several times she looked across at the *Thunderer* but saw only Hookey working on the deck.

Chapter Eight

Tamzin began her reply to Meryon with a flourish of Spanish guitar music. She had been postponing the tape to him, because this time she could not make up her mind how to start or what to say or not say. She was cleaning Cascade's tack in the kitchen and listening to the radio when the music started. Her hands soaping the reins slowed and fell still as she stared unseeing through the window, drawn into a kind of enchantment. She had never heard anything like this before; in its sweeping scope it seemed at the same time wild and noble, arrogant and gentle, but splendid altogether. Suddenly the idea came to start her letter with it. She reached for the tape recorder and changed the cassette with such haste that it almost made her slower; but the music was long and as her recording began slid into a second movement more splendid than the first. At the end of it, thinking one movement enough for someone calling himself tone-deaf, she stopped the tape while she hunted in the programme notes to find out what the music was.

"This is me, Tamzin. I never got my introduction to jazz, but how about that for guitar music? The man who wrote it was blind from three years old, the *Radio Times* says. He's called Rodrigo, and the music is the *Concerto de Aranjuez*, the second movement.

"I'm glad about Meg. The idea of her guiding you is the last thing I'd have thought of, she's so scatter-brained, and I'm not surprised about the croppers. Perhaps you could get a proper, trained guide dog if you applied for one; how about that?"

She knew the answer even as she asked the question. Anyone too stubbornly independent to go on a waiting list for corneal grafts would never accept a guide dog. She finished the tape with an account of Mrs. Venus's new venture and the shrimp picnic in the ferry hut. "Are you still out of bounds? I'd like to see Meg."

Days passed with no reply to this, although she had received and answered tapes from both Thomas and Simon. The summer holidays were slipping away; they were into September and the damsons were heavy on the branches of the vicarage tree. Already there were deep dews when she went to fetch the ponies from the paddock in the early morning, and the evenings were dark at half past eight.

It was because she had asked to see Meg, she knew, when he had been perfectly clear that their friendship was over, at least in the way that they had known it. She had hoped for too much from the understanding they had seemed to be rebuilding in their tape exchange. Playing his last tape over again, in her attic with the cats stretched in a patch of sun below the window, the thought came that she hadn't answered all his questions. "Who is this Simon bloke?" Meryon had asked.

It was a pity to waste a whole tape with one answer, but if they did make short tapes she hadn't one. It wasn't really waste, anyway, since you could go on using the same ones again as often as people sent them back.

"Hullo," she said into her microphone. "This is me. P.S. Simon is someone I am exchanging tapes with. He is eighteen and lives in London. I forgot to tell you in my last. Love to Meg and everyone, from Tamzin." She ran the tape through to rub off the rest of a letter from Thomas which was on it, and then thought wistfully, a little wickedly, of Meryon playing back all that silence. Oh well, she said to herself, packing it into its padded envelope, it's more than he's sent me, and what else can he expect?

She was surprised to get a reply back by return of post. Like her own, it was a message of few words and a long silence. "Hullo. It's me, of course. What does he look like? Mere curiosity. Yours, Meryon."

There was also by the same post a letter from Mrs. Fairbrass. Tamzin had gone through it quickly at breakfast and now, her house duties done, she was reading it again at her high south window.

"Just in case he's still being cagy with news, I thought I'd send you some. You ought to know what a success your Meg is, and the chances are he hasn't told you. He found out almost at once how much better he could get about with her, even allowing for frequent bumps and falls, which I don't have to tell you he completely ignored. Well, you know how once he gets an idea or an interest he always follows it to the limit? He got the idea that she could learn to be a real guide dog and that—of all things—he was going to teach her himself. I suppose it all keys in with the total independence idea, and at least it's snapped him out of his feeling of furious helplessness—wanting to get about but refusing to let anyone take him. I should have thought the idea of a blind person training his own dog was quite impossible. Perhaps it's the apparent impossibility that fascinates him.

"He says that, in a way, she's almost the perfect dog for his purpose, because she's already had basic obedience training as a sheep-dog, and has known him since she was a puppy; and he says even her friendliness, which failed her for sheep work, is an advantage in a guide dog. He heard a broadcast talk about them, and it said the old idea of guide dogs being one-man dogs is not held with, now, because one-man dogs won't let anyone else come near, even in emergencies—surprising, really, for Meryon to admit he might need anyone's help or that there might be an emergency! I have to admit that what he says is that if a dog gets too protective it could be dangerous to other people. But it's all a good sign, don't you think?

"He's being quite logical about the whole thing, really; working out exactly how many lessons Meg can cope with in a day without going stale, and how long they should last; and although he's clearly impatient to get on with them he sticks to the times he's decided on.

"What really would surprise you is the progress they've both made. He's been working with her in the house and garden, of course, where he knows almost exactly where he is and so where to make her turn 'left', or 'right', and where to check her and make her sit and wait. I can see the possibility of all that; but what happens when they go beyond the garden, if he still won't let any of us help?

"He's had a harness made at the shoe-repairers, to his own design ..."

Well, what will happen when they go beyond the garden? Tamzin asked herself, gazing through her window. She could see a small shower travelling, like a blown curtain, over the sea. There was sun to each side of it, dramatic against the dark cloud. Once, years ago, there had been rain in the front garden and none in the back, and she and Diccon had rushed backwards and forwards through the house pretending to be weathercock people ... She was only mentally doodling, thinking of these things, while she made up her mind about the important thing. Well anyway, she said to herself finally, I've got to exercise Cascade. I can think where I'm going when I'm on my way.

Her way took her to Castle Farm, because she wanted to tell Mrs. Merrow the news about Meg, the dog who had failed and then started again.

"Well, now, saints alive!" said Mrs. Merrow, on the verge of a joyful tear and sniffing a little. "If that isn't the best news I've heard since the sheep-dipping. It isn't every dog gets the chance to find out where its talent lies, is it?"

Irresistibly, Tamzin found herself imagining some dogs in banks who ought to be sailors, and some in factories who were cut out to be in law. But seriously, she told herself, animals did have different characters, and some were suited to one thing and some to another, it was true.

Mrs. Merrow found an apple for Cascade, and Joseph came through the yard on the tractor and stopped to pat him and to tell Tamzin about a new calf. Nobody would ever have thought that Joseph himself had been such a misfit when, in his earlier years, he had worked in ships' galleys.

"Well, I'm real glad about Meg," he said, "and I know Dad will be." Tamzin could understand this. Mr. Merrow had not wanted Meg to fail. He had no use for failed sheep-dogs, but he would be glad that she was succeeding in a different way—glad, too, that her success might mean a new freedom for Meryon. Joseph looked back as he turned to the tractor. "Will you come and see the calf?"

"Next time. I'm going on to see Meg and Meryon, now." She was surprised to hear herself say it, because she hadn't made up her mind until then. "Is it going to rain, Joseph?"

"That's blown away, now."

Riding from the farm she looked at the tide-creek which Cascade had jumped, and marvelled at his achievement and her recklessness. The garage man glanced up from attending to a motor-cycle as she passed, and she imagined him saying to its owner, "Well, they won't be expecting her, will they, if she hasn't made up her mind until now?"

There were mallows in the hedges and beside the ditches along the lane to Meryon's house; pale pink to deep rose, lilac to purple, they stood out conspicuously like little garden hollyhocks, a flower of late summer.

Tamzin hated the summer to be going. Holly berries were colouring already, and the mountain ashes were hung with their red harvest, which Meryon would not see.

Moving along the grass verge Cascade's hoofs were silent. Tamzin knew that Meryon was in the lane before he could have known that she was. He was at some distance, walking towards her with Meg in the harness he had had made for her. It seemed so odd that there should be no recognizing shout and wave, as there always used to be. In a way it emphasized the gulf there was now between them. She had drawn a breath to shout her own hullo, as she always had done, but something made her stop, and then pull up Cascade and wait.

Meryon was walking along the footpath at the side of the lane; not slowly and haltingly but with almost his old stride. Tamzin hardly recognized Meg. Certainly she looked the same but that steady purposeful walk had nothing of her old bouncing giddiness, unless it was the alertness that could be seen even at fifty yards distance.

What really held Tamzin's attention was a delivery van parked at the roadside between Meryon and herself. The driver must have gone through the gate to a house half-hidden in trees, and be intending to return fairly quickly because he had left his cab-door open; it hung outwards over the path, well above the height of a border collie. Tamzin looked at the situation with a growing sense of apprehension. How could any dog—even a trained dog, perhaps— know of this hazard? Meg could see the van all right and would almost certainly pass it with room to spare, as Meryon must have known or he would not have taken her along the lane; but unless the driver returned in time the door would hit Meryon head-on. It didn't sound much, colliding with an obstacle at walking speed, but Tamzin had once in a dreamy moment walked into a sign-post, and it had hurt very much.

Touching Cascade with her legs she rode on as Meg and Meryon came towards the van. There was no sign of a returning driver through the garden trees, and there was no time for thinking what to do. Tamzin rode across the path and reached to shut the door. Then she saw why it was open. The driver was slumped across the seat, a shoulder and one foot protruding from the doorway.

"Meryon, stop! There's something in your way—"

"You, again." He sounded exasperated but he had stopped. Meg was waving her delighted greeting but she stayed where she was. "Do you know why I didn't tell you about this? Because I want to be left to work it out for myself. I've got to work it out for myself—won't you ever see?"

She was exasperated, too. "Listen there's a van here—"

"All right—she knows about vans. It isn't the first time we've been out."

"But this one's door is open, and I can't shut it, and there's a man ill inside—must you be so DENSE? Do you *want* to walk into a door that Meg can go under?" She had swung out of her saddle and was standing in front of him blazing, although that could mean nothing any more. "Shall I go to the house for help or will you give me a hand to straighten this chap out? He looks awfully uncomfortable with his head hanging—there's a mark on it, too, as if he hit it getting out in a hurry. I bet he did."

"Certainly, nurse," Meryon said drily and lowered Meg's harness. "Sit!—Mr. Merrow taught her that," he added, in case she should think it worthy of praise.

She was hitching Cascade to the door-handle. "There's no need to be so self-crushing. I expect you taught her lots, as well. Now, if you lift his feet I'll get inside and straighten his head and shoulders. He doesn't seem hurt except the bang on his forehead. I could undo that collar—he might come to if he can sit and breathe all right."

"You said it," Meryon told her, as suddenly the driver flailed out an arm and began shouting.

"Help! Murder! Get your hands off, you dirty thief! A dog, too. Call her off! Help!"

"Shut up, you blithering oaf," Meryon hissed. "Don't you know when anyone's helping you?"

"Helping me off with the firm's money, I know—*help!*" the man yelled, seeing someone running down the path from the house in the trees. "Quick, call the police, I'm being robbed!"

"It's Mr. Baker," Tamzin said, looking up.

"What's all this?" Mr. Baker asked, in true stage policeman manner, running up full of agitation and anxiety.

"Highway robbery, that's what!" the driver was very excited.

"Nonsense." Meryon was hunting for Meg's harness.

"Waited till I was just getting out and then coshed me on the head. Came to with him at my pockets and his girl at my throat—"

"You leave my girl alone!" said Meryon.

"Swear it, they were, guv! Dog, too, and a horse for getaway. Take your life in your hands every time you go out, these days—bank robbery only last month—"

Mr. Baker straightened himself. "Look, man, this boy's my neighbour, known him years; girl vicar's daughter from Westling. Must've made a mistake, old chap—easy enough, I know. Helping you, I expect. Never mind, no harm done. If you've got that carpet, which I hope you have, I'll give you a hand carrying it up, and find a spot of stuff to put on the bump …"

Tamzin began to unhitch Cascade as the van-man went grumbling round to the back of the van with Mr. Baker. She paused a moment with the reins in her hand. "What was that you said about your girl?"

"Oh. Did I?" Meryon asked innocently.

"Well, I'll be getting along, then." She was in the saddle, Cascade fretting at his bit, his feet fidgeting to go.

"Er—Meg—she's doing pretty nicely, don't you think? For such a short time?"

"Very nicely," Tamzin said.

"Mrs. Merrow would be pleased."

"Very pleased."

"Funny, isn't it, how responsible she is in harness? Meg, I mean. The moment you take it off she's as wild and scatty as ever. You—

er—you wouldn't like to come along and see, would you? Just for a minute, I mean, of course."

Tamzin hesitated, a faint smile gone before it had really come. "Yes, I think I should, really. But just for a minute, of course."

Chapter Nine

"That's our old Meg, all right," Tamzin said, laughing. "You can't believe it's the same dog."

They were in Meryon's garden on a low stone wall where once they used to sit looking across the marshes and the castle to the sea. This was the first time they had sat there with their backs to that far green-grey view with the strange and mysterious light effects unique to Romney Marshes. Behind them, too, was Cascade, avidly snatching at the grass in the Fairbrass's paddock to get as much of the different taste as possible before going back to the familiar home flavours.

Off her harness, Meg was racing round and round the wide lawn, missing the big cypress near the side by a swerve and inches. Sometimes she stopped abruptly and threw the same speed into going round on the spot after her own tail. Then suddenly she stood wagging and waving, her lively eye roving until it fell on something that Mr. Fairbrass had left with a weed-box at the edge of a pansy border. With a rush and a pounce like a fox with a field mouse it was in her mouth.

"Present for you," Meryon said, hearing her teeth adjusting the balance of what she was bringing. "Probably a flower-pot or something—she's started this thing of having to make presentations to visitors she approves of. To date, it's been one cushion, two spoons, an ash-tray, a pencil and an umbrella."

"It's a trowel this time. Thank you, Meg!"

"She always stays around, handy, when I let her off; comes rushing round the house every now and then to see if I'm O.K. I like to leave her free as often as I can, she's so young, but she does seem to feel she's on duty all the time, whether she really is or not."

"I know," Tamzin said, "I know she's wonderful, and it's fantastic how she's learning—" Her voice broke off, leaving the sentence hanging.

"Go on. You were going to say 'but—'"

Tamzin was silent.

"Have you ever done an intelligence test?" she suddenly asked.

"Lord sake!"

"Well, have you?"

"Yes."

"High score?"

"Since you ask."

She turned on him. "Anyone'd think you'd bend some of that brain power to what you're doing now! Don't you ever *think* how unreasonable and dense you're being? Is there any sense insisting on doing something alone if it would be a better job with a helper? It isn't fair to Meg, it doesn't give her a proper chance. It isn't fair to your parents, they've had enough shock and worry about you. It isn't even fair to you—do you really only want a second-class guide dog?"

Meryon stiffened. "I like to do things by myself. No—that's an understatement—I hate being helped."

"You know what?" she said after a minute. "That sounds chicken to me. And selfish, too."

She heard him snort, his hands gripping the stone wall.

"Well, isn't it?" she demanded. "As if you were afraid to admit you could do with any help. And not giving a darn about fairness to Meg and everyone. Meg especially; she's failed once—don't you care if she fails again? She's the one they'd blame if you got hurt when you're out with her—if that van-door'd hit you to-day, for instance.

But she can only be as good as she's trained to be. Oh, I know it's O.K. in the house and garden, where you know where everything is," she hurried on, seeing how she had wounded him, "and I think the results are fantastic, really I do; but how can you teach her properly outside, when you don't *know* what's there?"

There was a long silence, in which Meryon stared stony-faced into the darkness that he lived in, and Meg lay in the sunshine and panted and grinned and sent him watchful glances, and Tamzin wanted to unsay what she had said and was afraid of saying anything else at all. Finally, "Well, perhaps I'd better be getting along," she said, for the second time that morning, and slipped from the low wall to the path.

"Wait," Meryon said, "and I'll tell you."

Hearing his voice Meg's glance swung round, eyebrows and drooped ears lifting.

"There wasn't only this independence thing. Oh, it's there all right—and the resentment at being treated like a child, or a half-wit. 'Does he enjoy listening to the radio?' Mrs. Harker asked my father yesterday when I was there. People thinking I'm fumbling and come rushing to help, when I'm *doing* something—not taking my word for it if I say no. I can ask if I need any help; I have to do things for myself if I can. O.K. I've got major adjustment problems, but I want to solve them myself." He paused. "You know all that, I daresay, and none of it applies to you. The only thing that applied to you was—dammit, I told you before—I wanted the best for you."

Tamzin looked at him, her heart aching. "I knew—I think I knew all along. It just couldn't have occurred to you that I knew the best for me, too."

Now there was nothing else to say because there was no need to say anything else. The why-did-you things they might have said no longer mattered. She leaned against the wall and watched Meg rolling, and Meryon's hand was against hers, and it didn't seem necessary to ask for or give any explanations. It was a terrible world, that could turn in a moment into darkness and grief; but it was a glorious world, too, that could have such understanding and courage in it.

"I liked your guitar concerto," he said after a while. "I ran it on to a tape of my own."

She was silent, and he went on, "Talking of tapes, you can answer mine in person, now you're here. That Simon bloke—what does he look like? Mere curiosity."

She smiled, remembering. "Five foot eleven and ginger." Then a laugh as she remembered more. "He thought I was 'rather tall and dark and probably frighteningly efficient', but I put him right about that."

"You're sure it was five foot eleven?" Meryon had a half inch to go, to that.

"It's what he said. But of course he's got a year's start on you," she said wickedly.

"In some things." Suddenly he said in the voice of someone very hungry, "What does the garden look like? Has the creeper on the house turned colour, or is it too early? Have the marsh sheep gone to the hills, yet?"

She saw the way it was, how he had wanted to know and would never ask, not even—or perhaps especially—his parents, for all the good family feeling there had always been. But now, now that her usefulness had been accepted, he would use it as freely as it was given. She narrowed her eyes into the sun and looked at things, as an artist looks, noticing detail.

"It's mostly roses in the garden, now—that very pale pink one on the south wall, and the gorgeous single yellow on the Dunsford side that has flowers like saucers."

"Mermaid, I like that one; but the pink is the one that smells— nearly the best of the lot." He looked as if he were listening minutely, but she knew he was seeing—in his mind's eye.

"A crimson one that looks like velvet, on this wall."

"That's the one that smells the best of all," he said.

"There's a peacock butterfly on it—velvet too—and Burma's stalking it." She looked at the house beyond its great cedar. "The evergreen magnolia still has a few flowers—like water lilies. Virginia creeper's changing colour from the roof downwards."

"Sap slowing down; it gets a bit sparse up there."

"The sheep are still on the marsh." She knew this without looking, but now she turned for the details. "Castle flock is lying in the shade of the walls, but there's a flock at Redshanks' Pool, changing pasture. Someone on a pony—Joseph on Patsy, I should think—driving them. The sheep look very white in the sun, you know how they do."

"I know. What else? Any shipping?"

Her long gaze roved. "Sailing dinghy with a red sail, off Dunsmere. Whose can that be? Tanker coming round Dungeness, very long. I always think they may break up on a sandbank somewhere, and the seabirds die of the oil."

"Remember when we had the seabird hospital, and you cried when they died?"

"But they didn't all die ... Meryon, the *Thunderer's* moving up the river."

"Gone adrift? Or are they moving her?"

"I can see someone on the deck."

"Going to his upstream moorings, then. You'd think she'd be more handy where she was, near the ferry, if he's doing her up, wouldn't you?" He had turned too, forgetting his blindness.

"It's Hookey who's doing the repairing," she said.

"The hell he is! You didn't tell me."

"It hasn't been all that easy telling you things. But now I'm at it—there was another man, not Jim; I saw him look out from the cabin. Well, I suppose there's no reason why there shouldn't be," she admitted.

"No. But I bet there's a reason why there was."

Looking at him she knew he was smouldering at the thought of not being able to follow up this tantalising trail—at the whole thought of his infuriating helplessness. Probably Meg, too, sensed the wave of exasperation; she came across and pushed her muzzle at his hand, flagging her plumy tail as she looked up at him.

"If only I had a bit more of Mrs. Venus in me," Tamzin said.

"Heaven forbid!"

"Oh, I didn't mean poison-pennery—just her genius for finding things out." To make him laugh she told him about the Snap-o-Matic camera and Smiling Morn, but nothing this time about recording the incident for Simon. Instead she tried Thomas, who was so much younger.

"Help me do a tape for Thomas! Cascade eating your grass as if it were his first blade for months, your father sawing logs under those pines, Burma playing with his ping-pong balls—"

"I think you're going to have to ring your folks and say you won't be back for lunch." He was grinning at her in his old way. "With all that, and a lesson for Meg as well. You know what you've taken on, don't you?"

Near to tears she nodded, and then remembered that a nod was nothing any more, and touched his hand.

"Let me tell you a funny tale," he said. "Do you know Mrs. March, who lives two houses away? Tall, rather managing woman, always wears those funny hats that look like chocolate shapes. Husband left her—I expect he didn't go a bundle on being managed. She discovered I was out alone with Meg and made herself responsible, clearly didn't trust either of us to look after ourselves. She started trailing us and in no time began issuing orders—'Turn right! Turn left! Stop! Cross now!'—talk about back seat driving."

Tamzin giggled, imagining it.

"But wait! The funny part comes. On Tuesday Meg and I were

walking down a quiet street in the town when suddenly she appeared, horrified that we were venturing so far, and began straight off, 'Turn right!' etc.—so busy looking where we were going she didn't look where *she* was going; fell over a step and cut her head and had to go to hospital for five stitches."

"We oughtn't to laugh, poor old thing," Tamzin said, laughing. "She meant well. But, listen, have you thought, you'll be safe from Mrs. March if I'm with you! Even if she thinks I'm no great shakes as a pilot."

He said, "There's a stationary car in the lane; let's go that way. Backwards and forwards past it, five or six times—make use of it while it's there."

She stared across but the lane was hidden behind trees. "How do you know?"

"Heard it, of course. It's a bats' world I live in, all sound and scent and touch."

Suddenly she remembered Simon talking about being "distracted by sight".

"I know which one it is, too," he told her, amused by the thought of the things that had become so important in his long dark day. "The old Vauxhall from Stone Farm; chap comes to check over the sheep across the lane. He'll stay about half an hour. We'd better get a move on. Hey, Meg!" The collie came bounding, giddily twirling, twisting herself into circles as he bent to fix her harness. The moment the strap was buckled she had sobered to stillness and stood waiting.

"The Merrows wouldn't believe it!" Tamzin scarcely did, herself. "We could go and show them, couldn't we, one day? Now there are two of us on the job." She was having to hurry to keep up with him, Meg set such a pace along the shingle drive; but he was walking with all his old confidence. He knew when he was at the gate and told Meg to wait. "The shingle feels different here under shoes—it's the grit from the lane mixed with it."

The collie looked to the right and left. Meryon spoke to her quietly, "Forward, left," and swung with her into the lane towards the parked car. Walking beside him Tamzin knew she should be feeling the same confidence but their whole undertaking, now that she had a part in it, subdued her as it had sobered Meg; and she, more than Meg, knew the size of it.

Chapter Ten

If Tamzin had ever imagined that her part in Meg's training would be a protective one, she quickly discarded that idea. She should have known. Meryon's way had always been to pitch into difficulties rather than try to avoid them. They patrolled the parked Vauxhall thoroughly enough for the farmer owner to look up suspiciously from the sheep once or twice, and finally return and drive off sooner than Meryon expected.

"No matter," Meryon said; "it gives us a chance to try something else. Anyway, this wasn't awfully successful, with Meg convinced you're no ordinary potty pedestrian but one of us."

"Well, I am one of us," she said, amused; "whether you like it or not."

"I know—but Meg isn't supposed to."

Tamzin had been playing jay-walker, emerging from behind the Vauxhall, standing in Meryon's way or coming up on a collision course so that Meg had either to take evasive action or stop and wave a friendly if puzzled greeting.

Meryon turned around, listening, and Meg watched him, one ear up and one down. "No other traffic; there can't be many lanes as sleepy as this. How are you at riding a bloke's bicycle?"

"I can, of course. Want me to be an ordinary potty pedaller?"

"My old crate is in the shed. You can phone your folks while I see if the tyres are O.K., and Meg can have a break."

A few minutes later, in the lane again, he was saying, "Bikes are a bit difficult. Windy days, wind in the trees, you can't hear them coming—can't even hear cars, sometimes. She's got a habit of swinging to avoid a bike so it could still get me. I want her to swing wider."

Tamzin nodded (Oh, remember! a nod means nothing any more, she reminded herself). "I'll shove a foot out at her, shall I?"

Soon she was pedalling up and down the leafy lane, under trees leaning across towards each other, while Meryon swung along using Meg's eyes. "Come as close as you can!" he called to her, "and don't slow down—other bikes won't."

Terrified of hitting him or Meg but committed to the job, she gathered speed and came past with a foot outstretched and waggling so that Meg must see it. Once or twice, trusting in Meg's forgiving nature, the foot reached far enough to give her a poke. The fourth time Meg began her evasive movement, firmly edging Meryon aside, before Tamzin was anywhere near.

Meryon was pleased. "That was absolutely first class! We must do it again, but not now." Meg knew that he was pleased and plonked her front paws on his chest.

"The best time to stop jumping is when a horse has cleared a really good one," Tamzin agreed.

"Horse! That's an idea. Cascade."

"Potty pony-rider? Can do. I'll throw this bike away and go and get him."

They did this test on a wider but still quiet lane that crossed towards the Hastings road. Meg was good about passing the pony—she had learned to keep clear of shepherd ponies—and she negotiated a couple of cars very neatly, pressing Meryon in close to the hawthorn hedge on its high grass bank. Bothered by the noise and size of a lorry coming from behind she stopped for a moment, looking over her shoulder. She was moving on when the lorry slowed and pulled up at the roadside.

"We'll let her pass it," Meryon said to Tamzin, "then back past you again."

As Tamzin waited in the saddle a second lorry went by in the same direction and drew up beside the first, the drivers talking across the gap in the road. Meryon heard it but he couldn't know exactly where it had stopped, Tamzin decided. Meg looked with apprehension at the monsters waiting so close together, so large and smelly and with their engines running. Baffled and disturbed she refused to go between them although there was room.

Watching, Tamzin could see that the collie was torn between her wish to obey and her fear of the lorries. Eventually Meg forced herself to take a step forwards, but panicked and doubled behind Meryon's legs. The drivers, if they did look into their mirrors, saw only a boy and a dog who had room enough to pass.

Tamzin held herself still lest the collie should think of her as a refuge, but steadying herself Meg found her own solution. Full of purpose and decision she turned and led Meryon across the back of the left hand lorry and up the steep grass bank.

He's got the sense to go with her, Tamzin said to herself; he knows she's really leading forward now, and not just shying.

Meg took him along the bank under the hedge—they were as high as the lorry's door—and then down to the road again in front. She had obeyed, after her fashion and as well as she was able in her fear. Tamzin could see that the dog was pleased, from the jaunty step and high tail carriage, and hoped for her sake that she would not be turned and made to face her bogy once more. The lorries settled the matter, moving off one after the other.

"I'll tell you something," Tamzin said, riding up. "You've got a responsible, thinking dog there. Did you know those lorries were side by side? She knew she had to get you past, and she thought out her own way when she couldn't make herself face yours."

"You know what I think?" he said as they walked on. "She wasn't afraid so much for herself as for me—I think she really knows I'm blind."

"Well—" Tamzin thought this was stretching probability.

"The time I first thought it was when I heard her jump off the sofa. You know she isn't allowed on there. She knows it, too. Never gets on when anyone's around—anyone who can see. Ma said she'd found her white hairs on it, though. I told you my ears had been getting pretty acute. Well, they must've got more acute than Meg realizes. She was soft on her feet as Burma, but when Dad came along the hall I heard her jump down. After that I started listening for her, and sure enough, she always sneaked up there when I was alone, and always slipped off when anyone came. Knows I can't see." He gave her a friendly slap. "It amuses me, though; I like to think she can be crafty as well as loyal! It makes her seem a rounder character, somehow. No one's perfect."

Tamzin had to laugh. "It would be awful if they were."

After lunch Meryon played a tape for Tamzin to hear. "From my favourite aunt, Dad's sister Lucy; you'd like her. She's in Algiers with my uncle. They cooked up this tape for me with the noises of Algiers. It's splendid value and quite funny in parts."

They did Tamzin's recordings after that. Meryon told Thomas the story of Meg and the sofa and Tamzin told him about the two lorries. Burma obliged with his ping-pong balls, batting them round the tiled kitchen with a cheerful noise and watched with a lofty expression by Meg who considered herself on duty. Meryon still had an old model steam engine and remembered well enough how to run it "with my eyes shut". Between them they got it running on the flagged path outside the kitchen door, where it produced a triumphant puffing. After a minute at the proper distance Tamzin held the microphone very close.

"It ought to have sounded like a real old style railway engine that time," she told Thomas.

Meg had been watching, cocking her ears and her eyebrows at the steam engine, but she soon got bored and began presenting Tamzin with offerings; a pebble from the drive, a garden kneeler, a plant-label that said *Hypericum Rowallane*.

They switched off the tape recorder and sprawled themselves with Meg and Burma on the warm grass. The Fairbrass parents were picking blackberries along the paddock hedges; Tamzin could hear their voices above the sound of bees.

"People don't give most dogs a chance, really," Meryon reflected. "No chance to use their minds. We take away their need to be intelligent about hunting and generally surviving, and give them nothing else to work out. They can think, all right, given the chance. Look at any working dog, guide dogs especially, that have to think for someone as well as about someone. Oh, they know you can't see, if only because you tread on their toes about the house. They know you wouldn't do that on purpose, don't they?"

Tamzin took hold of the paw that Meg slapped down on her hand spread on the grass. "Of course they know."

Meryon's logical mind was having second thoughts. "It's a nice way to imagine things; but possibly they just think we're half-witted," he said briskly.

Chapter Eleven

The training of Meg absorbed them through the first days of September. Both to himself and other people Meryon seemed really alive for the first time since the day of the bank raid, laughing and shouting about the house, teasing his mother and arguing with his father almost as in the old days.

Afraid of being a bore at home Tamzin tried not to keep talking about the training and to take her usual interest in village and vicarage life, but nearly everything came a poor second against the interest and difficulty of this new enterprise. Simon and Thomas complained about late, short tapes, but they were interested, too, and wanted much more news about Meg. Simon was of the opinion that the thing couldn't be done. "Who does this chap think he is? Setting up to train his own dog when sighted people take years to learn how to do it properly. But, honestly, I do think he's likely to have a pretty nasty accident one day, trusting himself to a do-it-yourself guide dog."

They did have their moments, such as the time a furniture van parked across the pavement, backed up to a gateway, and Meg went to walk straight under it. Meryon had slapped right into the side of it before Tamzin could shout from the corner where she waited on Cascade. As usual, he made good use of it, walking Meg backwards and forwards past the van until she was perfect at leading round it. "That's what I want. That's the training that Meg wants."

There was the time, in a back street of the ancient little town, that a man-hole was left open in the pavement with no one guarding it. This time Tamzin was walking with them and saw it in time to warn Meryon; the cover was propped against the kerb.

"See what she does," Meryon said.

Meg did not understand man-holes and would have skirted only the rim of it. At the last heart-stopping minute Tamzin's hand flew out.

He said, "We may never see another one open—I haven't, before—but we'll make the most of this one. Don't stand over it or she'll think she's going round you, not the hole."

The workman concerned, hurrying back, was as mortified and astonished as anyone would expect. "Only left it for a mo; my mate came over dizzy and I took him across to the pub."

Now that he had started seeing with Tamzin's eyes, Meryon could never have enough of her running commentaries about the things that were happening and the way things looked.

"The swallows are gathering already; they're strung along the telephone wires all down the lane. Summer's going."

"This one can go, for my part. It wasn't a summer to remember."

They were walking with Meg towards the sheep levels, a longer distance than they had attempted before. It came to him that he had sounded bitter and, to be honest with himself, he had not felt bitter for quite a time. "Tell me some more."

"The pears are ripening in Mrs. Lang's garden, you can see the red on them. There's a ladder in the branches … There are willow herb seeds floating from the little wood, and yet there's almost no wind."

"They only need a breath," he said.

"You could think they were a fleet of flying saucers, the way they look with the sun behind them—very bright and round. You could easily think they were miles away in the air and very big and fast, not close and tiny and just drifting."

He said nothing, seeing with his inner eye.

"A man with an Irish setter on the other side of the lane. It's looking at Meg but she isn't taking any notice."

"On duty," said Meryon.

"Midges under the trees, going up and down all the time as if they were string puppets. There's toadflax in the grass, like little yellow snapdragons, and harebells." She reached up to the hedge. "Blackberries. Open your hand."

She had almost forgotten Jim Decks and the *Thunderer*. She had completely forgotten Mrs. Venus and the Snap-o-Matic camera. From time to time school loomed in her mind as the end—a fortnight away—to the only really good and important thing, she felt, that she had ever had a share in. The minutes left to them were like rice grains in a famine, each one of value. There would be weekends still, but continuity would be lost, evenings would grow shorter, the weather might break up.

"No need to worry," Meryon said when she told him about it. "The way we've got on she's as good as trained, now. I often take her on roads when you aren't here, even into the town; didn't you guess?"

"I suppose so. You had her on roads before we were working together. I just feel easier when I'm there."

"You'd be surprised how ears fill in for eyes not seeing. I could do without aeroplanes, though. One comes over when you're listening; you've got to wait, especially at weekends when there's more traffic."

"There was the man-hole; you couldn't hear that."

"I know. And there are other things, not as dangerous but pretty inconvenient. The ford near Hole Farm. I'd forgotten it—wasn't looking out for it, anyway. You know there's a footbridge at the side? That meant nothing to Meg. The water's only ankle deep. She just went straight through, enjoying it, I expect. Well, you can guess we spent the next half hour crossing by that footbridge."

Tamzin could well believe it. She smiled to herself. "Let's stop and lean on the fence. You know where we are, with all the marsh

167

below us and the sea beyond. The castle with its tree growing on the top like a feather in its hat, and the ivy as thick as the walls. Sheep everywhere. And all those wild willows with their hair sticking out; it's pollarding does that. Four herons flying down the river …"

She was surprised, when riding home through the village and coming to where Smiling Morn's shop looked across the road to the vicarage garden, to see Mrs. Venus emerging from the vicarage back gate. It was a long time since she had pushed through the letter-box one of her scandalizing anonymous letters—which were anonymous only in that she did not sign them with her name, but always with the words *One Who Knows*. She made no secrecy of delivering them, indeed she had once been known to place one in the vicar's hands. Most probably, the Greys thought, she just did not like to commit herself by signing her proper name to anything, in case some exasperated neighbour should finally rise up and sue her.

Mrs. Venus came gliding up the street in the strangely invisible and self-effacing way which enabled her to discover much about other people before they were aware of her nearness. She smiled as Cascade pattered past her, and Tamzin said hullo and smiled back. It felt almost as if she were greeting a phantom. Turning in at her own gate Tamzin glanced uneasily over her shoulder to make sure that Mrs. Venus was still there, silently walking up the street.

"Mrs. One-Who-Knows has brought a letter," Diccon told her, looking up from the drain below the kitchen window. "I saw her push it under the door." He had trapped a useful lot of water by plugging the hole with grass tussocks and a stone, and was now introducing to it three toads which he had found in the garden.

"Why don't you go out on Banner, or something, instead of torturing those poor frogs?"

"They're toads, and they *like* water. Why don't you take Banner and me with you any more, if it comes to that? It isn't much fun riding alone."

Not fun riding alone? Tamzin thought about that as she took Cascade round to the paddock where Banner trotted up and down the fence whinnying his loud impatient welcome. She had always rather enjoyed it, herself; but she felt guilty about deserting Diccon and gave his pony a special petting. Banner's thick black mane stood up so high before it fell over that it shook and wobbled when he moved, like ostrich plumes on a hat. She smoothed it with her fingers, and it felt rough and silky both at once. He lifted his head round and rested it on her shoulder in the way he had, the long jaw-bones digging heavily through her pullover; and then there was Cascade, back from the trough and dripping water all over her arm. She gave them both a loving hug and ran back to the house.

Mr. and Mrs. Grey had the idea that they and their children were more or less equal members of the vicarage family. There had never been much "not-in-front-of-the-children" attitude; not much protection from the stark facts of human nature, and not much forbidding of mess and fun and enterprise. The children knew who in the village got drunk, which family was always fighting, which was lovingly fed by all the others because the father gambled; and they knew all about Mrs. Venus. She was, the vicar held, not so much a malicious poison-penner as a thwarted natural writer. Her burning interest was in people, their character and doings. Given a loving childhood and a sound education—neither of which she had had—she might have been a successful novelist, the vicar said, with his "there but for the grace of God go I" way of looking at things.

He was re-stringing tennis racquets when she came into the kitchen. This was one of his many unusual skills, which ranged from bees through picture-framing and water-divining to target-shooting, taking in a dozen other accomplishments on the way.

"We've had the best day ever! And went the furthest—down to the marsh. Next time we're going to the farm. The Merrows won't believe it when they see their failed sheep-dog."

"As long as they give at least half the credit to Meryon. Funny, though, isn't it, how often people and other animals have much more in them than one ever thought? Come and peg for me," he invited, pushing his chair aside. She lifted Schnooky off the next chair and on to her knee as she sat waiting. Her father pulled the string taut and she drove the bright steel bradawl into the string-hole, to hold it tight until the next line was ready. She and Diccon were used to the job and did it automatically.

"Who's Mrs. Venus blackening to-day?" She rubbed the backs of Schnooky's ears.

Her father was threading the next horizontal row, a kind of coarse weaving, over and under. "I haven't looked. It's on the table. One of life's little jobs I don't exactly rush at, any more—poor woman."

"I'll read it for you, shall I? You always said my pocket money was for washing-up and secretarial, but usually I don't get much further than typing sermon notes."

"Of course, read it. I know you don't talk about parish affairs. Though, bless us, Mrs. Venus will already have told four or five people exactly what she's written, I daresay. And what she's going to write next time if they aren't careful. Peg, please!"

Tamzin thrust it in the new hole. "Feels as if there's a photograph or something in the envelope. Did you know she's got a camera, now?"

"I had noticed, yes." Mr. Grey was too wise about this parishioner to say, "Nice for her to have a new interest," or anything like that. All her interests were devoted to perfecting that main interest.

"She got it with Sugar Snazzles. I was in the shop—it *is* a photograph, two, and a letter."

The vicar seemed absorbed in his threading of the racquet string. "Peg." But Tamzin too was absorbed and did not hear.

"It's of the *Thunderer.* There's Hookey on it, and that other man—I told you I'd seen someone else on board, didn't I, but I couldn't see clearly from the jetty. Jim wouldn't admit there was anyone else there."

"What does she say?"

Tamzin spread the letter on Schnooky's back.

"'Dear Reverend,

'You should ought to know, and my greavious duty to tell you, the hippocrites as go to your church on Sundays, enough to stop any righteous person doing same take that Jim Decks not as he go to church much but hippocrite all the same, I got a dictionary now with ten coupons and looked that word up'."

"Well, good for her about that, anyway!" said the vicar.

Tamzin went on. "'There's bad things doing in his old fishing smack I seen and heard but don't ask you to take my word no more, they say cameras tell no lies and I send you this picture, what I took sideways me looking up the river so they thought I was photygraphing the *Alice* coming down'."

"The real stuff foreign agents are made of," the vicar observed, pegging for himself. "What the communists are missing!"

"'Hookey is one as you would expect, but there is another as you see and my belief they got him prisoner I never seed him set foot ashore'." Tamzin looked up and said, "Well, if she never has, the chances are he never has set foot, I should think." She stared at the snapshot for a minute. "She's even had it enlarged. It isn't very good, but what can you expect with a Snazzles camera? Still, I keep thinking I know the face but I can't remember who it is. Do you know?" She passed it across.

After a moment's perusal her father passed it back. "No, never seen the man, as far as I know, and usually I do remember faces. What else does she say?"

Tamzin read on, "'You know what I think he's one of those French smugglers what Jim and Hookey are in with, everybody knows, and double crossed em. Been there a tidy time and now

Hookey say they going to move the boat up river'." Tamzin looked up. "He's moved it; I saw from Meryon's garden." She went on, "'That's to stop me looking I know, my cousin got a telescope but ent willing to lend so may not have more information for a while. The other snap you will see for yourself is that Marlene Carey what's no better than she should be, walking out with Peter Pope what pinched the tools from the garage two wrongs don't make a right, someone should be warned and hope you do it or there'll likely be more trouble'."

The vicar sighed. "What a pity she can't suppose that Peter's trying to go straight, now he's got himself a girl. A nice girl, too, young Marlene; getting over her flightiness and understands Peter; they'll make a good pair … Any more?"

"'Yours respectfully, One Who Knows'."

"Oh. Well, you might shove the peg in, then."

Chapter Twelve

———————◆———————

"You'll remember, one day," Meryon said when Tamzin told him about Mrs. Venus's photograph, "and it'll be Hookey's brother-in-law or someone. Anyway, it isn't really our business."

"Mrs. Venus thinks it's a smuggler who tried double crossing Jim."

"Scoop for her," Meryon said. "Keep her happy through the next six letters."

They were walking to Castle Farm; this was the day when Meg was to visit her old home. It was a showery morning and there was a smell of autumn that Meryon noticed immediately, especially from the damp stubble of cornfields by the high lanes. Now they were down on the Sea Road, where the sea itself had once been, with ships sailing into the little town that for centuries now had been stranded on its deserted cliff. Where sea-foam once boiled there was now the foam of fleeces as flocks grazed the ancient sea-bed.

The shower of the moment, with sunlight through it, was like trailing white satin over the marsh. Tamzin tried to describe it to Meryon, and added, "The cloud that's raining is over the castle; it'll miss us."

"I don't care if it doesn't. I like rain. So do you." He sounded almost happy, as if his new freedom and their renewed trust were all he wanted. In a strange way it seemed to hurt her more than his fierce pride had done; she didn't know why—perhaps because his acceptance of his blindness made it seem somehow permanent, unalterable; there had been more hope when he had raged against it.

"We're coming to the farm gate," he said.

"I was just going to tell you that! Your sixth sense beat me to it."

"Blind people don't have a sixth sense. They just use the other ones more. It's simple, really. But still I don't know when rain looks like white satin, unless you tell me!"

"You're laughing at me. It's my old trouble, being too poetic— making everything look like something else. But how can I show you what things really are like, if I don't?"

Suddenly he was serious. "Don't change! I didn't mean to laugh. I'll tell you something. I never saw so clearly with my eyes as I sometimes see with yours."

Secretly glowing, she tried all the same to be more matter of fact. "Blue smoke going up from the middle chimney—they're burning driftwood. Joseph's red jersey on the line. The geese have seen us. Elderberries nearly ripe on the bushes by the cowshed. Mrs. Merrow will be thinking about her wine making, I expect." She reached to snap a twig from a hazel tree and give it to him. "Next year's catkins! They're green already. It always astonishes me."

"I had the offer of an Institute trained dog, this morning," he told her as he paused to recall with his fingers the shape and texture of catkin buds.

"You turned it down, of course." She knew that he must have done.

"Of course. Anyway, I've got as good a dog as a guy could have." He put the little twig in his pocket and told Meg to walk on.

"She knows where she's going," Tamzin said.

The geese had warned Mrs. Merrow of approaching visitors. Coming out on to the sheep-nibbled turf that made the best kind of lawn around the thatched farmhouse, she called back to the open kitchen door, "Father! Joseph, Mike! It's Meg and them!"

There was a barking, a cackling, a shouting of greetings, and a bleating of sheep that scattered as the Merrows emerged and came across the turf.

"Well, saints alive and bless us all!" Mrs. Merrow was already dabbing the corners of her eyes. "Would you ever have believed it of our Meg, Father? Answer me that! Meg, Meg, love, you ent forgot your old missus?" Her hands went down to the dog.

The old farmer checked her. "Leave her be, then; can't you see she's working? You allus did spoil the working dogs, lass."

It wasn't only Mrs. Merrow. The farm dogs leapt around sniffing and barking, to be called off firmly by the old man and his son. Meg made what must, to her, have been super-canine efforts to stay on duty, aloof and untemptable, but anyone could see how distracted she was—so much of her old life to recognize, so much she didn't understand.

"She'll settle," Mike said. "Give her a minute. First time she's been back." He was a tall young man, brown and lean, his sleeves rolled up on strong arms.

"Kettle's on the boil." Mrs. Merrow dabbed a fresh tear that was partly of joy for Meg but more of grief for Meryon that she would never let him know. "Come in and have a cup. It's that nice to see you all, and her doing so fine."

Young Joseph was shy and quiet at first while the cups were going round with the fruit cake in the kitchen and Mrs. Merrow showed off her tame robin taking crumbs from her hand, to Meg's astonishment; but after the news-exchanging, when he was getting accustomed to the sight of Meryon with his clouded eyes, he opened out.

"You'll come and see the new calf? I say new—she's a fortnight old, now; her mother's the cow that lost her tail."

"Primrose." Tamzin knew all the names.

"Poor thing," said Mrs. Merrow, collecting cups and saucers.

"In the barn door she did it," Mike told them. "The wind got up sudden and slammed it as she was going out."

Tamzin had her tape recorder over her shoulder. "I never did get those farm noises for Simon and Thomas. It was the day we galloped off after Meg. Would the calf say something for us, Joseph? I know those geese will fairly yell."

Tamzin's tape scarcely stopped running for the next half hour as the sounds of Castle Farm went stringing on to it. Meryon's seeing hands were reminding him all the time of pigs' rough backs, cows' silkiness and kittens' softness, the hugeness of tractor tyres and smallness of bantam eggs, of wheat running through fingers—with a hiss that Tamzin recorded—and dairy-nuts, rough and oily and smelling of malt.

Once he got over the first shyness Joseph didn't mind being recorded at all. He made admirable running commentaries about the animals and the farm work and plans, talking and arguing with Meryon and Tamzin just as they used to in the old days.

"You don't mean you're still using this string contraption to shut the cowshed door, Joe!" Meryon's hand had found it.

"That's much easier nor a ordinary latch, I tell you. You just reach out and tug—no walking to the door—and the latch lifts; and this spring here pulls the door open—" his eye caught the distant Sea Road. "What a way to drive a car, then!"

Tamzin's finger went down to the stop switch, as it did automatically whenever the conversation wandered or dried up. She glanced through the cowshed door.

"Doctor, perhaps, rushing to some poor soul—" She had reminded herself of the day she wanted to forget, the crowd and the shouting, the screaming and the cry for a doctor. She hurried on, "A red car, Meryon, a bit like yours; really is wiping up the road."

He was listening; so was Meg. "Might be ours. It's a Rover, anyway. Coming in the gate, isn't it? Sounds different."

She thought he seemed uneasy; the Fairbrasses were all reasonable drivers. Then as the car swung round the track she saw the Fairbrass number plate. Meryon's mother was driving. She was out almost as the car pulled up, glancing round and seeing the three of them.

"Your mother's running!" Tamzin said, surprise and uneasiness in her own voice. Meryon knew and was telling Meg to go forward. Tamzin followed but Joseph melted into the cowshed, shy and apprehensive of something that he didn't understand.

"You've got everything with you? Sorry to be in such a rush but can you get into the car and let me explain on the way back?" The Rover's engine was still running.

"Dad O.K.?"

"Yes, oh yes—perfectly. But we must hurry! Tamzin too, of course."

He turned and shouted back to the cowshed. "Joseph! Urgent recall! Don't know why. Say we're sorry to your parents. See you!"

They were in the car and swirling in a circle over the short grass to the track again. Meryon was in the back with Meg and leaned forward to ask, "Well, what's all the now-or-never, Ma?"

The gears were running up to first. His mother kept her eyes on the road ahead. "If we can race time to it we may be able to get your sight back."

The news took the breath from both listeners. Tamzin reacted first. "I can't believe it—oh, drive quickly! Wherever it's to."

Meryon's voice when it came had the old dogged quality that no one had heard for many days. "If you mean grafting; I said I wouldn't go on a corneal graft list and I meant it, haven't changed my mind. I can't think what else you might mean."

Mrs. Fairbrass slowed with controlled exasperation behind a coal lorry, then called up all the car's acceleration to overtake on a short stretch of visible road. "Corneas—but not the list. Ben and Lucy. We never told you, but they bequeathed their eyes to you—they both did."

"Lucy! She was always my favourite aunt." He said it almost to himself. "But—she's *died*, you mean?"

"They both have."

The silence of shock could be felt inside the car. Meg, too, was aware of it and made a small whining noise.

Tamzin's hands gripped tightly round her knees as she stared ahead. Mrs. Fairbrass took the sharp bend at the bottom of the Strand Hill and changed down as the Rover leapt to the steep gradient. Meryon pushed back the upsurging obviousnesses—"They can't both have! But they were in Algiers. I don't believe it."—and said, "How? When?"

"This morning. They were coming home. Their plane crashed, in the Pyrenees. There weren't any survivors."

At the hilltop the car turned under the arch of the immensely strong stone Strand Gate that had stood there through six centuries. She went on, lightly, exasperatingly determined, "And if there's any nonsense from you, my lad, about turning this down, let me tell you—they gave their eyes to you and to no one else, and no one else is going to get an atom of good out of it."

"O.K. I understand. I suppose I asked for it." Then, "Dad—how's he taking it?"

"Well, sensibly. He wasn't really close to Lucy—there were nine years between them—but they got on well …"

"He's been on the phone since we had the news, not long after you left. We're flying to Barcelona."

"*What?*" It was Meryon's voice. Tamzin was still dizzily saying to herself, He's going to be able to see—if everything goes all right—oh, please let everything go all right!

"If he's been successful booking we leave at once, as soon as we can throw a few things together. It's because of the time limit for using corneas."

"What *is* the time limit?" Tamzin hardly dared to ask.

Mrs. Fairbrass wove the big car through the traffic of the little town's main street. "Six hours." She cut-in and was shouted at near the ancient church. "Four in some conditions. Not time to fly them to London. Little enough time to get them to Barcelona. But that's the only way."

Tamzin and Meryon and Meg all swayed as the Rover took the right-angled turn out of the street to a quieter lane. Meryon suddenly asked, "Does anyone know if the corneas—they might not even exist."

"There wasn't any fire. But that's about as much as anyone knew when I left. It's difficult to get much information over the continental telephone. The airline is helping; it seems they knew about the bequest. There's been a helicopter survey and a rock-climbing team went out at once to find the place. It's right up in the mountains, not very accessible I should think." She turned into the drive of the Fairbrass house and pulled up beside the useful Morris estate car that Tamzin's father had recently bought at a local sale. Tamzin stared through the window at it and then threw herself out.

"Mother! Dad!"

"Listen, love." Her mother's hands were on her shoulders. "Would you like to go with them?"

Too shaken to speak Tamzin nodded.

"Great!" Meryon was there with Meg.

"It will only be for a week because of school." Mr. Grey was transferring a suitcase from the Morris to the Rover. "Lucky thing everyone's passports were up to date."

Meryon's father was throwing in another case. "Plane leaves Gatwick at six. I booked Tamzin in: felt pretty sure she'd like to come. We'll just make it if everyone's ready in under ten minutes. Kit, can you pack in that time? If not, you must buy some stuff in Barcelona."

"Oh—what about Meg?" Tamzin suddenly cried. "And Burma? Cascade's here, too."

"The Grey–Fairbrass Travel Service thinks of everything," her father said calmingly. "Don't underestimate us. Meg and Burma are coming to the vicarage, and this won't be the first time I've ridden your pony, as you well know."

"Dad, you're unique. Mother, too. Can I take my tape recorder?"

"All right, but get into that car. Good luck, Meryon! I know you know there can be a dozen snags yet, but it could come off!"

"Thank you, sir! I know, all right."

Meryon gave Meg's harness lead to Mrs. Grey. "It's good of you! She's easy, really. One meal a day and exercise. So long, Meg! I'll be seeing you."

Chapter Thirteen

Y ou know what you said?" Tamzin asked him when they were snaking up the steep lane that was the shortest way out to the London road. "I'll be seeing you!"

"I know I did. It's just a figure of speech. But you can say it's an omen if you like!"

"And those dozen snags?"

"Snags are for getting over, round or under, aren't they? As far as I'm concerned, they can start."

She swung round, her hand on his knee. "Don't! It's like provoking them."

He laughed. "Whatever happens we aren't likely to be any worse off than now, are we? Even if we aren't any better."

Tamzin thought to herself, oh, we could be! She was frightened of flying. But she said nothing about that; only, a little weakly, "An hour ago—was it?—we were playing with a calf at Castle Farm." The things that could happen in an hour—in a minute, even; she remembered the minute in Dunsford High Street that had changed so much for all of them.

Once they were clear of the blind turns and narrow twists and out on the broad road, Jack Fairbrass threw information in snippets over his shoulders while zooming the Rover through September Sussex country that Tamzin longed to describe to Meryon. "Pretty well non-stop phoning since we heard … Fixed up all I can, I think … If all goes as we hope, eye operation in Barcelona soon after we

A WIND IS BLOWING

get there. Depends of course on corneas being found undamaged and got down from the mountains in time ... Good hospital there, standing by for emergency op.—got quite a name for corneal grafting ... Sometimes need four corneas for grafting two eyes, case they don't get a perfect specimen every time ... Poor Lucy! Ben, too. I liked those two—what I saw of them; always tearing off to some place. They'd be glad if it all works right, now, some good coming of it."

"It was wonderful, your thinking of phoning about me," Tamzin said, "in all that. I still can't believe I'm coming."

They were no further than Uckfield when the Rover began to misfire. The brief spluttering moments of failure in the smooth firing were like a kind of terrible heart failure to which Tamzin's own heart responded, painfully banging. She could scarcely bear to look at Meryon, as if—in some impossible way—he might notice her dread.

"Filter, do you think?" she heard him say, leaning an arm on the back of the driver's seat.

"Sounds like it. Or blocked jet."

"Lord! Now of all times," Kit Fairbrass said. Tamzin knew she was trying to keep calm against the thought of minutes going like water over a weir and the relentless deadline of aeroplane departures, not waiting even for a matter of sight and blindness.

"There's a garage along here. I'll pull in, see if they can fix it. She's losing speed."

Meryon's fingers were on the braille wrist watch his father had given him. "We'll be lucky if they haven't all gone, except a petrol wallah, perhaps."

"Another car there, anyway," Mrs. Fairbrass said hopefully. "Its bonnet's open—good sign—there must be someone who can—"

But there wasn't. Only Meryon's petrol wallah and the customer, a man—like his car—of some elegance.

"Just putting oil in this gentleman, that's all, sir. Sorry. Even if we weren't closed these filter jobs take time, have to drain the petrol tank. Do it tomorrow if you like to leave it?"

"Can you hire me something—a fast car? Gatwick. Plane leaves at six."

"Well, there you've got me again, sir; don't do any hiring, see."

Tamzin and Meryon's mother looked at each other, struggling with despair.

Meryon was unloading the boot. "Don't under-rate Dad. He'll high-jack something if there's no other way."

No one quite heard what Jack Fairbrass did do, but suddenly they were all throwing the luggage into the other car which was, Tamzin noticed gratefully, a large Citroen, probably very fast. Five minutes after they had limped in with the coughing Rover they were sliding out in the Citroen with a stranger driving. Elated by the giddy hair's-breadth of it Tamzin described the car to Meryon, at the same time half-listening, fascinated, to hard bargaining going on at the front. The hiring fee, it seemed, was to be on a sliding scale according to the fastest possible time of safe delivery.

The stranger clearly had every intention of raking in the highest stake and went for it enthusiastically and boldly. Slipping the wrong way down a quiet one-way street and once driving right through a country estate complete with deer and Highland cattle, he took chances of being challenged for the sake of short cuts. Of late middle age, he turned out to be an actor between jobs—"resting", as he put it—and prepared, even eager, to do anything paying. The breath-taking journey was further enlivened, not only by extraordinary tales of theatrical life but by three large ball-bearings which he kept in a saucer by his feet as a kind of self-imposed smooth-driving test.

"Every driver ought to have them, taught me a lot, hardly ever lose them, now—I musn't speak too soon—there! Right round that nasty corner without losing one."

The rumbling-grumbling sound of the rolling bearings made strange background music to talk of an unfamiliar world and to the team-work grovelling whenever a ball did go overboard, which Meryon enjoyed as much as anybody.

"Barcelona; I know it like my own yard," the actor said on hearing about the journey. "There most of one summer; we were filming *The Bulls of Vilanova*—a small part I had, that time. Don't go to see a bullfight." They were sweeping up to Gatwick now with time still in hand. "I tell you one thing, though. You must go to St. George's Fountain. You don't know about it? It's in the cathedral garden. People throw coins into it; but not just for luck the way they do into other fountains. They do it to bring blessings for the blind."

They were at the airport and the rush was immediately on again, people and luggage piling out, thanking the driver, paying up the bargain—"I'll keep an eye on your car, live quite near; here's my address."—Tamzin held out her hand with a ball-bearing in it. "You lost it coming into the airport. And I'll remember St. George's Fountain!"

The plane was called Echo Juliet. They caught her with fifteen minutes to take-off time, but she did not leave until another twenty minutes had crept by walking on everyone's nerves. Ground engineers were making a last minute check on her altimeters, Mr. Fairbrass found out and told them.

When it came the roaring shuddering race of the take-off took Tamzin's breath—the sudden smooth lightness when they were airborne, the fields and houses swinging away under them.

"What can you see?" The urgent question pulled the whirl of her thoughts together.

"See? Oh, it's like a toy—you could pick up the houses and buses and things and put them down somewhere else! *Meryon, we're really on the way to Spain!*" Then, "Hop gardens, with people working in them, getting smaller and smaller … oast houses … soon it will be the sea, and toy ships, unless we're too high."

"*Were* you afraid when we took off?"

"Yes—but I was so excited it hardly mattered. Everyone else in the plane looks so ordinary, as if they flew every day. Reading papers, writing letters—the plane's nearly full."

"Flying is supposed to be like war—hours of boredom between moments of fear," he said. "At least half the passengers can't even have a port-hole to see through, and if they have it may be cloudy."

Over France cloud appeared and thickened, but the evening sun made a dazzling snowfield of it. "Or a mountain range, where the clouds rise high. It's all shining, and the sunset's beginning to be pink." She saw his finger on the braille watch and looked at her own. She had been trying not to, after looking at it every minute for the first half-hour. "How fast are we going?"

"Five hundred miles an hour."

"Oh—can't we go any faster?" If she could have willed Echo Juliet to fly at a thousand—two thousand—she would have. Twenty minutes lost already.

"Not this plane."

Supper came on trays carried by a hostess with a smile which looked determined to stay cheerful whatever the circumstances. Tamzin tried not to wonder what terrible peaks might be under the world of pink cloud. It was the kind of surprise packet supper they would both have enjoyed on any ordinary day; everything in neat separate compartments or in tiny mysterious containers with the airline initials on the side. There was no tray for Meryon who, if their desperate race were not in vain, would be under a general anaesthetic this same night. Tamzin looked at hers, on the folding table that lifted from the back of the seat in front of her, and then she looked at Meryon.

He said, "I feel the same," knowing that she was not touching anything. "I'm just not hungry, are you? Even if there weren't a ban on my eating."

"I ought to have saved her the trouble of bringing it." She looked across the aisle. "Your parents are much more sensible."

"I think—all this—matters more to us than it can to them. Does that sound awful?"

"No. But I'm pretty sure it means more to them than we know. They're just older and wiser and—well, as I said, more sensible."

The hostess took Tamzin's tray without comment.

"Used to it, I expect," Meryon said. "She thinks it's air-travel nerves."

"And not all that far wrong; it's nerves as *well* … We don't look to be going at five hundred miles an hour."

The Pyrenees burst out of the cloud, wild peaks and ridges standing clear with the coloured clouds around them.

He heard her indrawn breath. "Tell me, what can you see?"

"I couldn't describe it! All the great mountains gliding so close under us. As beautiful as you can imagine and terrible. Crags—a thousand pinnacles! There's a precipice falling like curtains. It's like when the world began. The sun has gone—just the pink light left … Meryon, was it here? Where it happened?" Her eyes ranged the cruel landscape, searching against her will for a smudge she didn't want to see.

"No. It was in the Sierra del Cadi. More to the west."

The plane throbbed and droned, and moved gently up and down like something breathing. Tamzin could feel the throbbing through the back of her seat; it was as if she were hearing it with her backbone. The pink light had deepened to red and was painting the wings. The mountains began to look dark and very savage.

"We don't know anything, do we?" she said, in a kind of helpless wonder. "We're rushing through the sky to Spain—perhaps that *is* Spain, down there—and they may not even have reached the wreck, or they may have and know it isn't any use our coming; and we don't know."

"If only it didn't have to be Aunt Lucy," he suddenly said. "I really liked her."

Tamzin turned on him, wide eyes blazing. "You wouldn't have corneas from a stranger, though all of us tried to make you, and now you say if only it weren't Aunt Lucy! But I do understand," she suddenly added softly. "I keep thinking what it must be like for your father, too."

"At least *she* would be glad," Meryon said. "She was that sort. A great traveller. Probably, if she'd had a choice, she'd have chosen to go in a plane crash. The way great hunting men sometimes say they'd rather die in the hunting field than helpless in bed." He turned towards her. "Do you think I'm saying all that to make it easier for me?"

"No." She stared down at the incredible mountains, darkening under pricking stars. In the far distance a thunderstorm lit the twilight, flashing between dark cloud and sierra ridge. "It isn't going to be very easy for you, anyway, is it? So much has to go right."

"You needn't tell me. Everything has to go right. We have to land on time, not be diverted by weather or anything."

Tamzin stared with a shiver down her spine at the faraway storm.

"The salvage team must have got to the wreck in time and found the corneas undamaged," he said. "They must have got them to Barcelona in time and in good condition. And after all that the grafts must 'take'. Sounds fairly well impossible, doesn't it? But it could all happen."

"What if it doesn't?" She hardly dared ask him but she had to know. "Have you thought?"

"Yes. Of course. Nothing will be any different, if that's what you mean. I stay blind; and independent—except of Meg."

Chapter Fourteen

———◆———

Clearing the last great rocky massif Echo Juliet left the storm far out to her right and began the long down-slide to Barcelona. Tamzin was aware of a strange feeling of successive drops checked by gentle bumps as the plane lost height. Meryon was the first to notice the lowered speed because the engines sounded different.

Thankful about the thunder Tamzin peered down at the approaching earth. "It was all single lights down there. Now they look like constellations—earth stars. We're getting nearer to civilization."

"There are fungi called earth stars," he said. "They're like brown puff-balls."

The passengers were asked to fasten seat-belts for landing, and gave up their collecting of bags and cases, coats and books and papers, to do so. A sleeping child began crying at the disturbance. There was an announcement about the weather in Barcelona being fine and warm. Tamzin scarcely heard it. She watched the lights of the city coming closer, growing thicker, circling round them: and then the drop and run-in.

Everyone was on their feet. The doors were opened and warm night air rushed in. Tamzin wanted to shout out, "Stop, everybody, please! Let us out quickly! We're racing time." One couldn't do that.

After a specially-arranged rapid Customs clearance, they were out at last, into the unfamiliar evening warmth and the noise and bustle.

A car from the hospital was to meet them. Mrs. Fairbrass was the first to see it. A young woman standing by it came across towards them. She was fair and grey-eyed and looked very English.

"Mr. and Mrs. Fairbrass and Meryon? I am a secretary at the hospital. I was sent to meet you because I'm English. I'm afraid I have to tell you that the corneas haven't arrived yet. But don't be too disheartened. There's still time." The driver was opening the boot and car-doors. "We're going straight to the hospital so that everything can be ready when they do come in."

After the wild rush across a county, sea and continent the sudden slackening of tension felt as if something somewhere had broken.

"I'm Susan Wood," the secretary said as the big saloon began making its way from the airport. "The crashed plane is in rather an inaccessible place. They had to send rock-climbers. It wasn't possible for a vehicle, or even a helicopter, to get near. But the great thing is, there was no fire. A helicopter went in to wait at the nearest possible place."

"But surely, after eight hours, the time is already up?" Meryon said. He sounded more as if he were talking about quick-drying paint than his chances of seeing again; as if he had never believed that could really be possible and so was not greatly disappointed.

"It may not be," Susan Wood said. "If they were able to get the corneas within six hours or so—or even longer, up there; it's very cold—they'll be all right. We sent out a chilled container for the climbers to take with them. That can extend the time up to ten or twelve hours."

"There's still a wind blowing!" Tamzin said to Meryon.

"A wind?"

"Old Jim says, don't lower your sails while a wind is blowing."

With a siren on the hospital car the motorway speed limit did not apply: faster than any English wind they flew along the broad road from the airport. There was an exhilarating feeling of hope in the night rush, the warm air gusting on their faces, the lights flashing past. Even in the aeroplane there had not been this sense of speed, of the ground racing past them. Rather they had seemed to float, suspended, dawdling in the sky. There was the curious subdued panic of driving on the right, but Tamzin was expecting that and half enjoyed it as part of the whole reckless race with time. She would scarcely have been surprised if their driver had rushed through red traffic lights with hand on the horn and siren howling. He was a fervent little man, too short to see over the wheel without using a folded blanket, and he drove ferociously but skilfully, with gold teeth flashing.

The suburbs were quite unbearable—flying speed down to a stop–start agony of lights and horns and gear-changing, the driver drumming impatiently on the wheel and wriggling on his folded blanket. Then, in the Avenida de Jose, in the thick of the city and so near their destination, a total hold-up, not only of themselves but of all traffic. Heads reached from windows, drivers shouted, horns blared. The hospital driver jumped up on his seat and looked out of the sunshine roof, adding to the shouting. Then bouncing back behind the wheel he spoke quickly to the young secretary as he flung the gear into reverse and began a manoeuvre of such intricacy and swiftness that it hardly seemed possible.

Susan Wood turned to her passengers. "He says some crazy English driver tried a U-turn in the middle of the Avenida and has got stuck with a lorry! Or words to that effect."

Jack Fairbrass replaced a canvas bag that shot off the rear shelf over his shoulder. "I take it he knows a short cut. That's the main thing."

"What I'll have to tell Thomas and Simon," Tamzin said to Meryon.

Small back streets flashed by; people sitting at tables on the pavement, shops still open and doing brisk business, a burst of flamenco singing from a bar open to the street, smells of coffee, a child dashing across the road and saved from annihilation only by Gold-Teeth standing on the brake and throwing Tamzin, Meryon and Mrs. Fairbrass over the shoulders of the three in front. There was a fountain and trees, a man selling birds in cages—and suddenly the hospital was there and they were getting out, Susan Wood shepherding them up wide steps. A sudden quietness settled as the doors closed behind them to familiar distant echoes and hospital smell. The suspense and waiting were a burden, the secretary gone to announce their arrival.

"At least we're *here*," Tamzin said to Meryon. "Surely nothing can go wrong now."

The secretary returned with an obviously Spanish doctor; a man of late middle age with greying hair. There were brief introductions before the secretary left. The doctor's name was Macias. Blessings on him, Tamzin thought, for being able to speak English—why did English people never master other Europeans' languages as they did ours?

"You will be glad," said Dr. Macias, "that the corneas have been taken and placed in a cold container. Three of the four are undamaged. I have this over the radio."

Mrs. Fairbrass leaned towards him. "Are they here at the hospital?"

"I am afraid, no. We have some trouble. It is from the coroner."

"I wondered about that," said Mr. Fairbrass. "Certainly in England there is always an inquest after accidental death."

"In Spain, too. And no one may to touch the body without the coroner's consent. In this case we took a chance, as you say, because a delay for inquest would have made the corneas useless. But the coroner has heard of it, and although the deed was already done he has called a halt."

No one said anything, but the desperate weariness could be felt.

"I have this from the helicopter pilot, who awaits permission to proceed." Dr. Macias looked from one to another. "Now we go to speak with the coroner—to state our case. You are not too tired?"

"*Tired?*" It was Meryon's mother. She glanced at Tamzin.

"I could run a marathon!"

There was plainly no need to ask Meryon or his father.

"If you will come with me, we go in my car."

It was a smaller car than the hospital taxi, but they were one fewer and without luggage. Tamzin was anguished to find that the doctor was a slow and deliberate driver, looking both ways at corners and waiting his turn. But the drive was without incident, and they were at the coroner's house within fifteen minutes.

"He expects me," said the doctor, pulling on the handbrake, "but I think only me. I was not sure if you arrive in in time; they told me the aircraft was delayed."

The coroner's house was in a little street near—Tamzin noticed on a sign-board—the Parque de la Ciudadela. It was an old house, severe with small barred windows and stone walls and it stood high beside the pavement like a cliff. Somehow this was discouraging, as was the long wait after Dr. Macias had rung the bell. "The Gothic quarter of the city," he told Jack Fairbrass. "Very old." Tamzin tried to stroke a thin tabby cat that ran past but it evaded her hand and vanished down an even narrower street.

The heavy door opened silently—they had expected it to creak—and a man servant spoke to them in Spanish. Dr. Macias answered and after some further conversation they were finally shown in to a large room full of old Spanish furniture. White wooden shutters were folded back from the one window, and in front of this was a long aquarium with fishes of strange shapes and colours. Tamzin was describing them to Meryon when the servant returned and announced, "Senor Bassa."

An elderly man, the coroner walked with a stoop and had a look of aloof sadness. It must be because of his work, Tamzin decided, her spirits sinking—or had he taken the job because he was a melancholy man? There was more preliminary Spanish conversation, and then Senor Bassa turned to Mr. Fairbrass, whose smattering of the language had not been equal to these exchanges.

"It is not permitted to take from the dead person before the inquest. This is a grave offence, punishable by the law."

"Senor, my sister and her husband gave their eyes to my son, who lost his sight in defence of law. If we had come to you first it would have been too late."

The coroner nodded. "This may be so. Still it is not permitted."

Kit Fairbrass suddenly stretched out a hand. "But, Senor, the corneas have been taken! May they not be used now?"

"Madam, this is like a person who has taken jewels saying, 'May I not use them, now that I have taken them?' This cannot be allowed."

A hopeless quiet hung in the room until Dr. Macias launched into an impassioned plea in Spanish. Unable to look any longer at the sadness of the coroner's face Tamzin turned instead to gaze at the remarkable aquarium. A fresh silence fell and she turned again to find the coroner looking at her.

"Are you fond of fishes, Senora?"

"Well, yes—I mean, I had a tame dolphin a little while ago. I know they aren't fishes, of course," she added, seeing an eyebrow go up.

"This must be a very seldom thing in English waters. Tell me."

There was no *time* to sit talking about fishes and dolphins, she cried out to herself, but heard her voice saying, "It was a wild one, a female. She came into our bay. I called her Simo."

Suddenly the hard face moved into a smile of surprising sweetness. "You have this from the great Pliny, his *Natural History*, no?"

"It was from Pliny, but my father found it."

"An honest girl. Tell me more about this dolphin. I am extremely interested."

Thinking, now, that his stoop had come of long hours peering at his aquarium, she said, "I used to ride on her. She came when I called. She had a mate who stayed further out."

Meryon suddenly said, "I expect she won't tell you, but Tamzin saved her from being caught."

Senor Bassa stroked his long sad nose with a forefinger. "This I think must be quite a long story. I should much like to hear it, for I too have studied dolphins."

Gazing at him despairingly Tamzin said nothing. She simply hadn't the heart to sit telling the story of her dolphin to this merciless man who would let a boy stay blind for the sake of a letter of the law.

Senor Bassa straightened himself, the stoop nearly disappearing. "I understand. This, he is your boy-friend as you call it, yes? You do not wish to speak of Simo to me when you grieve that I keep your friend sentenced to blindness. A coroner sees much sorrow and must harden himself, or he would not be able—how you say?—to carry on. But there must be understanding, too, you agree?" He turned to Mr. Fairbrass. "I cannot, of course, give official permission to use the corneas, even should I wish; but an understanding is different and need not go further. Doctor Macias!"

"Senor!"

"My telephone is in the hall. You may speak over it to your helicopter. Also to the car which is to meet it. Possibly also to the hospital. Hurry, man!" he exclaimed, although the doctor was all but hurdling the Spanish furniture. "There is no time for wasting."

Jack Fairbrass had risen to grip the coroner's hand. Mrs. Fairbrass to Tamzin's astonishment was in tears, which seemed to embarrass Senor Bassa. Releasing his hand he turned to Meryon.

"Young man."

Meryon drew himself erect. "Sir!"

"You will take your chance with this cornea operation. It is a chance, as you know. After it you may see, or you may stay blind.

There is not yet much experience in these things."

"Thank you, sir, I understand."

"It is good to have such aunt and uncle, may their souls rest in peace!" The coroner crossed himself. "The young senora, too—it is a very special girl who can tame a dolphin."

"She is a special girl, sir."

"I am glad you know it. I wish you know it always."

Now he turned to Tamzin. "You will be in Barcelona for a few days? It would give an old man much pleasure to have more talk of dolphins. Your good friends will bring you to take coffee with me, and you will tell me about Simo!"

Suddenly Tamzin ran across the splendid crimson carpet and threw her arms around the stooped shoulders.

Chapter Fifteen

Dropping with exhaustion Tamzin had been taken to the hotel where Jack Fairbrass had arranged bookings for the three of them. There was no longer any need to stay alert.

Meryon had gone straight into the theatre. Even now, in the night, the long, complicated operation would be in progress. After leaving her comfortably in her room with a tray meal ordered Mr. and Mrs. Fairbrass had returned to the hospital. They would tiptoe in, they said, and see if she were awake when they returned; but there would probably not be much more news. She was to try to go to sleep. There was a whole week still for being awake.

Even though she had not eaten in the aeroplane Tamzin could not do more than taste the tray meal, exciting and unusual though its offerings would have been except on this night.

A bath was refreshing. She sat at her window staring out at the lights of the city, of shipping in the nearby harbour, wondering exactly where the hospital was. The night air was soft and warm; it had strange stirring smells. All those people hurrying along the streets when an English town would be asleep; they did not know—incredibly—that a fight was going on in their midst to make a blind boy see.

She tried not to think about it. She thought instead about Old Jim and the strangeness in the *Thunderer*; she wondered what Mrs. One-Who-Knows would be photographing next with her Snap-o-Matic, if Smiling Morn would really smile when Meryon walked into the little shop seeing (Please, God, let him come home seeing!), and whether Hookey Galley still kept his prisoner (she nearly remembered, then, who that face reminded her of) in the old boat's cabin … Perhaps that was the hospital, over there—that tower of lights. But flats and hotels were towers of light in Spain, no matter how late … She went to the table and took her tape recorder—she must do something to stop thinking about what was happening in that great building—she ought to be glad it was happening after all the terrible set-backs, not worrying herself to death.

"Hullo, Simon, this is me, Tamzin. There's so much to tell you, even at this stage, I need a mile of tape. What it'll be like by the end of the week …"

She was nodding half-way through the tape, more tired than she thought. With an effort of will she kept her eyes open long enough to switch off and reach her bed.

The room was full of sunshine when she woke. There was a tray with fruit and coffee on her bedside table. Someone must have brought it in, but she had heard nothing. She couldn't believe that she had let herself stay sleeping when Mr. and Mrs. Fairbrass had come in on their return from the hospital. Now she was suddenly bursting over with new energy, rushing to gaze out of her window at the splendid morning city while pulling on a white dress and sandals and snatching apricots from the tray. The window was a French one opening on to a balcony. As soon as she was passably presentable she swung it open and stepped out to lean over the wrought iron balustrade.

Tables were set out on the wider balcony below, among tubs of scarlet hibiscus. Two morning glories had rushed to the tops of supporting pillars and launched out to swing their blue trumpets into space. Someone looked up at her and waved.

"You're there! I'll come right down."

Finding them after dashing down too far and rushing up again, she swirled into the empty chair.

"We hadn't the heart to wake you," Kit Fairbrass said. "It's all good news, so far."

"Yes?"

"Operation over, everything O.K." Mr. Fairbrass said. "Nothing now but the wait."

"You mean he'll be able to see?"

"We should know for certain in five days, when the bandages come off; but Doctor Macias will have some idea of how things are in three days."

"And listen!" Mr. Fairbrass said. "They did both eyes. They almost never do, because it's a long operation—two hours just for one eye. Four hours of unbroken concentration would be too much for most surgeons, and working most of the time down an operating microscope."

"But Doctor Macias did it?"

"He and two other surgeons," Jack Fairbrass told her. "They laid a team on for Meryon, because it was his one chance. We rang up early this morning and the Ward Sister said it all went perfectly. They didn't even need to use the third cornea, so it was rushed to another hospital and used for someone else."

"Oh, I'm so glad! When can we go and see him?"

"This afternoon; and twice a day after that."

The waiter was hovering under a dangle of morning glory. He needed only a nod of encouragement to bring more coffee and fruit and a basket of rolls so crisp that their crusts were audibly crackling. There was butter in a blue bowl and a yellow hibiscus flower in a wineglass full of water.

"I'm still not really hungry," Tamzin said. "I'm too excited to live! But listen to those rolls."

"None of us ever listened so much before That Day," said Kit. "I wonder if we'll go on noticing all the sounds when—if Meryon sees again?"

Tamzin gazed at the shining roofs, taking in the hurrying street noises, the blare of a ship's siren, bells clanging in towers, voices shouting, someone singing … "I think I shall, if I go on with tape letters, and I want to do that."

Jack Fairbrass had arranged to hire a small blue Renault for the week, and the first thing they did with it was essential shopping; bank and post office, stationer's for cards and writing paper, midge-oil for Kit who attracted all insect life, and for Meryon huge red peaches and a jasmine in a pot for the glorious scent it had and to remind him of the Sussex garden. After the shopping the car-seats were hot as radiators. Kit spread a sheet of brown paper from a parcel and sat back limply.

"Oh, I never was so *sweaty* in my life!"

Mr. Fairbrass put a packet on Tamzin's knee. "Something for you; we thought you'd be short of them this week, of all times."

"Cassettes for my recorder! Oh, wonderful—thank you both!"

"Nipped into the shop next to the florist's," he told her, "when you were getting the jasmine—which I should think took all the pocket money I cashed for you."

"No, there was enough for stamps, and still a bit left."

"An hour to lunch and time's our own. You girls have any place you specially want to see? The harbour, Tamzin?"

"Could we—do you think we could go to the cathedral? To find St. George's fountain?"

"The man with the saucerful of ball-bearings!"

"Yes. He said people went there to ask blessings for the blind."

"It shall be done even as you say, oh maiden. But—dead serious—I'm in favour. There may be something in it, who knows? More things in heaven and earth …"

There was a golden light on the cathedral stones that was not all from the sun, but was in the stones themselves. Looking up briefly at the two great bell towers soaring into the sky, Tamzin followed Kit and Jack Fairbrass into dimness that was like walking into a forest. The nave was very wide, giving an impression of a way through the forest. Her head and shoulders covered by a filmy square Kit had found for her, Tamzin knelt with them in silence and felt very small and still.

There were in the cathedral magnificent renaissance carvings, added, Jack Fairbrass had earlier told her, for the Chapter of the Order of the Golden Fleece; but nobody wanted, on this day, to see the sights. The three of them went out to walk through the cloisters—severe Gothic arches garlanded in cool green leaves, enclosing a tree-shaded garden. Surprisingly a small flock of geese lived here, consecrated, an American tourist told them, to St. Eulalia.

The fountain to Tamzin was like a kind of Mecca to which she had travelled, a pilgrim from afar. She dropped in her coin, watching its sliding oblique descent, and thought her thoughts, prayed prayers and wished her wishes. Two other coins had gone with hers, and all three were for Meryon.

"I must put two more in, for Simon and Thomas."

After that they sat in the peaceful garden for a few minutes, and Kit made some sketches, and Jack watched, and Tamzin switched on her tape recorder so as to keep for as long as she liked the limpid sound of the water, and the chattering geese, and the birds hidden in the leaves, and soft Spanish voices as two girls went by.

It was while they were sitting there, quiet in the shady garden, that Tamzin knew in a flash of realization whose the face was in Mrs. Venus's photograph, the man in the *Thunderer*'s cabin. She knew where she had seen it before. It was the face of the man who had thrown ammonia on the day of the Dunsford bank raid. There was no doubt at all about it.

The realization was a severe enough shock to drain her face of its normal warm colour; she could feel it, like a cold hand stroking.

No one noticed—Kit studying her drawing, leaning back on warm stone and Jack shutting his eyes in the sun.

Why was he in the *Thunderer*? Or was he, still? She pondered Jim's involvement and threw out the idea that he might have had anything to do with the raid. Outside the law he certainly often was, especially—as with many fishermen on that coast—in the matter of smuggling, which they considered to be honest free trade, the goods paid for in the country of origin at the fair market price; but robbery with violence—that was not the way of Sussex fishermen.

It was difficult not to be preoccupied on the way back to the hotel. Well, you can't *do* anything, she told herself finally; not here and probably not at all, so stop aching on about it, or Mr. and Mrs. Fairbrass will think you're sickening for something and be sorry they brought you.

She had herself fairly well in hand by the time for lunch, which was on the balcony again shaded now from the burning sun, and found herself hungrily enjoying strange and delicious things among the hibiscus trumpets. There was a cold soup, spicy, with raw tomato in it—refreshing as a mountain pool; and then, because she had never had it, a real Spanish paella, its saffron tinted rice full of sea creatures enough to keep Jim Decks fascinated through a long description—she tried to memorize them for him. A huge flat basket had piles of peaches and apricots, grapes with the bloom on them, oranges with leaves on them, pomegranates with long stalks just as they had been cut.

"Do people have a siesta, still?"

Mr. Fairbrass was examining an orange leaf. "Older people. They say it's dying out, as a custom. But the shops all close until teatime."

"It seems an awful waste of time," Kit said.

"That's why it's dying out, I suppose. But of course everyone keeps open and working far later."

"What about the hospital?" Tamzin asked.

"Don't worry! When you're ready we'll go."

Meryon was waiting for them—"Watching the door with my ears!" he said. His eyes were bandaged, as they would be for several days, the rough black hair looking blacker against the dead white, but he seemed relaxed and content. "Well, there it is, there's nothing more anyone can do; just wait. It's a marvellous feeling, really."

You can't tell him about The Face, now, Tamzin told herself, and spoil all that.

"What's the wonderful smell, that's like jasmine?"

"Jasmine!" she said. "It's growing in a pot, trained round in a little circle." She put it in his hands.

"Eyes feel all right?" Kit asked.

"Pretty decent. Peaches, somewhere?"

"Proper bloodhound you're getting," his father said. "Shall I put them in your bowl? They seem to have given you lots of fruit, already."

"Marvellous nurses here—give you anything!" He put the jasmine on his table. "And the doctors—well, what can you say about chaps like that? ... They're going to take a look at the grafts in three days. Bandages off in five days, with normal luck, but another five or so before they let me out."

"What d'you mean by normal luck? Anything particular likely to go wrong?"

"There's always a risk—a fairly remote risk—of infection, isn't there? And as they did both eyes I suppose that doubles the risk. I think if it did happen," he added in the matter of fact voice he used for these things, "it would be a bit of a disaster—put the lid on my ever seeing again ... Still, it *is* remote; thousands of operations are done without anything going wrong." He reached for and bit into a peach with appreciation. "Don't find them like this in England, do we?"

"Did you know the third cornea was used in another hospital?" his mother asked.

"Yes. For a chap who got a splash of molten metal; worked in a foundry. He's doing O.K. too, they told me just now. Aunt Lucy would be glad. Uncle, too—but I bet it was her idea. You wouldn't believe the precision job this corneal grafting is," he went on after a pause. "Doctor Macias was telling me a bit about it when he came round this morning. They use minute needles—four millimetres, think of it!—and either fine strands of virgin silk or mono-filament nylon, working through an operating microscope. Wish I could have seen it! Still, you can't be the patient and the audience, I suppose. Another thing, this is the first time, Doctor Macias says, he's even heard of grafts on both eyes at once."

"But you, being an obstinate fellow, have to have preferential treatment and, for all I know, make medical history," Jack Fairbrass said. "Isn't that just life all over? When do they let you get up?"

"Tomorrow. It's not the op. that makes them keep me in bed now, but all that anaesthetic. What's the ward like, Tamzin?"

She looked round it. "Roomy, but only four beds. No one in the bed next to you. Light blue walls, big windows, open with white Venetian blinds down on the sunny side. It all looks light and clean and airy."

"Now I can see it—as good as. And you—what are you wearing?"

"The white cotton thing; you know it. Hair tied back, it's cooler."

"Ma?"

"That jungly dress, and the copper necklet."

"I always liked that. I can see you both now, in my mind's eye. Dad, I reckon you're just wearing the old flowered waistcoat with ruffled silk shirt and plum jacket, bullfighter hose, Bermuda shorts and buckled shoes as usual?"

"How could you guess?" his father drawled.

Chapter Sixteen

No one talked much, in those next few days, about Meryon's chances; not even Meryon himself. It was better, somehow, to leave the hopes and doubts unsaid; everyone knew they were there.

Tamzin's other preoccupation, about the man in *Thunderer*'s cabin, was almost worse in a way, because it was not shared with anyone at all, nor could be until she was home and could see Jim.

Kit and Jack Fairbrass kept Tamzin and themselves on the move, so that there was not much time to stir up under-surface anxiety into a state of gnawing worry. On the mornings when they attended the inquest and funeral she was left at the hospital with Meryon. They sat on the balcony of his ward and she described the view of the city and told him about the great port, full of shipping, which they had explored the day before; about the old zig-zag market and shopping streets, the *Ramblas*, where every kind of business and trade flourished, and you could buy cage-birds, fruit, books, clothes, or a Spanish guitar.

"People sitting everywhere under the trees along the pavements, and stalls of lobsters, and flowers—even bicycles and washing machines; shoe-shine men fairly telling the street how dirty your shoes are, to shame you into having them done! No one in a hurry, strolling just for the fun of it and to meet friends; you have to imagine sun through leaves and thousands of sparrows cheeping and people talking and buying and selling things. But oh, the sticky heat! You feel you want a bath every ten minutes or so."

"Bet you envy me my air-conditioned ward!"

"Do you know, I *enjoy* the miseries, in a way; they seem part of being abroad. We're always hungry, of course—nobody seems to eat much until very late at night, and I'm fainting with hunger and sleepiness by then. But I still don't want everything to be the same as at home."

"That's the stuff explorers are made of."

She said, "I bought two little furry bulls, one for Diccon and one—just for fun—for you, because they feel so nice. Open your hand—if you don't like him when you see him you can give him back to me, or if you only like him a little we can share him, a week at your house and a week at mine."

"He's a fighting bull," Meryon said. "I'll keep him near the jasmine and he can fight for me if any germs come around."

"St. George is looking after the germs," she said.

"So you went there! What did you ask him?"

"I'll tell you when the bandages are off—when they're really off, not just for tomorrow's inspection."

In the morning they took coffee with Senor Bassa, partly in fulfilment of their promise and partly to occupy the desert of time until the eye examination had been done and they could talk again with Dr. Macias. The coroner proved to be fascinating company, now that no point of law was there between them. He had a considerable knowledge of oceans and ocean life, and the kind of loving understanding of his own aquarium that good gardeners have of their gardens. He knew more about dolphins than Tamzin's reading had even brushed, but still he wanted to hear all that she could tell him about Simo, the dolphin who had come when she called and singled her alone for special allegiance, out of all the swimmers on that shore.

They left Senor Bassa with invitations pressed on them. "It would give me happiness to show you the great things of our city; my home is yours, any one or all of you—and the young man also who defended the law."

"That goes for us, too," Jack Fairbrass told him. "Kit and I would be really delighted to have you stay with us. Who knows? Tamzin's Simo might honour you with a personal appearance!"

Dr. Macias did not keep them waiting. He understood the stress there is in not knowing. They were shown into his room immediately, but the most searching glance at his calm face showed no one what news he had to tell.

"It is the third day only, and early to know very much, but all is as it should be at this stage."

The three who had come to see him waited on, their eyes on his face.

"There is no infection present; and although this may still happen, the most dangerous period is over. Every day is a day gained towards a perfect result."

Kit's voice, very small and quiet, asked, "When might he be able to see—anything at all?"

"This is a gradual thing," the doctor said, moving the pad on his desk an inch aside. "He sees already the light as a mist. When we take away the bandages in two days more, he may see shapes of things. After this we shall require to keep him in hospital here for a further week, when he may return home to be in the care of his own medico. Steadily then the sight should continue to improve. In his case—there is much in his favour—perhaps as near to full vision as—how do you say?—makes no difference."

Tamzin was looking at him, her eyes very bright, but she was seeing the new dinghy leaning to the wind, and Meryon was at the tiller, and she was somewhere, too …

Jack Fairbrass was shaking the doctor's hand and saying something, but Dr. Macias had worked his miracles too often to have his head turned by them. "The boy would like to see you, I know. Come, I will take you."

Between the morning and evening hospital visits, on that day and the next, Mr. Fairbrass drove them in the Renault far out of the city and into the mountains. It was his first duty, he said, to pay his respects to Ben and Lucy, and so he would drive up into the Sierra del Cadi, as near as he could to where they had paid with their lives for Meryon's sight. Kit and Tamzin could come too if they wished, but there would be rough roads, high and giddy; there had, even, the week before, been an attack on a lonely road by bandits.

"Of course I have grandfather's pistol with me—I always do when I'm abroad—but it hasn't any ammo. I don't expect they make any for it, nowadays."

Tamzin and Kit didn't seem to mind about anything except being left by themselves at the hotel, so presently they were all heading northwards out of the town, leaving behind the streets and town houses. Now in the country there were tall white houses with blue and green shutters and steep pitched roofs; they had overhanging eaves and flowered balconies. Then the good hard roads were left behind and finally the last of the regular traffic.

"Now there will only be the odd crazy adventurer, like ourselves," Jack said, and the car was climbing, climbing, in third gear.

On the south-facing slopes there were apricots ripening in small levelled plots. Jack Fairbrass stopped the car to buy some from a boy with loaded baskets. They were warm from the sun and very sweet. It was good to sit on hot rock and gaze at the tawny distances; a country glowing with green and gold and russet, and always there were the mountains.

"Still low enough for olives," Kit said. "Look at those women shaking the trees with their long poles. How they can wear all that black—down to their ankles—in all this heat." The olive trees had twisted trunks and delicate silvery leaves. There were golden maize cobs spread out on the rocks, mellowing to ripeness in the sun.

Cooled, the Renault pushed on higher, through woods of cork oak, chestnut and beech, the road unsurfaced now and very rough.

The little stone farmhouses clung dizzily now to the mountainsides, and always there was a stream nearby rushing headlong, overhung with shrubs and trees covered in old man's beard. Some farms had tall round towers. They were built, Jack told them, as a refuge in the days when Barbary pirates ravaged in from the coast.

"People say there are wild boars—and bears—in the high forests," Kit said. But they saw only mountain cattle, and on little shelves of land working oxen and farm families picking stones.

The road grew quite appalling—second gear all the time—with passing places notched into the rocks and corners fit to make the heart fail. "A road without visible means of support," Jack said, and Tamzin looked down giddily over sheer drops hung with trees.

Now they were above the oaks and into the regions of fir and pine. Up here every turn threw at them its breath-taking view, the full glory of the crags. Tamzin saw an eagle planing over the slopes; and still in the shaggy uplands there was the occasional lonely farmhouse and—incredibly, Tamzin thought—Coca-Cola advertisement. At one farm Jack stopped the car again—"To cool her and us"—and because her Spanish though poor was better than Jack's, Kit talked to the young woman who brought them bread and cheese and oranges.

"She says the plane came down about three kilometres into the pine forest. The road doesn't go any nearer. She says if we climb up behind the farm we come to a clearing where a woman from the village is herding cows, and we can see the place from there."

"Did you ask her about the bandits?" Tamzin asked, but Kit said she couldn't remember the Spanish for it.

Wind-bent pines shaded the hot hard trudge above the farm. The high crags grew ferns and mosses that loved the mists and hanging clouds. There was no view until the forest opened and there was the world. The glory of it was a shock. It took away words and breath as well. There *were* no words for it, Tamzin thought, unless they came from the Book of Genesis.

In the immediate foreground were the cows the young woman had spoken of, grazing mountain grasses which the mists had kept green while lowland pastures dried to brownness. They were tawny cows with bells that clunked musically in the clear air as they moved. An old woman in the usual black sat knitting as she watched them, at ease on a hump of stone in the shade of a pine tree.

Finding his voice Jack murmured, "The top of the world, and not far from the edge."

He took his field glasses from their case and ranged them in silence, over the eagles' eye distance. Then he handed them to Kit. She had seen where he had brought them to rest and found the place herself. When it was Tamzin's turn she could only look briefly at the scar in the green forest, where the wing of an aeroplane shone white in the sun.

The old woman was watching them, and they walked across the springy turf to her. Tamzin looked at the cows with special interest while Mr. and Mrs. Fairbrass tried out their halting Spanish, but the old woman was not as easy to understand as the girl at the farm.

"I think she wants to look through the field glasses," Kit said.

Jack gave them to her with his wide smile and some comment about the marvellous view, and they watched to see how she would take the wonder of it, unfolding vast and clear to her eyes.

The old lady, after some muttered twiddling, had the glasses trained to suit herself, straight down to the village where she lived. Presently she began smiling and laughing to herself, and there was a rich chuckle as something funnier than usual met her eyes.

"All this superb view of no account at all," Jack whispered, "beside the neighbours' doings!"

"She said—I think she said—the mountains are hard and lonely," answered Kit as they walked back over the alp. "I did remember the Spanish for bandits, though, and asked her. They were on the same road we're taking!"

"That's fine," Jack told them. "It's the one place where they won't be; they'll be miles away, now."

The scramble back down to the car was harder on the leg muscles than the uphill climb had been. Kit looked with brief longing at the little stone farmhouse when they reached it. "Tea—or something—would be nice, but there isn't time; we've a long way to go. Perhaps we'll see the apricot boy."

The young woman came out of her door and smiled at them as Jack turned the car. He said, "Astonishing the grace of these mountain people. I thought when she brought our lunch, never have I seen three oranges on a plate placed so gracefully on a table."

The road down seemed to be hanging in the air. The heat grew as they descended and Kit and Tamzin, in their cotton dresses, felt themselves sticking to the backs of their seats. Every turn brought fresh stupendous views. "It's like coming down in an aeroplane," Tamzin said as the car swung round a hairpin, "circling to land—" and as she spoke three men leapt out of the pines at the roadside waving their hands.

The Renault screeched to a halt. The men were shouting at them. They were rough and wild looking. Coldness gripped in Tamzin's stomach. So this was it. And no good screaming with only the eagles to hear. If she lived through it this would be something to tell Simon and Thomas …

Jack Fairbrass got out of the car and walked to the men. There was much shouting and gesticulating, and suddenly he started laughing. The men turned and vanished into the trees and Jack came back to the car.

"Three roadmen—would you believe it? There's been an avalanche round the next corner and half the road's missing. We're to drive very carefully—as if we weren't all the time!" He got into the car, then turned and looked at the two white faces. "To think I forgot grandfather's pistol!"

Chapter Seventeen

D r. Macias himself telephoned the hotel with the news. Coming back to the others on the balcony Jack Fairbrass could scarcely stop himself from standing on the table in the middle of the breakfast cups and telling all the hotel, as well as all the people in the square below.

"Rang us the first moment—bandages just off. He can see—he isn't blind any more, Kit! Tamzin, he can see! Not all that clearly, yet, of course—that'll come—but better than Doctor Macias expected. Like someone looking through tears, he said—what on earth are *you* two crying for? Get your handbags or whatever you carry around, and into that Renault."

Meryon was looking out of a window in the large light sitting room for mobile patients. He turned with his old grin. "Hullo, you lot! Gosh, I never remembered how beautiful you all are—even you, Dad!"

"Less cheek from you, boy!" Mr. Fairbrass said gruffly.

"All right, give us a kiss, Ma! Tamzin, too. You're wearing that blue dress," he said to her, "that you had on the last time I saw you. Makes it seem as if nothing had happened at all."

"How much vision at this stage, old chap?" his father asked. "We gathered it wasn't likely to be much."

"Better—much better, I think—than anyone expected. Pretty good. A bit misty, as if we were in a fog. It clears gradually, they tell me; might be weeks. But I'll say, it's fairly well marvellous to me!"

"Did you know you're in the Spanish papers?" Kit asked him. "It's the first time a double graft has been done successfully, they say, but they add that the degree of success won't be known until to-day! There's even a photograph, with the bandages on, of course. You didn't tell us you'd had a press photographer in."

"Didn't I? Must've been thinking of something else. There's a lot to think of."

"Cambridge!" Tamzin said.

"The main thing, of course; nearly everything else springs from that. But sailing again! Have we still got the dinghy, Dad?"

"Certainly we have—been keeping it for you, naturally."

"Seeing what's doing in the *Thunderer*, Tamzin."

She nodded—a nod meant something, again—but kept to herself the matter of the photograph.

"Only thing is—will Meg be awfully disappointed? Her great work ended."

"You'll just have to start sheep, or something, old man, to keep her occupied," his father said, grinning.

"Sheep were what she *wasn't* good at," Kit reminded.

"Strap a little brandy barrel on her back and send her out after lost hikers on the marsh," Tamzin suggested, giddy with good news. "Or just keep her as a good, honest, well-trained, beautiful dog."

Meryon pulled a handful of Get Well cards from his pocket. "You wouldn't believe the fun I've had reading these. Bit hazy, of course, but I can make them out. Even one from the coroner bloke who nearly stopped everything. Several just arrived from England—this from your folks, Tamzin; nice, isn't it? Burma's and Meg's paw-prints on it, too. And a naughty one from Jim; wherever did he find it?"

"Will they let you out for a celebration dinner, to-night?" his mother asked.

Meryon shook his head. "No chance. Not this week. Risk of infection, I suppose. Never mind, what's a week in a lifetime?"

"We'll just have to bring a bottle in," Jack Fairbrass said. "Or two—or three—if we can get the doctors and nurses to join us. We've got a telephone call booked to Tamzin's family this evening; they'll be champing to hear the news. She goes back tomorrow evening, of course."

There was one more mountain drive, this time as the guests of Senor Bassa and in his Fiat estate car. It was up a much more frequented but just as giddy route, the road thrashing this way and that in a quite heart-failing manner as it tossed off the same stupendous kinds of view that the bandit road had done.

The Fiat had a sophisticated radio with speakers both in the back and front. The coroner was a musical man and the car was filled with Mozart at his most joyful. Sitting in the front with Senor Bassa Tamzin was in a whirl. "What with my ears popping and my eyes on stalks and music coming from all sides, I don't know where I am!"

"This is how I enjoy to drive," the coroner said, "slowly and with music."

Well, if this is slowly, Tamzin thought—and the next thing they were reversing to a passing place to make room for a bus, of all things on that road, and the big Fiat was so near the edge of the precipice that nothing could be seen except space. Buses were not allowed on the edge, the coroner explained, and told how once he had met twenty-four of them, all on a railway workers' outing and accompanied by military vehicles. "I had so many times to reverse, and always to the edge, that I was not—how do you say?—too keen."

There was much horn-blowing on the corners—"The only way to save yourself"—and a prim comment as they passed a pair of lovers coming down in a mini-car, "To take kisses on this road is not good."

Well, anyway, Tamzin said to herself; even if I *wasn't* too madly distracted to record it all I haven't any tapes left, so I'll just have to try to remember. Was there ever a week like it in the *whole* of my life?

The next day, her last, she spent an hour alone with Meryon. He was allowed now on the balcony leading from the patients' sitting room and they leaned together on the balustrade looking over the city, as so often they had leaned and looked over the marsh. There was so much to say, but they said almost nothing. Presently he put that in words. "I don't have to ask you what you are wearing—that yellow dress is a new one, isn't it?—and you don't have to tell me what the world looks like, any more. The things we do have to say are too far down."

She thought about that in the plane going home, and knew how true it was. But there was something else to add to it, and that was that the things they did have to say didn't need to be said; they both knew them.

On this solitary flight she was afraid again, perhaps more afraid than on the flight to Spain, because now it seemed terribly important to stay alive. The plane droned on above thick cloud, rising and falling a little, and the young woman sitting next to her kept talking about the disappointments of her Spanish holiday, and presently Tamzin's eyelids wouldn't stay open any more.

"Mother—Dad—both of you! Oh, I'm so glad to see you!"

Arms were round her in the crowded airport reception room. "Meg's in the car, too, but we thought Burma wouldn't enjoy it. He's going to miss our vicarage cats when he goes home."

"The news is all over Sussex, now!" her mother said. "The local rag has a column. And who do you think told them? Mrs. Venus."

"No!"

"She's branching out," the vicar said. "Our Harbour Reporter. She always gets all the news before anyone else. There may be something we can build on, there."

Driving home along dark lanes flaring with headlamps Tamzin was vividly awake. It would hardly have been possible to share the back seat with Meg and be anything else.

There was the whole fantastic week to tell about, and leaning half on Meg and half over the seat-back she told it all, even to the morning glories and the thin cat and the old woman herding the cows.

"And when he comes home next week he may be seeing quite well, no more living in the dark! And there'll be Cambridge, and everything as it was always going to be."

The vicar said over his shoulder, "Remember the Ancient Mariner?—*At one stride comes the dark*. I thought about it after the accident. Now it's nearly, *At one stride comes the light*."

"And what about Meg?" asked Mrs. Grey.

Tamzin gave the collie a hug. "Surely she can just be a pet, now, like other dogs?" Then she remembered what Mrs. Merrow had said. "We'll think of something. There are all kinds of things a dog can do. Aren't there, Meg?" After a minute she added, "I suppose there's no news about the bank robbers? No one caught?"

"Yes, two men, the day before yesterday," her father said, "but not the man who threw the ammonia, and no money. They were arrested in Hastings; hadn't gone far, had they? Perhaps Mrs. Venus put the police on their trail—I musn't make fun of her, poor soul!"

"Dad, talking about Mrs. Venus; have you still got those snapshots she sent you?"

"I think so, if only in the W.P.B."

"I thought I'd have another look at the *Thunderer* one."

"The *Thunderer*'s gone to sea," Mrs. Grey told her. "Would you believe it?"

"*What?*"

"Two days ago. With Jim and Hookey. No one seems to know where. Young Jimmy is looking after the ferry."

"If you want my opinion," said the vicar lightly, "they've gone to escape from that Snap-o-Matic." But Tamzin didn't even hear.

Chapter Eighteen

"B ut, Jimmy, if they haven't got any nets on board what are they doing?"

Young Jimmy was mending his own nets; they hung like great dark cobwebs from the roof of the ferry hut. He wasn't really young except in relation to Old Jim, whose age nobody seemed to know, not even himself.

"I didden say they ent got no nets on board. I say they ent got no nets, which they ent. Mebbe they got somebody's else's nets on board."

Tamzin straightened out a knot for him. "Is that other man with them, the third man?"

"Third man?"

"Jimmy, you're hedging. You know there was someone in the boat."

Young Jimmy had not the shrewd sharpness of his father, but he had not his ruthlessness, either. He was a kindly man, as slow to anger as he was believed to be in the uptake.

"That's good news about Meryon Fairbrass," he said, shuttling his wooden needle in and out of the broken net. "I'm real glad to hear he's got his sight back. That his dog you got there, is it?"

"Yes. I'm looking after her until he comes home. She's scatty, but so obedient now, you'd hardly know she's scatty."

"True you wouldn't—sitting there still as a doldrum."

"When they went to sea, Jimmy, did they say anything?"

"They said they was going to sea, gal."

"They didn't say when they were coming back?"

"Beats me you should be that interested, gal, when you got your boy-friend back from blindness to think of. If there ever was miracles, there's one."

"But, Jimmy, it's because of him that I *am* interested!"

Young Jimmy turned and looked at her, sitting there with Meg beside her. "Listen, gal—keep out of it, just you keep out of it."

"I haven't much choice, now, have I, the way things are? School tomorrow—I've missed a week already. But Meryon will be home next week-end."

The hand with the netting needle paused again. "How well will he be seeing?" It seemed as if Jimmy really wanted to know.

"Pretty well, I should think, except for details. He won't need Meg to guide him, anyway."

"And how well will he be in himself, gal?" Again the urgent inquiry, as if it mattered to Jimmy. "Strong and steady, like?"

"Of course, Jimmy. Why not? He's kept as fit since the accident as he always did. And this wasn't the kind of operation that pulls you down; he didn't have to stay in bed or anything."

The needle shuttled through the mesh again. "That's just as well, gal; I'm glad about that."

Tamzin thought a good deal about Jimmy's questions—and his evasion of hers—during the difficult first days of term. The first week back was always difficult, but this time the pace of the days just before with the worry of the present and the excitement about the future made concentration almost impossible.

When her father had found it for her she studied the *Thunderer* snapshot very carefully and was as sure as anyone could be, after a single terrified glance on a distant afternoon, that this was indeed the man who had blinded Meryon. But until Jim came home from sea there was nothing that could be done. She could not say anything

217

that might betray him, until she had seen him for herself.

In the evenings, before settling to homework, she had Meg and Cascade to exercise while the shortening daylight lasted, and usually Diccon and Banner went with her. There was a letter from Meryon nearly every day, written in his own familiar firm hand. Optimism was running high for him, now, with sight strengthening daily and freedom increasing as the risk of infection diminished.

"We went up into the Cadi and saw your old woman herding the cows. The first thing she did was ask for Dad's field glasses! I feel now I should like to learn Spanish. Actually, languages were a thing I could well have started in the blind days; why I should hanker now, when there are so many other things I want to do, I don't know."

Another letter began, "This morning I went out on my own as the parents were shopping. I went to the cathedral to find your St. George's fountain, and dropped a thank offering in. Those splendid geese, they reminded me of Castle Farm, though I expect they're far too holy to be thought of in the same breath with Joseph's gaggle. Everything I look at is so full of colour and light. Is it just Spain, or is it me?"

Towards the end of that week the vicar announced to his family, "I've offered Mrs. Venus a job. And what's more, she's accepted."

The family gazed at him over teacups.

"Our parish magazine home reporter. All she really needed was a genuine outlet, I do believe I'm right about that."

"Gorblimey and sink me for a coghead!" said Diccon, who had been spending more time with the fishermen lately.

"Well, yes, me too," said Tamzin. "And whew! Quaking queens and great galigaskins."

"You're going to censor her, I take it?" his wife asked, never greatly surprised by what her husband did.

"Certainly, full editorial rights and all that. She knows it, too. I had to explain that she will now be writing for a different, wider public; straight news items, and illustrated by her own camera, too. I shall pay her expenses and a little over. She was very pleased; even, shall we say—" he looked for a word and found one of Tamzin's, "thrilled."

"Oh," said Tamzin. "Well, I hope the rest of the parish is, too."

"We also made an agreement," the vicar said, "that she devotes all her spare time to the magazine reporting and stops sending letters from to-day. She quite understood and considers herself under contract as a commissioned writer. My goodness, she's half a head taller already."

On the Friday evening Tamzin found Mrs. Venus at the vicarage door, a notebook and ballpoint in her hand and her Snap-o-Matic over her shoulder. Drawing herself up with pride and dignity she announced, "Good evening! I represent the parish magazine. I am hoping you will grant me an interview—look, ducky, I want to put in a piece about Meryon coming home, flying in tonight and that."

"Why, yes, of course," said Tamzin. "Come in and I'll tell you about it."

"Pity I can't get a photygraph," Mrs. Venus said, "but I'll take one of Meg, instead. I got some little flash-cubes, now—lord sakes, I'll be living on Sugar Snazzles till I reach my hundred and that's a fact, never get through them sooner."

Tamzin was getting used to wild excitements and fears and griefs and sudden reprieves; she slept all through the night when Meryon was flying home.

When she was with him, the next morning, and they had marvelled together about the things that had happened, and Meg had acted so crazily that the Merrows would have shaken their heads, and Burma had walked down the garden as if he'd never been away, Meryon said, "Funny thing, I slept most of the way over. Must be getting used to the incredible."

"Me, too," she said. "It's old age creeping on."

He laughed. "I want to look at everything! Come with me? Don't forget it's months since I saw any of it. And I'll tell you one thing; you'll never know the absolute marvel seeing is—no one who hasn't been blind ever could know."

"A long time ago," she said, "soon after the bank raid, I did try to find out what blindness was like. Partly because of you and partly to understand about Simon and Thomas. I went blindfold for a day. It was so awful, I dream about it sometimes. But still it wasn't the same as being blind, because I knew I could pull off the bandage at any time I wanted."

When she had got over her wild welcome, Meg was bewildered and at a loss to know what to do. Here was Meryon, who relied on her for everything, somehow steering himself around quite fast and accurately. And why did she have no harness on? Clearly worried she rushed in whenever he moved and pressed herself close to his leg, looking up anxiously at him.

"All right, old girl! Have your harness." He grinned round at Tamzin. "She can wear it less every day, until she gets used to the idea."

Any local passer-by looking through the trees into the garden would have seen exactly what he had often seen before; the girl from Westling and the blind Fairbrass boy with his guide dog.

Meg was very relieved and happy, glancing up as usual but now with dancing eyes and lolling tongue. Her world was back to normal.

The thing that gave Meryon the most delight to re-examine was his old hearse, the Emma, sharing the double garage as usual with the red Rover, now back with her filter trouble diagnosed and corrected.

"Absolute perfect nick!" he said glowingly to Tamzin, while Meg sat on guard in the doorway. "Just look! Some parents would've got rid of her, in the circs, but mine looked *after* her. And how." He lifted the bonnet. "Take a decko at this engine." Lovingly, and not for the first time, she had its unique qualities pointed out and explained to her; she had never mastered the difference between a gasket and a manifold and still didn't, but there was no need to tell Meryon this. She helped him to find the foot-pump and bring up the tyre pressures, and she held the torch while he filled up the radiator and investigated the states of oil and petrol.

"I can't get over your seeing well enough to do these tricky things."

"Tricky? Topping up a radiator?" He laughed. "But I *can* see well, isn't it great?" He slapped the Emma's shiny bonnet. "There she is, all ready for the road, the good old girl. Let's go and lean on the wall, the way we used, and look over at the marsh. I'll get Dad's field glasses."

The days of leaning with their backs turned were over now, gone down into the past.

"I came here on my own, at the crack," Meryon confessed. "Had to do a quick gloat. But I can gloat some more—as long as you like. Was there ever a country like it? Even the high Pyrenees?"

There was no answer. He turned and looked at her and saw her face pale. She was staring away to the sea, beyond Cloudesley Castle. A fishing smack rode at anchor there in the full morning sun.

"What is there about an old smack to make you look like that?"

"It's the *Thunderer*."

"I see. With the stranger still on board?"

"The stranger," she said slowly—"the stranger is the man who threw the ammonia. I'm almost absolutely sure."

She told him about the photograph while he stared through the binoculars.

"*Thunderer* all right. Odd place to put her hook down. She can't be waiting for the tide, it's already running."

"She's been at sea a week. I've wanted to see Jim ever since I remembered the face. I had an idea he guessed as much and stayed out for that reason."

"Of course, he may not have the chap on board, now," Meryon said, adjusting the focus. "I wonder why he ... Tamzin, they're looking at *us* through glasses. Pretty sure of it. Your eyes are better than mine—they always were—see what you think."

She took the glasses; a nervous finger turned the central ring. "You're right. It's Jim. What else could he be looking at? There's only the castle and the sheep and this garden up on the cliff. I think it's us ... Meryon, they're lowering a dinghy."

"I suppose the answer to that is, where else could they be making for but Cloudesley Castle? And if so, why? How many in the dinghy?"

"Three," she said, longing to lie and say two.

"Emma's ready. Coming to find out?"

The glasses swung down. "I don't want you to go—please don't go!"

Chapter Nineteen

"Y̶ou can't have any idea how great it is to be driving again," Meryon said, as the old hearse sailed between the hedges like a ship in the narrows. "No need to look so worried; I can see a lot better than some drivers—that number-plate, for example—"

"That's not what I'm worried about."

"Meg will look after us—won't you, girl?" She banged a paw on to his knee on hearing her name. "Look," he went on to Tamzin, seeing that she was silent, "if Jim and Hookey *have* got this chap, they've had him a long time. And they would seem to have kept him under their four thumbs quite easily. Why should he suddenly break out now?"

She shook her head. "I don't know! I don't know why Jim's got him. I don't know anything, except the awfulness of what he did before."

"Rather not come?"

She shook her head again. "I'm coming."

"Sure? You know I've got to go, don't you? Oh, I'll be O.K.—I just know Jim wants me out there, and I've got to find out why."

He pulled in at the Sea Road garage for oil and petrol, and the garage man recognized Tamzin and stared at the hearse with the collie dog lying on the coffin-platform and shook his head. She could imagine him saying to the mechanic under a baker's van, "Well, if they think there's a cemetery down this road they'll have to think again, won't they?"

Turning on to the farm track the Emma rolled and dipped, more shiplike still. There was no hurry. Meryon stopped at Castle Farm to look in—*really* look in, Tamzin said to herself, marvelling—and be hugged by Mrs. Merrow and congratulated by the others. Mrs. Merrow laughed and cried at the way Meg still guided him, pressing against him in her worried and responsible way.

"That dog's grown as many years as it's been months," Mike said. "Done her good, that's what you have."

"It's been mutual," Meryon said.

"They tell me you're going up to Cambridge, son," the farmer said. "And what'll you be doing with Meg, then?"

"I'm not sure; still thinking about it. Depends on her, a bit."

In five minutes, on the marsh track again, the Emma's nose was headed for the castle.

"That Thomas of yours," Meryon said. "He'll be too young to have a guide dog … I was thinking of Meg."

Tamzin was gazing at the castle. The sheep clustered near it turned their heads to the approaching hearse.

"Look—look—they're at the castle—Jim and Hookey." Her hands were gripping the edge of her seat.

Meryon swung the Emma round a pot-hole. Meg, standing on the coffin platform, swung with the hearse as a sailor to the ship. "Fine—I do hate hanging around—don't you?" He sent her a sideways look. "Still worrying? Don't! I'm not going to throw away a decent life this time."

"Can you see it's Jim and Hookey?" She wanted impossible reassurance of his sight.

"No," he said honestly. "Faces beat me at this distance. Third man anywhere about? Left him aboard, I expect. We'll find out he's a French smuggler or something, and feel pretty silly, I expect."

The bare poles of the *Thunderer* showed above the beach banks beyond the castle, swaying gently to the swell—fingers writing on the sky. Into Tamzin's mind, like pebbles, the words from Omar Khayyam dropped—*The moving finger writes: and, having writ, moves on* ... It was as if they were in a play, the two of them and the dog, and had a part in it, and did not yet know what that part was.

Meryon parked the Emma neatly, reversing off the track beneath the castle wall.

"Jim—Hookey—it's good to see you!" Meg was pressing close as they walked over the short grass.

"Never thought you would, lad, that's a fact," Jim said, dealing him a severe friendly blow on the shoulder-blade. Hookey's hawk-face flickered its characteristic greeting scowl and returned to normal—a far less frightening state.

They were moving towards the castle gate, a crumbled hole in the great curtain walls.

"Got a nice liddle game on the boil," Jim told him, rubbing his hands. "Ever seed a cat play with a mouse? Hookey and me we got a mouse—ent we, Hookey? Speak up, you gawpin' great codfish—in a hole and all, as is right and proper."

"Jim! You've got somebody in the castle vaults."

"You watch me whistle of 'im out. Real funny, this'll be. I ent got no pity for them as deals in blinding."

The whistle pierced the soft October air and echoed coldly inside the castle walls. Tamzin pressed herself against the side of the gateway and stared at a dark patch in the turf against the round inner keep. This was the present entrance to dim tunnels where ammunition had once been stored—where Tamzin and her friends had played terrifying childish games through years of coming out to Cloudesley Castle. She had not been down there for a long time and remembered with a shiver.

The edges of the dark hole blurred as a shape of head and shoulders rose from it; then the whole man, standing there, squinting in the sun. Tamzin felt fear in the pit of her stomach when she saw

225

the face that she had seen twice before—in a photograph and in a crowd on Dunsford High Street.

The man came towards them as they stood by the broken stone gateway. He had a confident, bold stride, swinging his long arms. But as he looked from one to another of them the confidence ebbed very slightly, giving place to a baffled wariness.

"Hey, Cutter! Come on then, mate, what's eating yew?" Jim called softly. "All them weeks waiting fer the weather and the ship and the man what can fix ya, and whadjer do but pedal backwards!"

"Got the money?" Hookey snarled at him.

The man they called Cutter jerked his head back.

"Fetch it, then. Doncher wanter take it with ya?"

For a second Cutter looked at them with a malevolent cunning that Tamzin had not known achievable to a human face. "I get it," he said, and turned back towards the vault. It had not been possible to say if he had recognized Meryon, who now that the man was out of close hearing swung to face Jim and Hookey.

"I'm not going to play your cat and mouse game with you. The three of us and Meg can easily throw him into the Emma and take him to the cop-shop. Why not, in heaven's name?"

"He don't deserve a quick end, that's why," Jim said, as Cutter disappeared into the vault. "Hookey and me, we coulda throwed him in at any time, since fust came he looking fer a sneak-out to France. Right in the cats' basket, that were! We played him on, weeks—dint we, Hookey? Speak up, you ole gizzard—mending the boat, waiting fer this and that. Waiting to lure the others, we was. Cops got them," he added sadly, "though we nearly had 'em. But by then we was saving up Cutter fer you. He think you can get him through—or did until he seed you! Let him suffer—same as he caused others."

Meryon gazed at the place where the man had disappeared. He knew the tunnels, their dark, damp twists and unexpected drops. "There's another entrance to those vaults—do you know it, Jim?

The far side of the keep. He's taking rather a time—"

"'Course I know it; knowed it when you was in your pram. And what of it, hey? I like to see him run a liddle, arter we kep' him all that time. He can't get a hunnerd yards without he fetches up to the ear-'oles in a tide-dik, unless he goes by the sheep-track. An' if he do that us can catch him smartish in Emma."

A dark shape lifted for a moment on the top of the outer ring wall, quick and black against the bright sky. It resolved itself into a frantically climbing man, sliding out of sight below the broken rim, on the further side.

"Sink me if he ent a-climbing of the wall!" Jim exclaimed. "Never thought he had it in him."

Meryon swung on his heel. "Meg!"

The collie sprang to alertness, tailing her master closely. The others were out of the gateway nearly as quickly. A sharp ivy-branch scored a mark down Tamzin's cheek. Hookey banged a knee and swore expertly. Meryon turned an ankle on loose stone and surprised himself and Tamzin by his own expertise in this line. Only old Jim leapt neatly from stone to stone shouting triumphant vengeance, convinced that he could run as fast as anyone and eager for the chase. Now that Meryon had temporarily lamed himself no one could run as fast as Cutter. No one, that was, except the collie.

"Meg!" Meryon looked at her, willing her. "Meg! Go fetch him!" His arm swung out to the running Cutter. But Meg looked at him in a misery of bewilderment; there were no sheep where he pointed; what could he want her to do?

The man turned at a sharp angle, running down a line of reeds.

"He come up agen the tide-dik," Hookey shouted, half-way to the Emma. "Beating along to the sheep-gate."

That way were the sheep, huddled now against the gate and pressing each other, frightened faces turned to the running man.

Meg's ears went up. Meryon looked at her; she had been trained to work sheep, hadn't she? Even if she were no earthly good at it.

"Meg! Come by!" It was the shepherds' old command.

From a standstill, in a stride, the collie was galloping—streaking flat over the turf in the way of good sheep-dogs. Whistling two clear short notes Meryon sent up wordless thanks for having listened and watched so much when the farm dogs were working—thanks, too, that his crazy collie dog in some way seemed to realize that here was her chance of chances to redeem her reputation.

The sheep knew sheep-dogs and looked to her, seeing her as an animal in authority. She was round behind them before the man had been able to run clear of them. A dash for freedom brought him back with teeth at his ankles. He was of the flock, and he would be driven with them whether he wished to be or not.

Two short and a long, Meryon whistled, and Meg tightened her bunch, dashing from side to side and all the time forwards; and in the middle of the scared sheep was Cutter, running with them and shouting, "Call your blazing dog off! It's savaged me!"

"Jumping gin bottles!" said Jim, wonderstruck beyond any other words.

Hookey was waving his arms and cheering like a spectator at a cup match as the sheep came surging forwards to be penned by Meg, at Meryon's long single whistle, between the Emma and the castle walls.

"Bit me leg to the bone!" Cutter shouted from the middle of the flock. "I'll sue you for it, I'll have you—"

"Certainly," said Meryon, "you can talk to the police about it; you'll have plenty of time, I expect. Now, get into the hearse. No need to panic," he added as the man's eyes opened. "We don't all go in for murder and mutilation. It's just the best transport I can offer you."

A sudden fresh breakaway had the man back with Meg at his ankles.

"Better get in," Hookey said laconically. "That boy ent as soft as he looks." With a lightning snatch he had the leather case from Cutter's hand. A further snatch and it was in Jim's clutches. "Thass fer the cops, that is, boyo!"

Helping Cutter in with his boot Jim shouted, "Down you go!" seeing at last a chance for some enjoyable mouse-baiting. "Down on the corfin platform—see him, Meg! Thass right, matey, much better not try any nonsense. Now, cross yer hands!" He glanced along the hearse to Meryon in the driver's seat. "Loverly corp he make, don't he?" A dried-up yellow chrysanthemum caught his eye on the Emma's floorboards. The old man picked it up and placed it between the folded hands. Then Hookey and he roared out laughing, settling themselves one on each side of the prostrate figure.

"*What* I'll have to tell Simon and Thomas," Tamzin said.

Jumping in, Meg sat at the prisoner's feet, and her tongue was lolling and her eyes were sparkling, but she had a perplexed look all the same. Tamzin noticed it, looking back from her seat beside Meryon.

"Perhaps she doesn't know what she is, any more," Meryon suggested, changing up through the gears. "Sheep-dog, guide dog or police dog."

"*What* are you going to do with her, when you go away?"

He grinned at her. "Perhaps we might share her, like the little fighting bull? Term-time at your house, holidays at mine. But, after this morning's work, I've got an idea the Merrows might be rather keen to have her back as a sheep-dog. Anyway, she's got a future now, hasn't she?"

"That's three of us," Tamzin said, and smiled, so that the Emma swerved a good step into the grazings before she settled to the track once more.

APPENDIX:
THE AUTHOR'S
NOTEBOOK

LION   BRAND

6^{D.}

MEMO BOOK

A John Dickinson Product

232

APPENDIX: THE AUTHOR'S NOTEBOOK

*A*Wind is Blowing* is dedicated to Arthur William Ashman, a blind Norfolk man who trained his own guide dogs. Monica Edwards visited him and made notes during or after the visit. These notes form the basis of Chapters Ten and Eleven of the book, where Meryon trains Meg the sheepdog.

The detailed description of Barcelona in Chapters Fourteen to Seventeen was taken from the diary of Monica Edwards's friend Betty Pullan, the wife of the Edwards family's doctor Ted Pullan and mother of Amanda Pullan. Twenty years earlier the author had (unsuccessfully in my opinion) used another second-hand location description for the Dorset setting of *No Mistaking Corker*. Family friends the Webbs had tried to persuade her to visit the area but she was content to use their descriptions instead. It is a mark of how far she had come during those twenty years that it still seems surprising that Monica Edwards never visited Barcelona.

Brian Parks, 2009

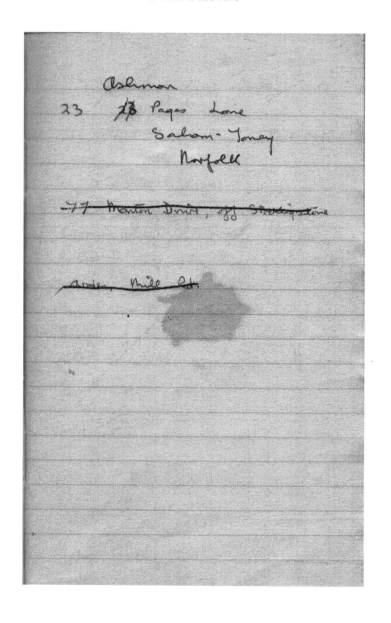

Ashman
23 1½ Pages Lane
      Saham-Toney
         Norfolk

~~77 Manton Drive, off Stockingstone~~

~~Arden, Mill St.~~

~~Tailboard of lorry sticking out.~~

Say Right, Left, None, Post Office

Dog that eats corners
Walking on road
Brooms, shovels, on road, Chaps
wanted to café, 'No, that's just what
I want!'
In & out heaps of leaves.
Heaps of tarmac, then stood with
hearts in mouths expecting him to walk
into things

~~While still.~~

'By gum, they made a good job of that
dog at the school!'

Courage & confidence.

I'm an outside man, I'm not interested in handicrafts.

Helpers — perhaps they don't want to go out when you do. You're independent, & follow.

People getting up to help — I just hate it.

Wife — There's a car starting up road — shall we go that way. Go back & forth 5 or 6 times — make use of it while it's there. Right, left. Then presently there's another car.

Rather have a child. — One-man dog. If I can't have this one I won't have any — pup that came to his feet.

Harness made at harness-maker's —
or cobbler's — over £3 — cobbler
charged 10/-.
D- strap, strengthened by turning &
stitching leather. Buckle each end.
3. rings — 1 ☐ in middle —
2 square rings for D strap.
D- lead.

Always, a move in front of you, in
thinking.
Elects herself as a guard dog, too.

Keep in Kennel, or she'll feel she's
on duty all the time.

Footbridge. Dog wanted to go straight
over though water — up to man's knees.
Once I find obstacle like that, I
keep on. Dog must do what you

~~want to do.~~

Know you can't ~~see~~, because you
tread on their toes almost because —
they know you wouldn't do that on
purpose.

'Come on, let's go to the pigs.'

Wait. (at road)
~~Forward left.~~
Forward right (when he hears car
has gone)

~~Bicycle — a little more difficult~~
~~Dog swings to avoid bike, but is~~
~~could get you.~~
~~Windy days — trees — difficult to~~
~~hear bicycles, even cars.~~
Go by church bells, dogs barking,
smells.

Airplane comes over when you're
listening — you've got to wait,
esp. on a Sunday when lots of
traffic — gets ted off my wife
because he always takes that
road — 'that's what I want.'
That's the training that the dog
wants.

2   Lynis, stopped to talk.
Dog didn't want to go between them,
came round behind his legs. Then
she took 'em round & up the
lane.

From across pavement.
Car across pavement, waiting in
gate.

Andorras
Sierra del Cadi . . . Ripoll

Bandits, earlier

Roadmen rushed out. Dusk,
Main roads, very rough, not surfaced,
appalling roads, 2nd gear all time.
Apricots

Shrubs & trees covered with Old Man's
Beard.
                        chestnut &
One leaves the oaks & beech trees &
climbs into the regions of fir & pine.
County glowing with green & gold &
russet. Always the mountains

Farms (red roofed) clinging dizzily to
mountainside. Streams.
Vultures soaring among peaks

Tall white houses with flowered balconies,
blue & green shutters, steep pitched roofs,
overhanging eaves. The white everywhere
except for red roofs & painted shutters
& balconies. Higher houses stone, red roofs.

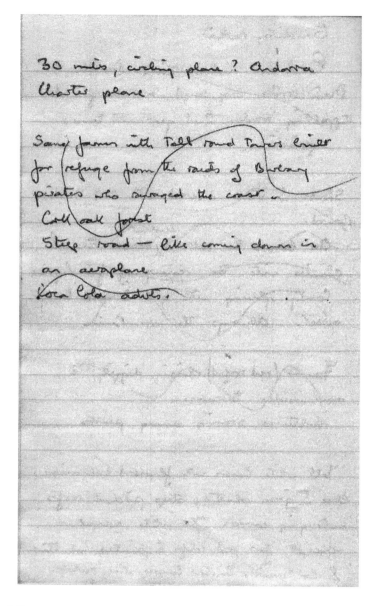

30 mins, circling plane? Andorra
Charter plane

Same farms with Tall round Towers built
for refuge from the raids of Breton
pirates who ravaged the coast.
Cork oak forest
Steep road — like coming down in
an aeroplane
Coca Cola adverts.

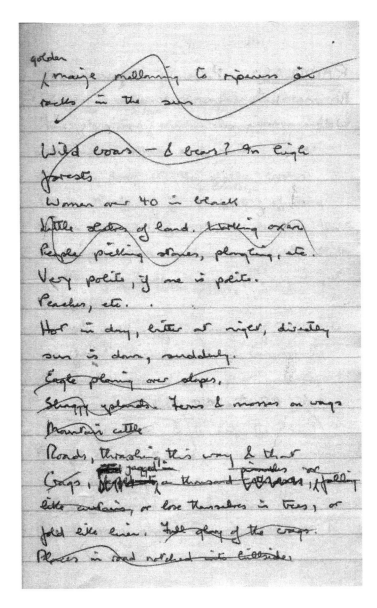

golden
{ maize mellowing to ripness in
sacks in the sun

Wild boars — & bears? An eagle
forests
Women over 40 in black
little plots of land. toiling oxen
People picking stones, ploughing, etc.
Very polite, if one is polite.
Peaches, etc. .
Hot in day, bitter at night, directly
sun is down, suddenly.
Eagle planing over slopes.
Stingy vegetation ferns & mosses on ways
Mountain cattle
Roads, threshing this way & that
Gaps, jagged, a thousand pinnacles or falling
like curtains, or lose themselves in trees, or
fold like linen. Full glory of the crags.
Places in red notched into hillside,

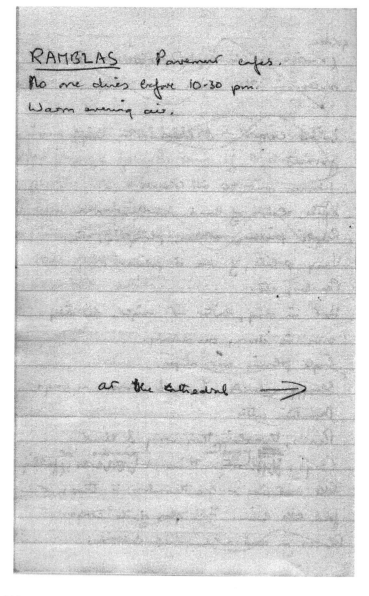

RAMBLAS   Pavement cafes.
No one dines before 10·30 pm.
Warm evening air.

at the Cathedral ⟶

Barcelona

Shopping & strolling place, the Ramblas.
Fine plane trees [2 rows] shading down the middle
with smaller streets each side, where
you can buy at the stalls, books,
trees, sheafs of flowers, [a florist,] cages of song-
birds, newspapers of most other countries, fruits,
a bicycle or a washing machine. Bootblacks
heckle for Trade, disparaging your feet
in public. [Trays, tables, guitars,]

People walking [round] for pleasure of it & to
see friends. Sunshine through leaves. No
hurry. Sparrows chirping, people conversing.
St. George's Fountain; coins thrown into
basin, for luck, & to cup the blind.
Peaceful cloisters [round] tree-shaded garden.
Two bull-rings.

Olive trees; twisted trunks & delicate silvery leaves
Peasant women shaking tree with long poles to
loosen the olives.

245

Pullars: lend field glasses to old
woman sitting in threshold, knitting, & minding
cows. Tried to talk to her. She turned
glasses on village exiles & began
smiling & laughing to herself. Superb
view of no account beside neighbours'
doings.

'At the top of the world & not far
from the edge'

Terrific winds across mountains & valleys.
Betty (hmst) had to drive on high
precipice roads because can't stand
heights & had to keep eyes on road.
Road without visible means of support
over sheer drops hung with trees

<u>Food</u>

"Never have we seen 4 oranges on a plate
placed so gracefully on the Table."
Rice & baby lobsters: mussels, in low
oval dish. Delicious.
Omelette.
Squid. Paella.

GIRLS GONE BY PUBLISHERS

 Girls Gone By Publishers republish some of the most popular children's fiction from the 20th century, concentrating on those titles which are most sought after and difficult to find on the second-hand market. Our aim is to make them available at affordable prices, and to make ownership possible not only for existing collectors but also for new ones, so that the books continue to survive.

As well, we publish some new titles which fit into the genre, including our Chalet School fill-ins, all professionally edited. Authors on the GGBP fiction list include Helen Barber, Elinor Brent-Dyer, Katherine Bruce, Monica Edwards, Amy Fletcher, Adrianne Fitzpatrick, Antonia Forest, Elizabeth Goudge, Lorna Hill, Phyllis Matthewman, Jane Shaw and Malcolm Saville.

We also publish non-fiction titles which are lavishly illustrated in black and white.

For details of availability and when to order, see our website or write for a catalogue to GGBP, The Vicarage, Church Street, Coleford, Radstock, Somerset, BA3 5NG, UK.

https://www.ggbp.co.uk/